ON THE BANKS OF
THE RIVER OF HEAVEN

OTHER BOOKS BY RICHARD PARKS

The Ogre's Wife
Hereafter, and After
Worshipping Small Gods
The Long Look
To Break the Demon Gate

ON THE BANKS OF
THE RIVER OF HEAVEN

RICHARD PARKS

PRIME BOOKS

ON THE BANKS OF THE RIVER OF HEAVEN

Prime Books
www.prime-books.com

ISBN: 978-1-60701-226-9

TABLE OF CONTENTS

INTRODUCTION
by CHARLES DE LINT

I had a bad moment when it seemed as though the magazine *Realms of Fantasy* was going to be cancelled.

I like the magazine as a whole—it's one of the few where I read pretty much all of the fiction; it always has a good feature on some artist; there's the Folkroots column; and what's not to like about the amusing ads for chain mail and wenches' outfits? (At least I find them amusing.)

But I would have missed it the most because, except for collections such as the one in hand, it's my principal source for new short stories by Richard Parks.

I first discovered Richard's work in *Realms of Fantasy* except I didn't realize it at the time. I have to admit that I don't pay a whole lot of attention to by-lines in magazines and anthologies. I'm just looking for good stories. But when I was reviewing Richard's first collection, *The Ogre's Wife* (2002) for my column in *The Magazine of Fantasy & Science Fiction*, I was surprised to find that I already knew a lot of the stories. A quick check of the copyright page told me why: I'd read them in *Realms of Fantasy*.

Ever since then, whenever a new issue hits the stands, I always check to see if it has anything by Richard in it. If it does, the first thing I do when I get home is read his story. Sometimes twice.

The reason for this is pretty simple. I could just say it's because he's such a wonderful short story writer, but that doesn't tell you anything. There are lots of very fine short story writers around. Our field appears to be particularly blessed with them: writers like Richard who deliver well-written stories, peopled with characters we can relate to, and stories that not only have a beginning, middle, and end, but move us as well.

Some of them also have Richard's somewhat rarer gift of being able to mix humour and drama within the same story without diluting the impact of either. A great example of this is "The Finer Points of Destruction" in which an ordinary joe gets a series of visits from the Hindu goddess of destruction, each appearance destroying another of his possessions. The humour never undermines the more serious exploration of interpersonal relationships, both among humans and among the gods.

A very few of writers understand as Richard does that the supernatural should create a sense of wonder, though he can also turn that around giving us gods and the figures of folklore in very human, down-to-earth terms. I also love the way that sometimes when I'm reading his work it feels as though he's channelling some ancient bard—maybe a Celtic one, as when he writes about selchies in "Skin Deep," or an Oriental one as he tells us the story of a monk meeting one of the Celestial Maidens of Heaven. You'd swear these stories were hundreds of years old, though like the best folklore, they still seem fresh and relevant in the present day.

But the real reason Richard is one of my favourite writers is because, like Peter S. Beagle or Parke Godwin, he's never disappointed me. Ever. That's not so common in any field of writing. No matter how varied the setting or subject matter, no matter how much I think I don't like a certain kind of story, Richard wins me over in just a few pages. Heck, usually in just a few paragraphs.

Take "The Twa Corbies, Revisited" in this very collection. A story about a pair of ghouls? It's not something that was high on my wish list. But by the time Prince Malthan, son of the ghoul king, is beginning his quest to understand what it means to be human, I was riveted. It might actually be one of my favourites in the book.

⸺✦⸺

There's another quality to Richard's work that bears mentioning—it's why I find myself rereading his stories with the same enthusiasm that gripped me my first time through the narrative—and that's the depth that underlies even the simplest of these stories. There's the sense of a Zen koan about them. Underneath the more straightforward narrative of the plot lie other narratives that the reader appreciates through intuition rather than rational understanding. They put the reader in a certain state of mind, the way a koan has no correct answer, but rather directs us to a particular method of viewing the world.

Maybe I'm reading more into it than Richard intended, but it doesn't matter, because the resonance is still there for me.

⸻

If you're already familiar with Richard's work you'll have an idea of what to expect from these stories, and I can assure you, you won't be disappointed.

If you're new to him, *On the Banks of the River of Heaven* is a perfect introduction to his work, and I envy you that buzz of delight that we all get when first encountering something this good.

Charles de Lint
Ottawa, Spring, 2009

ON THE BANKS OF
THE RIVER OF HEAVEN

The fish in the River of Heaven—known to mortals as the Milky Way—are both immortal and elusive. For many years they fell through Kaiboshi the Herdsman's nets until the year his wife, Asago-hime the Divine Weaver, made him a gift of a special net, finer than gossamer and stronger than iron. With this he caught the Celestial Fish easily enough while the Celestial Ox that was his primary responsibility grazed peacefully nearby and the Celestial Otter watched from the river.

Kaiboshi did not eat the fish, of course. Fishing was just a way to pass the time until the seventh day of the seventh month should come again.

Kaiboshi had just hauled in one more wriggling net of fish when the Celestial Otter, who until this point had done nothing but watch, stuck his head out of the water. "Herdsman, give me a fish, please," he said.

Kaiboshi frowned. "It is your role to chase the fish, not to catch them."

"And so I have done, for eternities past counting," Otter said. "Is it strange that, after all this time, I might want to know how it feels to actually hold one?"

Kaiboshi, who knew quite a bit himself about wanting what he could not have, carefully removed one of the Celestial Fish, its scales iridescent with stars, from the net and handed it to Otter, who carefully took the fish in his paws and examined it with what Kaiboshi could only interpret as awe and wonder. After a bit Otter put the fish in its jaws, though only tightly enough to hold it. With this he happily paraded for a time along the banks of the river, head held high.

During all this handling the fish just gasped, as any other fish would do, though in the case of a Celestial Fish this was no more than a polite reprimand, as one might clear one's throat to remind another that someone is waiting on them.

"Hmmm? Oh, of course. Please excuse me." Otter placed the fish back in the water and released it just as Kaiboshi emptied his net. There was a swirl among the reeds near the shore, then calm again. Kaiboshi gathered up his net and took it to a nearby tree branch to dry. When he returned to the shore both the Ox and the Otter were waiting for him. Or rather Otter was waiting; the ox simply had not moved.

"I wish to thank you," Otter said.

"No need," Kaiboshi said. "It was little enough that I did."

"Perhaps to you," said Otter. "But it meant a great deal to *me*, and so I must repay you. Is there anything you desire that is in my power to grant?"

Kaiboshi thought about what he wanted. "Tomorrow is the seventh day of the seventh month. The Master of Heaven has decreed that on this one day of the year I may cross the Bridge of Birds to visit my lady Asago-hime, and thus I am soon to be reunited with my love. The rains have prevented us seeing each other for two years now, but surely we will not be denied a third time. I wish only to see my love; there is nothing anyone can grant that I desire more than this."

Otter sighed. "I understand. Yet I consider myself in your debt from this day forward, so if you ever do think of a way I might be of use to you, seek me here at the river."

With that the Otter slipped back into the water and disappeared with barely a ripple, off again to pursue the elusive fish. Kaiboshi the Divine Herdsman watched the ox graze until night fell, and then he slept and dreamed of his love.

⟨⟨⟩⟩

On the seventh day of the seventh month as it had for the previous two years, it rained. And it rained. The cranes still came at Kaiboshi's bidding to stand by the shore and form the base of the bridge. Next came the geese and the ducks and other waterfowl, who fared well enough creating the platform and first few degrees of arc for the bridge. After that, however, came the hawks and crows and sparrows and smaller birds, and the rain beat down on them incessantly, and their wings became sodden and would no longer support them and a bridge, too. The cranes held on gamely as the river swelled into flood, but their skinny legs began to tremble. Kaiboshi reluctantly concluded that the enterprise was doomed, and he dismissed the birds with thanks rather than risk seeing them fall in the river after the inevitable collapse.

Three years now the rains had come on the appointed day. For three years the Bridge of Birds that was his only way to cross the Celestial River had been unable to form. Kaiboshi began to wonder if he was cursed, but more he wondered if Asago-hime had started to forget him. He sat down on the banks of the river and let the rising waters chill his feet as he indulged in a bout of melancholy, since he knew of nothing else he could do.

"Three years is a long time to be apart from the one you love," he said aloud. "Even for an immortal." He turned once more to the Celestial Ox, patiently grazing in the rain. "You could decide to graze on the other side of the river, you know. The Master of Heaven would have to allow me to follow you there."

The Ox merely turned its broad posterior in Kaiboshi's general direction and munched on a patch of sweet grass. Not that Kaiboshi could find it in his heart to fault the creature for this; the other side of the river was largely built over by the Master of Heaven's grand palace and those of many of the other major gods, and those who had gardens kept them behind high walls. The grazing there was, from an ox's view, very poor. Thus they were segregated according to function: Asago-hime to the palace, where she wove night and day to make the clothing and tapestries of the gods. Kaiboshi to the lands opposite across the river, where the wild creatures ran free and the grazing was best. Kaiboshi understood and accepted this, except for his separation from Asago-hime. That separation he had never been able to accept, save for the fact of their yearly visits. Only lately even that comfort was denied him.

Kaiboshi pulled a flute from his pack, the flute he had carefully carved and polished as a present to Asago-hime two years before and had yet to give to her. "She'll forget me," he said. "I know it. The curse will continue, the rain will come, and she will forget me."

"Unlikely," said a voice that was not Kaiboshi.

Otter stuck his head out of the swollen river near Kaiboshi's feet. "Pardon the intrusion, but Asago-hime is quite unhappy, on account of the rain. She said so."

Kaiboshi frowned. "How do you know this . . . oh. Of course. You can swim the Celestial River."

"Since the river is my home, it would be strange if I could not," the Otter said. "And I have just come from a sheltered cove beneath the window to the room where your lady resides. If the thought gives you comfort, know that she is just as miserable as you are, if not more so."

"I do not wish for my lady to be unhappy, and yet I do want her to miss me when I am not there. Oh, if only we could be together always, things would be so much simpler."

"I doubt that," Otter said. "It is my understanding that, when you lived with Asago-hime, both of you shamefully neglected your duties. The Celestial Ox wandered where it would, including the gardens of any god foolish enough to live on this side of the river. And your lady wife avoided her weaving to the point that the gods were becoming rather threadbare. Is this not why you were separated in the first place?"

"We had each other," Kaiboshi said, smiling faintly. "We had little need of anything or anyone else."

"And that's the problem in a nutshell," Otter said, "when so many other people need and depend on you."

Kaiboshi rested his head on his knees, looking glum. "You sound like the Lord of Heaven."

Otter shrugged. "One can understand his point of view without necessarily agreeing with everything he's done. What's that you're holding?"

"It was a present for Asago-hime, and I can't give it to her. Unless . . . Otter, can you take this flute across the river to Asago-hime? Would you?"

"Of course I can and would. I am in your debt, as I said. Yet the water would likely ruin it. Perhaps, if you were to find something dry to wrap it in?"

Kaiboshi found and cut a length of sturdy bamboo, just longer and wider than the flute. From this he made a watertight case and placed the flute inside, then tied a loop of cord around it. This Otter allowed Kaiboshi to place around his neck and then Otter set out across the river. Kaiboshi watched him dwindle to a spec on the vast water and disappear. Kaiboshi sat back down on the banks of the river and watched the spot where Otter had vanished while the Celestial Ox, perhaps remembering a more succulent patch of grass elsewhere, wandered off.

⸻◆⸻

When Otter reached the other side of the river, he went straight to the little sheltered cove he had spoken of, where, indeed, the window to Asago-hime's rooms opened over the water. Otter could hear the clack-clack of Asago-hime's loom as she wove. The noise was rather loud, so Otter was forced to shout to be heard.

"Asago-hime? May I speak with you?"

The Divine Weaver appeared at the window. Otter did not consider himself any judge of what the human immortals called beautiful, but he was forced to admit that there was a pleasing esthetic quality to Asago-hime's face, and her long black hair set it off marvelously. "Who calls? Is that you, Otter?" she asked. Her voice sounded somewhat husky, and, looking closer, Otter could tell that her eyes were reddened.

"Yes, Lady. Have you been weeping?"

"The rains kept my husband from me yet again. It is almost more than I can bear," she said. "Yet the cloth must be woven, and I must get back to it."

She started to turn away, but Otter called out to her again. "Tarry a moment, Lady. I bring a gift from your husband, and I cannot enter the palace. Can you come down to the shore?"

Asago-hime's countenance brightened immediately. "Oh, certainly!"

Her weaving apparently forgotten, Asago-hime disappeared from the window, and it was hardly a moment before a door near the base of the palace wall opened and she hurried out in layered blue kimono that rippled like water and glowed like the sky. For a moment all Otter could do was stare at her, impolite as that was.

"A token from my husband?" Asago-hime prodded gently.

"Hmm? Oh, yes. It's here . . . " Otter took the loop from around his neck and pushed the bamboo case to the shore where Asago-hime could reach it. She pulled it open and took out the flute.

"Oh, how lovely!" She immediately set the flute to her lips and proceeded to weave music as easily and surely as she did cloth. Otter could do little but stare and listen until the song was finished. "I've wanted to play more but lacked the means. It is good to know that my husband has not forgotten me."

"Forgotten? In truth he thinks of little else," Otter said drily. He hesitated then. "This is not my place to say, but Kaiboshi was kind to me, and I would not see more misfortune come to him. His worry at being separated from you may cause him to neglect his duties."

She smiled a little sadly then. "Otter, I know full well what My Lord is feeling. It's one thing to be attentive to one's assigned purpose when there is always something to look forward to, but what does either of us have now? The rains haven fallen on our assigned day for three years now. They may fall for another three . . . or three hundred."

"That *is* unfortunate . . . and somewhat strange," Otter said.

"Strange or not, it is the way things are. I would not wish Kaiboshi to neglect his duties, but I also cannot wish that he forget me. You are a kind creature, Otter, but you play in the river and chase the Celestial Fish, and nothing else is required of you. How can you understand how I feel?"

Otter thought of the one time in eternity he had held one of the Celestial Fish. "Perhaps at least a little," Otter said. "As you say, my duty is to chase fish in the river, not to command the rain that flows into it or even the water that flows *in* it. Still, if I can be of help to either of you, I will."

Asago-hime bowed in polite thanks to Otter and returned to the palace to resume her weaving. Yet every now and then, if one listened carefully, one would hear the clack of the loom grow still and be replaced by the long, mournful notes of the flute.

⇒◆⇐

As the Divine Year progressed there were rumblings on the Plain of Heaven that had nothing to do with rain. Twice now the Celestial Ox had to be shooed out of one or another god's garden, and the last several batches of cloth from Asago-hime's loom were all of pearlescent white, beautiful beyond reckoning but suitable only for weddings or funerals. Since there were precious few of either in the Heavens, the cloth began to pile up to no good purpose.

So things stood as the seventh day of the seventh month approached yet again, and as the time grew even closer, one day Otter surfaced to find the Lord of Heaven standing on the banks of the Celestial River, staring across the water. The view was lovely, but he was not smiling.

Otter knew that this was not the best time to approach, but it was clear enough what was on the Lord of Heaven's mind, and Otter's obligation to Kaiboshi would not let him remain silent.

"Is it my lord's will that Kaiboshi and Asago-hime be punished yet again? Will you separate them forever this time?"

The god scowled. "What would you have me do, friend Otter? They neglect their duties yet again, despite their agreement with me, and

I must bear both blame and responsibility for this. I may be Lord of Heaven, but I am not the master of my own daughter's heart."

"Isn't it right that this be so?" Otter asked, curious.

"Above all else, the Celestial Plain is about *order*, friend Otter. Love is not orderly. It comes as it will, and it leaves chaos in its wake. It is dangerous."

"Does that include your love for your daughter? You do love her, I know."

The Lord of Heaven sighed. "A father's love for his daughter is part of the Celestial Order, but so is her obedience to him. Instead Asago-hime chose Kaiboshi over the man I had chosen for her. To my regret I indulged her in this, and now all the Heavens pay the price of her obstinance to this very day, not just Asago-hime and Kaiboshi."

"That is only because the rains have kept them apart for the last three years," Otter said.

"And why do you think that is? Or do you believe it a coincidence?"

"It did seem strangely persistent," Otter said. "Yet, considering the effects, I had not thought it in your interest to cause it."

"Rain is the dominion of the Rain God. And again you see the fruit of my daughter's whims."

"I don't understand," Otter said.

"Asago-hime chose the Celestial Herdsman as her husband. To spare the Rain God's pride I did not let it be commonly known that he was the man I originally intended for her."

Understanding dawned. "Ah, but I rather fancy that *he* knew. If it is his jealousy that causes him to interfere, why don't you simply command him to stop?"

"From making rain? That is what the Rain God *does*. While it is true that his timing shows a vindictive streak I didn't know he had, that alone does not violate the tenets of his area of responsibility. I can no more command him to stop the rain than I could punish spring grass for being green. On the other hand, that my daughter's bargain has turned out poorer than she or my son-in-law hoped is no excuse for not honoring that bargain."

Otter bowed low. "Certainly not. Yet you would agree that, if the rains were to hold off for a year or two, the situation might improve without drastic action on anyone's part?"

"No doubt, but I think it will rain this year too."

"What if it doesn't? You have no great wish to inflict any further suffering on your daughter. Indeed, such might even be counterproductive." Otter saw the scowl deepening on the Lord of Heaven's visage and hastened to add, "Not that I would dare to hint that the Lord of Heaven's judgment is either unfair or unwarranted. Still, if there was an alternative . . . ?"

"I have said I will not interfere. What can you do?"

"Perhaps nothing," Otter conceded, "but why not give me until the seventh day of the seventh month to find out? Since this situation has been going on for the better part of the last four years, a day or two more would surely do no harm."

The Lord of Heaven appeared to consider this. "As you wish," he said finally. "Until noon on the seventh day of the seventh month, but not a moment longer." He turned away from the river then and strode back to his palace, leaving Otter behind in the river to ponder how in all the world he could stop the rain when he couldn't even catch a fish.

"It is the Rain God's jealousy that makes him keep Asago-hime and Kaiboshi apart. I know of no cure for this, but it's possible that, if I were to talk to him, he could be persuaded to see reason," Otter said.

This seemed like a perfectly sensible plan to Otter who, despite or because of his playful nature, was himself an eminently sensible creature. He set out at once for the Rain God's home, which was at the top of a high mountain near the headwaters of the Celestial River. It was there that Otter immediately ran into two problems. The first was that the streams rushing down from the mountaintop into the river below were cascading downward even faster than the Celestial Otter could swim, which was very fast indeed. The second difficulty was that the slopes of the mountain were haunted by the Rain God's daughters: wild-haired, mischievous sprites who delighted in turning the slopes of the mountain into mud and slippery stones. After Otter's third failed attempt he wound up belly-flopping nearly a league down the mountainside on an impromptu mud slide to be deposited once more into the Celestial River with the loudest and highest splash that Otter had ever made.

Now, mudslides were one of Otter's favorite things and he could not remember a better one than that prepared for him by the Rain God's daughters, but he realized after that third attempt that, fun as this was, he was not going to be able to reach the Rain God this way. He had to think of another path.

Otter puzzled for a while, and when the solution came to him, it seemed so simple that he wondered why he hadn't thought of it sooner. He could not reach the Rain God, but the Rain God's more powerful twin brother was the River God, and he was quite easy to reach . . . at least for an otter.

The River God in his true form was a great water dragon who lived in a cave near the base of the Rain God's mountain, where the waters first flowed into the Celestial River. The River God was also of a generally agreeable nature when he wasn't in flood; perhaps he could be persuaded to intercede with his more moody brother, especially since the Rain God was dependent on the River God for his water in the first place. The main danger was the giant whirlpool in the River God's cave, but Otter knew a stone path that would let him avoid that.

"At least," thought Otter, "there's no harm in asking."

Whatever Otter meant to do, he knew he had to do it soon if there was any chance of repaying his debt to Kaiboshi. Evening was already approaching, and the next day was the seventh day of the seventh month, when once more, the rains would surely come.

Otter swam quickly against the current and soon came to the place where the waters emerged from the mouth of the River God's cave to meet the runoff from the Rain God's mountain, there together to form the body of the Celestial River. He dived under the water there and followed the current until he finally surfaced in a large quiet pool.

There was a distant dull roar that Otter recognized as the maelstrom, and before he dared swim much further, he slipped out of the water at place where a narrow ledge ringed the pool. Every so often along the cave's wall were rock crystals that glowed like torches, giving weak but adequate light. Otter followed the ledge along the underground river until he came to the place on the far side of the cave where the vast whirlpool churned.

The maelstrom was even larger now than Otter remembered, reaching from one side of the river to the other. The water that escaped it flowed on toward the cave mouth and out into the river, but Otter knew better than to try to swim anywhere near the thing. The currents there were overwhelmingly strong and unpredictable.

The ledge here connected with a larger cavern that served as the River God's palace. Crystalline formations grew from floor and ceiling, serving as pillars and creating chambers within the cave. Otter peered into the crystalline palace but saw nothing. He looked around the cave ledge. "Hello? River God? It is I, Otter."

A spout of water ejected from the center of the whirlpool, and just before it was about to splash into the stone ledge by Otter's feet, it transformed from water into what now appeared to be a handsome young man with jet black hair and dark eyes. It was not often that Otter had seen the River God in his human form, and he didn't recognize him until the man spoke.

"Hello, friend Otter. What brings you to my palace?"

Otter, now that he recognized the Lord of the River, bowed low. "I've come to ask a favor of you, Divine One."

The River God smiled. "Very curious. No offense, but what does Otter require other than the freedom of the river and plenty of fat fish to chase?"

"Ordinarily, My Lord, nothing at all. I'm here because of an obligation I owe to another."

"And who might that be?"

"The Divine Herdsman. Kaiboshi."

"Ah, that one." The River God stopped smiling. "Ask if you will, but I'm not inclined to do anything to the cowherd's advantage."

Otter blinked. "I am surprised to hear this. Has Kaiboshi offended My Lord in some way?"

"Offended? Say rather he possesses something that by right belongs to me, though that need not concern you, friend Otter. Just understand this, and do not take it personally if I refuse your request. Now, then—what is it you wanted of me?"

"To intercede with your brother, the Rain God, so that tomorrow the Bridge of Birds may be formed as the Lord of Heaven decreed."

The River God laughed until the cavern rang with the sound of it. Otter merely waited, feeling a bit confused and uncomfortable, until the sound died down enough for him to be heard again. "Clearly I have said something that amuses you, My Lord. May I ask what that is?"

"Oh, friend Otter," the River God said, wiping tears from his eyes. "Where do you think my brother acquires the extra water he needs to make so much rain across the Plain of Heaven in the first place? Why do you think this whirlpool practically roars with the volume of water flowing through it?"

"I supposed he got the water from you, as the river is the only source of water in the Heavens," Otter admitted. "But I did not know the whirlpool had a part to play in this."

"Underneath the whirlpool is a stone channel that forces water from my domain up to the top of my brother's mountain. I supply it gladly, since he's making it rain on *my* behalf. Now do you see why I was laughing? In your innocence you've asked me for the one favor in all the Heavens that I cannot and will not grant."

"I see, but I do not understand," Otter said. "How is the suffering of the Divine Herdsman and the Divine Weaver to your advantage? I had not thought you cruel by nature."

The River God glared at Otter. "Cruel? Nonsense. I merely seek what is mine by right, as I said."

Otter blinked. "You seek guardianship of the Divine Ox?"

The River God sighed. "The Ox? Oh, Otter. Go back to your fish; these matters are clearly beyond your understanding."

"It's true that I'm an ignorant creature," Otter said. "But that is not by choice. If you will not grant my request, then at least teach me the reason. If it is not the Ox you covet . . . oh."

The River God nodded, smiling. "Now you see. By keeping that lout Kaiboshi and the exquisite Asago-hime apart, I've made certain that Kaiboshi's bargain with the Lord of Heaven will not be kept, and so he will be forced to separate them permanently. And then Asago-hime will be mine, as the Lord of Heaven intended all along. It pains me to cause my beloved any grief, but she will forget her silly infatuation with that oaf in time. I will see to that. Now do you understand?"

Otter thought that, perhaps, he did understand. Finally.

"I had intended to repay my debt to Kaiboshi, but not at your expense, My Lord. No doubt you will make a splendid husband, and your plan is a marvel of cunning simplicity. Was it difficult to obtain your brother's help?"

The River God stroked his chin thoughtfully. "In truth, it was my brother who knew of my frustrated affection for Asago-hime, and he first broached the idea. He's always been the clever sort, and as he said, all he needed was my water to make the plan work."

"Quite ingenious," said Otter. "Yet, if your patience is not yet exhausted, may I ask how did you learn that Asago-hime was intended for you? The Lord of Heaven was quite discreet about his choice."

"Again I must thank my brother," the River God said. "He confided this knowledge to me, though how he obtained it himself he could not say. I think he protects his sources."

"As surely as he protects your interests," Otter said, bowing low again. "As you've already said, these matters are beyond my own poor brain. I had understood the situation differently. Doubtless I was mistaken."

Otter turned to go, but the River God stopped him. "Wait, friend Otter. What do you mean? What were you mistaken about?"

"I must have misheard the Lord of Heaven this morning. Water in my ears or the like. It is nothing."

The River God frowned. "What did he say?"

"Well, I *thought* he said that Asago-hime had been intended for your brother, the Rain God. But that is quite impossible, isn't it?"

"Yes, of course," said the River God, and his eyes were glowing.

"Clearly I was mistaken. Else it would be your brother who really stood to gain if the marriage between Asago-hime and Kaiboshi was dissolved. Is that not right?"

"Yes. Of course," the River God said, with just a bit more emphasis. His eyes were still glowing, and the antlers of his true dragon form had sprouted on the River God's broadening forehead.

"In which case your clever and cunning brother would have been playing you for a fool, and that notion is ludicrous beyond all reason," Otter said, backing away slowly.

"Yes. Of course!!!"

The River God's words changed into an incoherent roar of rage, and stones crashed down from the ceiling. In an instant he fully transformed into the mighty River Dragon. Otter was already across the cavern and poised over the entry pool. "Thank you for your teaching, My Lord," he shouted. "You needn't see me out. I know the way!"

With that he plunged back into the water and swam as only an Otter can swim with the current at his back, until he was well away from the cave of the River God and the Rain God's mountain.

<hr />

The seventh day of the seventh month dawned cold and stormy. Lightning flashed across the sky, and the winds howled, as indeed they had for much of the night. Otter found Kaiboshi by the river looking, if anything, more forlorn than the last time Otter had seen him. An occasional cold water spray from the river drenched him, and he didn't bother seeking shelter.

"I can stand no more, friend Otter," Kaiboshi said. "I will cross this river today if I have to wade it."

"Being immortal, you won't drown, but you know as well as I that the terms of your bargain will not allow you to cross, save by the Bridge of Birds. You will be swept from one end of the river to the other and back again."

"What else can I do?"

"Summon the Bridge of Birds, Herdsman," Otter said. "After all, it is time."

Kaiboshi waved an arm at the angry clouds, the flashing lightning. "Against *this*?"

"The wind will howl," Otter said, "but birds are masters of the wind. It will not deter them. Nor are they so high that the lightning will strike them in preference to better targets. Summon the birds. Go visit your wife."

"But . . . the rain?"

"It will storm, but it will not rain, Master Kaiboshi," Otter said. "Not this day. Note that the darkest clouds and the worst of the lightning surrounds the Rain God's far mountain. I believe it will stay there."

"Yes, but what does this mean?"

Otter shrugged. "A family dispute, I believe. It need not concern us. Summon the bridge."

Kaiboshi looked doubtful, but he summoned the birds as was his right under the agreement, and they came. First the cranes to form the anchor pillars at each end, then the waterbirds, then the birds of the air and forests, all obeyed and took their assigned places. They threw their songs back in raucous defiance of the heavens, and the bridge held.

There was an occasional drop of water that might have been blown off the top of the river by the wind, but there was no rain. Slowly, as if unable to believe his good fortune, Kaiboshi crossed the bridge of birds. He started carefully, testing each step as if all was an illusion that might collapse at any moment. Then he moved faster and faster until he practically ran across the roadway of feathers to the opposite side. Freed of their burden, the Bridge of Birds burst asunder and scattered, each to their assigned place on the Plain of Heaven, until the following morning when Kaiboshi would summon them again.

Otter watched the bridge become birds again and fly away. "All debts settled," he said happily.

"I gather the brother gods Rain and River are doing the same even as we speak," said a new voice. "I think we have you to thank for this, friend Otter."

Otter looked up to find the Lord of Heaven scowling down at him. "Well, considering the alternative . . . ." Otter began, but the expression on the Lord of Heaven's face made him think better of it.

"My daughter will be pleased," the Lord of Heaven said, and his scowl lessened somewhat, "and I guess there's some virtue in that . . . if she knows what's good for her."

"It's all they wanted," Otter said simply. "And since I don't wish to neglect my own duties, I really should get back to chasing those fish . . . "

"Stay a moment, friend Otter," said the Lord of Heaven. "All actions have consequences, and yours can be no different."

"I suppose that's just," Otter said, and he sighed. "What is my punishment?"

"I said 'consequences,' friend Otter. Whether it turns out to be a punishment or a reward is not up to me."

The Lord of Heaven reached down into the river and swirled the water with one finger, and in that swirling a figure took shape. One long and lithe with dark brown fur and darker eyes.

"Her name is Kawauso-hime," the Lord of Heaven said.

It was just a name, but with the speaking of that one word Otter finally understood fully and completely why Kaiboshi waited by the river on the seventh day of the seventh month, why the River God and the Rain God were currently lashing at each other both over and under the mountain. He understood why what Kaiboshi and Asago-hime shared was so dangerous, and why he, like them, would never, ever, give it up.

"Do I belong to her or does she to me?" Otter asked, though he didn't really care which. He just wanted to understand.

The Lord of Heaven shrugged. "Both. Neither. That's something you'll have to work out for yourselves," he said.

After the Lord of Heaven was gone, Kawauso-hime looked at Otter with mischief in her eyes. "Who are you?" she asked.

"I'm Otter," said Otter when he could find his voice again. "Do . . . do you like to chase fish?"

"It's one thing I like to do," Kawauso-hime said, showing her fine white teeth. "We'll start with that."

And, in flash of fur and a splash of the Celestial River, they were off.

THE FINER POINTS
OF DESTRUCTION

Jack Kimble was alone in his apartment early Friday evening when the Hindu Goddess of Destruction manifested inside his ancient tv. The tv was, not surprisingly, destroyed.

Jack rolled off the couch and onto the floor, covering his head with his arms at the first shower of sparks. Considering the age of the tv and the general tone of his recent luck, the explosion wasn't much of a surprise. It was only after the clatter and tinkle of flying glass finally subsided that Jack looked up and got to the surprising part.

Kali Ma crouched in the small opening of his tv cabinet, her taloned feet resting on a mess of smoking wires and broken glass like the body of a fallen enemy. Her skin was blacker than obsidian, her red eyes large and terrible. She was naked except for a necklace of miniature skulls that Jack thought must surely be plastic until one of them clicked its yellowed teeth at him. Jack had an impression of immense size, even though she barely had to crouch to fit into the space formerly occupied by the now pitiful remnants of his tv.

Jack, a Southern Baptist when he needed to fill in the blank marked "Religion" on a form, didn't claim to be an authority on Hindu cosmology, but he had at least heard of Kali, and he knew this was that same goddess because she announced it to him.

"I am Kali Ma," she said with a voice like rusty knives being sharpened. "Called Endless Night, Wife of Lord Shiva and Goddess of Destruction. Mortal, who are you?"

Jack heard a croaking sound, and finally realized that he was making it. Once he knew that, it was a little easier to try to arrange the croaks into something resembling words.

"Jack . . . Jack Kimble. Ummm. Pleased to meet you?"

"Of course," Kali said, as if there had never been any doubt of that. She stepped down from the smoking remnants of the tv and onto the ugly green carpet. She peered down at Jack, still cowering in front of the threadbare sofa.

"You may rise now," Kali said.

Jack wasn't so sure he could, but his knees, while wobbly, didn't quite buckle as he got to his feet using the arm of the couch for support. He thought of all the usual things a person might be expected to think at a time like this. That he was dreaming. That it wasn't really happening. That he was hallucinating. Then his bare foot encountered one of the sharper pieces of debris from his former television.

"Owww!!"

Jack sat back down on the couch again and carefully examined his left foot. A bright sliver of glass protruded from beneath his big toe. He carefully teased it out and then used his handkerchief to stop the bleeding. When he looked up again, Kali was still there, standing with her own bare feet on broken glass. Jack wasn't sure, but he thought that she was scowling. With her face it was hard to tell.

"On your feet, mortal. It's improper to sit in the presence of divinity," she said.

Jack noticed where Kali was standing. "Doesn't that hurt your feet?" he asked before he thought better of it.

"I am the Goddess of Destruction," Kali said calmly. "How can anything related to my sphere of influence harm me? Now get up before I get angry."

Jack didn't know the answer to that. He barely understood that it was a question. He did understand that a creature calling herself Kali was standing in his living room, and whatever else he might do, he did not want to make her angry. He got back up off the couch, being more careful where he put his feet this time.

"That's better. So. I suppose you're wondering why I am here?" the goddess asked.

Jack hadn't quite gotten to that part, to tell the truth, but he realized that, indeed, that very question had been next on his agenda.

"Yes Ma'am," he said, as politely as he could.

"You may address me as 'Kali,' " she said. "I'm looking for my husband. As I already mentioned, his name is Shiva. Have you seen him?"

"No one's been here except me for some time now," Jack said. Which was the simple, painful truth. "May I ask why you think he'd be here?"

"Because this is the place he will be, if not at this moment," Kali said, as if the answer should have been obvious. "If he's not here now, then I'll come back again and again until he is."

"Uh, excuse—"

Jack wasn't even sure what he was about to say, but whatever it was quickly became moot. Kali vanished in another shower of sparks, leaving Jack alone again with the wreckage of his television. He pinched himself, just for the sake of argument, but it wasn't really necessary. His toe still hurt from the glass and had started to bleed again. He went looking for some antibiotic ointment and a band-aid and then, because the glass was still a danger, he cleaned up the wreckage. First he put on some shoes, then picked up the larger pieces, none of which was really that large. There was nothing of the tv left that was too big for the trash can. When he was done, he sat back on his ratty old couch and stared at the place where his television had been.

Figures . . . If a goddess was going to appear to me, it would be someone like Kali. Why couldn't it have been Venus? Goddess of Love and Beauty? That'd be worth a dead tv.

It was the first coherent thought Jack had managed to put together since Kali had left, and it was a complaint. Jack was a little ashamed of himself but couldn't say why. After all, a real, living goddess had manifested in his den. How often did something like that happen? Yet he didn't feel especially honored, or much of anything else. Numbly, Jack stared at the empty place where his tv had been for a little longer. Then, because he couldn't think of anything else to do, he put on a jacket and went outside.

The jacket proved to be a good idea. There was a little nip in the air. Fall was always late coming as far south as Medias, but now, near the end of October, it had finally put in an appearance. Jack put his hands in his pockets and walked, not paying a great deal of attention to direction. There were other people about on the sidewalks near downtown: young couples, a skinny old man walking his dachshund. Jack noticed several people in running gear and realized he was near Municipal Park. For want of a better plan, he decided to go that way.

There was a young man sitting on a park bench beneath one of the old oak trees. He was glowing as if being consumed from the inside out by a blue fire. That was the first thing Jack noticed, but the second thing he noticed was that no one else was paying the glowing man the least bit of attention. The old man walking his dachshund allowed the dog to lead him up the sidewalk beside the bench without even breaking stride. A young couple walking past were too busy looking at each other, Jack assumed, but that didn't explain why none of the other people taking advantage of the waning daylight in Municipal Park were paying the man any attention at all.

Jack paid attention. The man appeared about thirty and wore a yellow nylon track suit. He was, by Jack's estimation, of Indian or Pakistani descent and quite good looking. Closer, Jack could see that the glow was not just a blue fire as he'd thought earlier, but a rippling weave of deep indigo and sky blue, and all shades in between. Every now and then it rose in little flame-like tongues behind the man as if creating a backdrop.

The glowing man watched Jack approaching, and when Jack was no more than ten steps away he smiled. "So. You're the one," he said. His voice sounded more Oxford English to Jack's ear than Indian.

Jack blinked. "Beg pardon?"

The man just went on as if he hadn't heard. "Which one was it, by the way? Tara? Shodashi?"

Jack finally understood. "Kali."

The man frowned. "Ouch. Bad luck, that. Still, it could have been Matangi. You got off lucky, by comparison."

"Matangi . . . ?"

The man sighed then. "Sorry, I should have realized you're not of our Perspective. Matangi is a goddess of decay. She tends to make things go to rot and ruin."

"Am I addressing Lord Shiva?"

"That is correct. You are?"

"Jack. Jack Kimble." It was the second time that day Jack had introduced himself to a god. He was feeling a little dizzy.

Shiva apparently noticed, and slid over on the bench. "Sit until you're feeling better. It's not exactly proper, but I'm not as big on ceremony as some."

"Th—thank you." Jack took a firm grip on the armrest and lowered himself to the bench. It was several long moments before his head stopped spinning.

"How . . . how did you know I had met another deity?" Jack asked finally.

Shiva shrugged. "For that matter, why did you happen to come to the park today? You think that was coincidence? As for knowing, you obviously spotted my Divine Aura. That made you either a holy man or someone recently in contact with divinity. Since I know all of my wife is looking for me I guessed the latter rather than the former. No offense."

Jack felt his head spinning again. "None taken. Ummm, all of your wife? Did you mean to say all of your *wives*? You mentioned other goddesses besides Kali."

Shiva shuddered delicately. "Please. I have one wife only, and her name is Parvati. Or Shakti, or Devi, or something else depending on who you ask. However, she has ten aspects that I know of, and Kali the Destroyer is one of those aspects. Kali appeared, but it could just as easily have been any one of the other nine. Have a row with Parvati and you're having a row with *all* of her, so to speak. So. Kali was looking for me, yes?"

"She said that you would be where she was, sooner or later. I think she meant my apartment."

"Thanks for the warning. I will simply avoid your apartment, and that's it for Kali. Now if I can just avoid the other nine I'll be all right for a while yet."

"But . . . she's going to come back!"

"Oh, count on it," Shiva said, and then he disappeared as swiftly as Kali herself.

Kali did come back three days later, only this time she manifested in Jack and Cindi's wedding picture. It was the only picture of them together Jack had kept after the breakup, but now it was nothing but broken wood and shreds of paper and jagged glass.

"You've seen him, haven't you?" Kali said.

Jack nodded as he stared glumly down at the remnants of the picture. He started to pick up the pieces. "Yes. He was in the park. I'm sure you can find him there."

"I'm sure I can't," Kali said primly. "I thought I already explained about that."

"But he was there! He's never been here. What's more, he told me that he never intends to come here!"

Kali shrugged. "What he intends does not matter. It's what he will *do* that concerns me, and I tell you that he *will* come here. It may take ten years or ten thousand, but he will bring his physical incarnate self to this spot."

Ten years?

The thought of ten years of repeated visits by the Hindu Goddess of Destruction was horrible enough, but just about as much as Jack could get his head around. Ten thousand years might as well have been a billion, so far as he could tell, but ten years? That was a time frame he could understand.

"Until next time, then—"

"Wait!" Jack found himself shouting before he even realized that he was going to.

Kali glared at him, but she did not disappear. "Why should I?"

"Please, I have a question—Is it really necessary that you destroy something of mine every time you appear?"

"Goddess of Destruction. Manifesting on the physical plane," Kali said slowly and carefully, as if talking to someone mentally slow.

"But if this keeps up, pretty soon I'll have nothing left!"

The goddess shrugged. "It's not like you have so much now."

Jack was a little offended but had to admit that Kali wasn't wrong. His apartment wasn't so much spartan as bare. Aside from the couch and the now-empty tv cabinet, there was a rickety dinette table with one chair in the kitchen area, one bed and a half-empty closet in the bedroom. The bathroom had no more than the bare essentials. It wasn't really that he was so bad off as all that; his medical leave plan wasn't generous but it was adequate. The real problem was that, after the divorce, he hadn't been able to muster enough enthusiasm to care about his surroundings very much.

"That may be true but I did have some . . . attachment to that picture."

"Yet no longer to the woman whose image was holding yours? Spare me, Jack Kimble. If the picture was more important than the person it deserves to be destroyed."

"It's not like that!"

Kali raised one fierce eyebrow. "Indeed? Then where is she?"

"Look, things just didn't work out for my wife and me. Sometimes everything you can do isn't nearly enough. Some people can't be together."

In Jack's years as a marriage counselor he'd come to know the truth of that, but he never thought he'd be applying that bit of hard-won wisdom to himself and Cindi. Then again, he'd never thought that all the horrible things that had happened in his life recently would happen.

"If destiny was as guilty of even half the crimes you humans lay on the poor thing, even I would not have destruction enough to punish it," Kali said drily.

Jack sighed. "Even so, if I understand you correctly, once you've destroyed everything, you'll no longer be able to manifest here anyway."

Kali's gaze narrowed. "Perhaps. What's your point?"

"My point is that it might be to our mutual advantage to find an alternative."

"There *is* no alternative. Shiva will come when it is time, and not before. If I knew exactly when that was," here Kali looked just a tad wistful, "then I would come to meet him then and limit the destruction of your material possessions, such as they are."

"Thanks for the thought, anyway," Jack said. "It was very kind of you."

"No, it wasn't. I am Kali!"

To make her point, just before Kali made her exit she destroyed the California Pottery bud vase Jack had inherited from his mother. Once more, Jack was left to pick up the pieces.

Jack found himself back in the park with Shiva the next evening, as he rather suspected he would be. Despite everything that had happened over the last year, Jack knew that his instincts were good . . . most of the time.

Shiva shook his head, and the blue flames surrounding him danced as if they'd been fanned. "Well, of course she destroyed your pot! You're lucky she didn't bring down the entire building on your head."

"For giving her a compliment?"

"For Kali, praising her kindness is not a compliment. Now, if it had been Tara," and here Shiva sighed, "what a sweetheart." He paused then and went on, thoughtfully. "As, too, is Kali. In her way."

"That's a side of Kali I'm not seeing," Jack said, but then he seized on something else Shiva had said. "Would you meet with one of the other goddesses, if I could find them? Tara, perhaps?"

Shiva shuddered. "Certainly not; I'm avoiding all of them. Besides, you do not find the Mahavidyas, at least not the way you're thinking of searching. In this particular instance they find you. The same way they're trying to find me."

"Since you brought up the Mahavidyas, I meant to ask you something. I've been doing some research—"

"Time to kill, I see. What is it you do, anyway?"

"I'm . . . retired," Jack said.

"It's not wise to lie to a god," Shiva said. "Or, for that matter, to yourself."

Jack turned a little pink. "All right, then. I'm on paid medical leave . . . probably permanently. I used to be a counselor."

"What sort of counselor?"

Jack hesitated. "A marriage counselor."

Shiva smiled a faint smile. "Oh, I do love a proper irony. Were you any good?"

"I used to think so," Jack said honestly, "until I lost a pair of clients, and then my own marriage crumbled. Up until then my track record was pretty decent."

"You lost them? How?"

Jack didn't know why he was telling Shiva any of this. Not only was he a god but Jack didn't even know him that well. Still, as a former counselor he understood the value of a good listener, and Shiva seemed to be very good at listening. Jack wondered if, perhaps, the deity known as Lord Shiva did a lot of listening. "It was . . . a murder/suicide. The husband shot his wife and then himself. I'm afraid I lost my way after that. Cindi left me soon after. I can't say that I blame her. I'm a loser."

"Why? How were you to know that this man's anger was a mask for something greater?"

"It was my job to know," Jack said simply.

"Then you made a mistake," Shiva said reasonably. "Humans do that. You're human."

"Look, thanks for trying to make me feel better—" Jack began, but Shiva cut him off.

"If such a thing made you lose your way, you must not have been very certain of your path to start with. Make no mistake, Jack Kimble: I'm not trying to make you feel better. I'm simply pointing out the obvious. That's required rather a lot when dealing with mortals."

"It's not my fault I'm not a god," Jack said.

Shiva shook his head. "Why not? There is no blame, no consequence, no mistake or mis-step that can't be laid squarely at your own feet if you choose to own it. Did you kill that couple? No. Did you persuade the husband to do so? I'm thinking that the answer is also 'no.' The husband made his choice and chose badly, and he will answer for it one way or another. It's not your concern. Now then: did you drive your own wife away? Most likely, and that *is* your concern. What are you going to do about it?"

"I wish I could believe there was something I *could* do."

"Believe it or don't believe it, but not doing so will make your life more miserable than it needs to be. If you're so fond of accepting blame, start with that."

Jack changed the subject. "I've been doing some research since Kali's last visit, as I said. I would like to state the situation as I understand it. Will you do me the honor of correcting me if I'm wrong?"

The god shrugged. "My temporary temporal imperatives are not currently prohibitive."

"Pardon?"

"I have some time to kill."

"Oh, right. Anyway, according to the story, when all this started you were—pardon me if this gets too personal—having sexual congress with your wife Parvati."

Up until that point Shiva had never looked more than slightly amused at anything Jack said, but now he actually grinned. "Congress? How many of us were there?"

Jack sighed. "Well, considering what happened with the Mahavidyas, that's probably not a bad question. But, more to the point, for some reason you became upset with Parvati."

"Why was I upset?" Shiva asked.

Jack blinked. "I don't know. I read this from more than one source, and none of them said exactly why. I assume they don't know."

"That's your second mistake. The first was going to such secondary sources, rather than spending your lifetime properly pursuing true understanding."

"If I did that I wouldn't have a place to live within a week," Jack said drily. "So what's my second mistake?"

"Whether anyone knows why I was angry or not totally misses the heart of the matter. It's enough that I *was* and now *remain* angry. That drives the event to which you just alluded, yes? The Mahavidyas?"

Jack nodded. "You were leaving Parvati in a huff, swearing never to return. To prevent this, Parvati separated into ten distinct aspects, now called the Ten Goddesses of Wisdom. The Mahavidyas. Kali I've met, but there were nine others including the ones you mentioned: Tara, Matangi and Shodashi. They covered all the exits, so to speak, and everywhere you went you were confronted by at least one of them. After which you allegedly came to your senses, realized that the Divine Masculine and the Divine Feminine were properly inseparable, and Parvati returned to her singular form and your own good graces."

"More or less true," Shiva said. "Given that language is such a poor conduit of meaning. What's your point?"

Jack took a deep breath. "My point is that, if this has already happened, why is it happening again, and in *my* apartment? No offense, but is this going to blow up in my face every time you and your missus have a tiff?"

Shiva laughed.

It started as such a low rumbling in the god's belly that, at first, Jack thought the deity sitting on the bench was getting hungry. Then the sound traveled up Shiva's body following what Jack assumed was the chakral order until it seemed to explode from the crown of his head. For a moment the other people about in the park hesitated, some looking about as they'd lost something but couldn't quite remember what. Others resumed their stride without missing a beat. Jack, for his part, had to put his hands over his ears to keep from being deafened. Then, as if the sound had to escape properly or the god himself would be torn apart by it, Shiva leaned back on the bench, opened his mouth, and *roared*. Jack swore he saw leaves falling but, for the rest of the mortals in the park, the moment seemed to have passed without much more notice. Jack realized that, no matter how much he personally knew better, to the rest of the world the Lord Shiva was just someone laughing on a park bench.

It was at least a full minute before the great quaking laugh began to subside and, except for the occasional chuckle, Shiva grew still again.

"I'm sorry," Jack said finally, "but what was so funny?"

For a moment Jack thought Lord Shiva was about to explode again, but his mirth remained under control, if barely. The god paused to wipe tears from his eyes. "You are, and bless you for it. To favor your own petty inconveniences over the experience of a physical manifestation of a cosmic universal symbology? That is so charmingly *human*. I haven't had a laugh like that in some time, so as a reward I'm going to explain something to you, unworthy as you are. But first I have to ask *you* a question: didn't you think it just a little strange to be caught in the middle of a divine marital spat that supposedly happened millenia ago?"

Jack blinked again. Considering that the Hindu Goddess of Destruction had recently manifested in his tv set, anything "a little strange" had become hard to spot. Still, now that Shiva had mentioned it . . . "Yes. A bit strange."

"To understand this, Jack, you have to learn to think, not in terms of space and time, but in proper symbolic space, which is wholly without the vector of Time," Shiva said. "See, this didn't happen millenia ago. It's not going to happen in some distant future. It's not even happening *again*. The trick to it is that this is *always happening*. That's what it means to be a god and operate almost solely on the symbolic plane of perspective. Yes, in the mortal universe time passes; even the gods pay lip service to that notion while we're visiting, as I am now. But in terms of my relationship with Parvati? Doesn't apply."

Jack felt the remnants of his universe collapsing around him. "This goes on forever?"

Shiva grinned. "And here we are again. I know you're trying, but try harder: There is no 'forever,' Jack. There's only an eternal *now*. Get with the program, please, but first I want to ask you another question: why are you no longer with your wife?"

"I told you. After I lost those clients—"

"You lost your way. Yes, I know. Did your wife lose her way? Or did she just lose patience with *you* and need to get away? I'm guessing the latter. For what it's worth I'm going to give you some advice, not as a god, but as a male who has been married for, in human terms, quite some time—both halves of a couple need to be apart now and then. Gods and mortals alike. Parvati understands that, in her own way, though she's never going to indulge me overmuch and that's the truth. Do you know how we came to be together?"

Jack frowned. "Honestly, I don't think it ever occurred to me that gods would need a courtship. Doesn't it just . . . happen?"

Shiva smiled. "In symbolic perspective, that's not far wrong. But from my perspective as the husband of Divine Parvati? Hardly. In fact the whole matter was rather touch and go. You see, I'm an ascetic god by nature. Oh, it's true. I meditate on higher planes and deny the flesh and those are my favorite things to do. To be blunt, I wasn't interested in either physical or symbolic union, even to one as bright and beautiful as Parvati."

"So how did it happen?"

"Parvati defeated me."

Jack frowned. "In battle?"

Shiva shook his head and he smiled. "In love, Jack. She said: 'If this is the only way I can be a part of your life, My Lord, then let it be so.' She became an ascetic with me. She meditated on higher planes. She denied the flesh. Her flesh, my flesh, all of it. She shared my austerity, because she knew how much it meant to me. Well, to reveal a contradiction, after that I couldn't keep my hands off her. Still can't for long, come to that. So. Have you spoken to your wife lately?"

Jack sighed. "She's not my wife anymore."

"Funny how mortals are very seldom certain except of the things that bring them the most unhappiness. If I were you, I'd work on that. So. Are you ready?"

Jack blinked. "I don't understand. Ready for what?"

"For us to go meet Kali at your apartment, of course." Shiva sighed, and the leaves in the park, already turning fall colors, seemed to fall in sympathy. "I can't stay mad at her for long anyway, since I never have, will, or do. And you did make me laugh, Jack. Sometimes it's good to talk to someone who knows how to listen. Even for a god."

Jack wasn't sure what to expect when he unlocked the door and led Lord Shiva into his apartment, but he didn't have to wait long. In an instant there a small explosion, flying debris of what had been a rather shoddy coffee table, and the goddess Kali, looking every inch the Goddess of Destruction she was, appeared. She didn't say anything but, with surprising dexterity, kicked Shiva hard in a stomach.

"Oof!"

Shiva went down and landed on his back on Jack's threadbare green carpet. In an instant Kali was poised triumphantly on Shiva's chest, her taloned feet drawing rivulets of divine blood. Jack took a step forward before he even realized what he was doing, but then Shiva spoke, and Jack froze in his tracks.

"Give us a kiss, luv," Shiva said.

"'Give us a kiss' indeed!" snarled Kali. "After what you put us through? Your hide is mine now. Or were you hoping maybe Tara would be the one?"

"Tara would do the same and you know it," Shiva said calmly. Jack wondered how he was able to speak so clearly and easily with an angry Goddess of Destruction perched on his chest, but it didn't seem to bother Shiva a bit.

"Compassionate Tara trims her toenails," Kail pointed out. "I don't."

Shiva grinned. "Well. There is that. So. Aren't you going to thank the nice mortal for bringing me home?"

Now Kali turned her gaze on Jack and for a moment he thought his heart had stopped. "I won't break anything else of his," Kali said. "To expect more reward than that would be impertinent."

"Umm, are you all right?" Jack asked Shiva, but it was Kali who answered, and though at first Jack thought it must be his imagination, her voice had changed. She sounded almost . . . gentle.

"He's fine. We're all fine. Time to rejoin."

"Must I?" and that was Kali's voice as Jack had always known it.

"We always do," said the gentler voice. "We always are." And then the Goddess of Destruction, Kali called Eternal Night, sighed.

Kali changed. Her bulging eyes and lolling tongue now seemed less fierce, and then her face altered completely. Nine times in succession, Jack was certain, but he didn't have the presence of mind to count. When it was all done there was a beautiful young woman demurely straddling Shiva. That is, Jack called her beautiful for want of a better word.

Shiva smiled up at Jack. "You know all those supine figures in all the paintings of the Mahavidyas? The ones the goddesses are standing on? It's me, Jack, in every one. I mean, what choice did I have?"

"None, My Love. Same as always," the radiant woman said, smiling, and Jack thought his heart would break, because he knew she was leaving. She, and everyone she was. Parvati. Kali. Cindi. All of them. Now she did look at Jack.

"Thank you," she said, and then they were gone. No muss, no fuss, no explosions. Just . . . gone. After a while that might have been long or short—Jack was never really sure—he went looking for his broom again. While he cleaned up he thought about what had happened, because he could do little else.

Sometimes it's good to talk to someone who knows how to listen, Jack. Even for a god.

Despite divine gratitude, Jack wasn't sure that he'd really done anything. After all, symbolically speaking Shiva and Parvati were always together, and always separate, all at once and all the time.

Still, in this particular eternal 'now' they were together because of him. Perhaps that was nothing, but Jack was no longer sure, in symbolic terms or otherwise. The promise of that uncertainty was just enough to start him whistling as he worked to set his little corner of the universe back to rights.

A PINCH OF SALT

No matter what stories you've been told or what you'd like to believe, the fact is that a mermaid can never forsake the sea, at least not for very long. Forget the gills and the tail—there are ways around those obstacles. Usually those ways are of the magical sort, with conditions and taboos and other rot, but even that is beside the point.

Just think of human beings, whose blood is only distant kin to the ocean waves, measured in a pinch of salt. Consider how we yearn for the sea, travel on the sea, live by the sea, swim and splash in the sea, even feed off the sea like pups at the teat. Consider this, and think of a mermaid's bone and blood, solidified foam and the endless night of the abyss. Consider all of this, and you'll understand why the mermaid Aserea, after seventeen years of a very loving marriage to Jal the Fisherman, simply walked down to the beach one bright summer day, regrew her gills and fine, iridescent tail, and disappeared forever.

You must understand that Jal didn't do anything wrong. He didn't beat Aserea, or spy on her as she bathed, or any of the other conditions that had been placed on his happiness. He was kind and caring and Aserea loved him deeply. The problem was that Aserea was a mermaid, the sea called her back, and when she could no longer resist the summons, she obeyed. Leaving Jal to grieve and their sixteen year-old son, Makan, to rage.

"Why didn't you tell me that Mother was a mermaid before now?"

"What business was it of yours before now?" his father asked calmly enough, mending his nets to try and take his mind off his loss. That didn't help, of course. He'd been mending his nets on the very day he had first spied Aserea, washed up on shore and helpless after a storm. He'd saved her life and in her gratitude . . . well, that is old business and need not concern us here.

"What business? She was my mother!"

Jala worked his marlinespike deftly. "And you would have been born of a woman whether she was once a mermaid or not. Besides, your mother and I agreed that the fewer people in the village who knew of her origins, the better. She was here, and that was enough. Now that she isn't, you're entitled to know why."

For several moments Makan could do nothing but stare at his father who, all the while, continued to mend nets with a sort of brooding intensity that might have made Makan hesitate to say what he said next, if he'd been of clearer mind.

"Don't you feel anything? Don't you *care*?"

The marlinspike hesitated on a bit of cord, then resumed its work. "'Care,' the fool says . . . You try to spend every moment with the woman you love, year after year, knowing to the core of your soul that each and every moment might very well be the last and all your tomorrows come to be drowned in those depths. Try that, Son. Try it for one sodding day."

"Father—"

The bung had been pulled and Jala wasn't stopping now. "Pray, you who understand so much—what would you have done, knowing that your mother paid for every moment of your happiness with pain and longing? Would you ask her to stay? Would you tell her to go? Find the balance for me between one cruelty and the other, because your poor father never could. But you didn't have to, did you? Oh, no. You swam in the ocean and climbed the trees and hills and learned to notice and chase after the village girls, and never once—once!—suspected that perhaps, just perhaps, the world did not revolve around you."

"There must be something . . . " Makan began, but Jal stopped him.

"Nothing. Your mother is gone. Think of her as one dead if it helps. She'll probably do the same for us." He finished his repairs and tossed the heavy net to his son, almost knocking the young man into the sand. "I suspect that it's time for the yellowheads to be running off Snakepit Island. Take that net out and see if you can catch any."

"What are you going to do?" Makan asked, regarding the net with distaste.

"I'm going into town and I am going to get drunk. Feel free to do the same when you're older. It won't help, but you're my son and you'll probably do it anyway. If you mention your mother to me again in that tone you'd better be prepared to fight me."

"I won't, don't worry," Makan said, sullen.

His father sighed. "Don't promise what you can't fulfill," he said, looking wistfully out to sea. "That's why I didn't ask you to promise. Neither am I going to ask you to swear to what I'm going to ask now."

"What is it?"

"Aside from your thick skull you're basically a decent young man, and that being the case, sooner or later you're going to fall in love. It can't be helped. I only ask that you try not to fall in love with a mermaid. For both your sakes."

———◆———

Jal had been right about the yellowhead. They were schooling in large numbers and the surface of the water was nearly boiling with them. Makan was just about to cast his nets when he was startled by the sound of a woman singing. At least, he thought it was a woman. The voice sounded at once female and like nothing he had ever heard. The sound was enticing—it wanted something from him. Makan wasn't sure what that might be, but he wasn't really thinking about it.

"If the song is coming from Snakepit Island, then some poor woman has been stranded there and needs help. I had best look into it."

Makan reluctantly put his father's newly-mended net aside and steered his small craft closer. Snakepit Island wasn't a lot more than the tip of some submerged mountain. Its shores were steep and craggy and there were very few places to make landfall. Not that there was much reason to do so—there was little vegetation and what meager fresh water there was came in runoff down the central peak and varied considerably from year to year. The island was fit only as a rookery for seabirds and the colony of adders that had given the island its name. They had established themselves there somehow or other in the distant past, feeding mainly on the smaller birds and the occasional egg.

While the island itself was of little use, the waters around it were a favorite spawning ground and news of the yellowheads' presence would not be a secret for long. Makan knew he needed to make his catch and head home before the fishing grounds became too crowded to work easily. Still, he had to check on the singer first.

As he got closer to shore he finally saw her, perched up on the edge of one of the lower island cliffs, perhaps no more than ten feet above the crashing waves. The poor thing had apparently lost her clothes in the wreck and she was, so far as Makan could see, completely naked.

He lost sight of her for a while then which, he thought, was probably for the best. The approach to shore was difficult, even for one who knew the way, and Makan concentrated on keeping his skiff off the rocks as he steered it through a crevice in the side of the island and into a very small, sheltered bay. Makan tied up his boat carefully and climbed up through a crack in the rock that was the only exit out of the landing.

The woman was perched on the low cliff where he'd seen her last, her legs tucked beneath her as she sang. Her back was to him and Makan realized he had never seen so much bare female flesh in his life, including that of his mother and even the more adventurous village girls. For a moment all he could do was stare. Such was his preoccupation with the curve of her hip and the play of the light across her back that it was several seconds before he realized that she didn't have legs tucked beneath her. She had a tail.

"Mermaid!" he shouted.

The creature jumped almost a foot into the air and landed a bit awkwardly. She tried to scrabble back toward the edge of the cliff but in a moment Makan had taken two long steps forward and grabbed her wrists.

"Let me go, you oaf!" She tried to bite his hands but Makan pulled her wrists apart and held her at bay, her arms outstretched. It was difficult, though; she was much stronger than she looked.

Now that she was facing him Jakan noticed what he hadn't before—besides the obvious—that she was young. Probably, at least by appearances, no older than he was. And that she was very beautiful. Her hair was black and very long, and her eyes were a shade of green he was certain he had never seen before. It was hard not to stare at her, but he made the effort.

"I don't mean you any harm. I'll let you go after I've asked you a question. I just want to know if you've seen my mother."

The question seemed to startle the mermaid nearly as much as his sudden appearance did. She stopped struggling and looked at him more closely. "Your . . . mother?"

Makan nodded. "She's a mermaid, too."

"Oh. I guess that explains it."

"Explains what?"

She sighed. "Why you're not *dead*, of course. When I saw you coming I expected you to steer your craft onto the rocks off shore trying to reach me, and drown."

Now Makan frowned. "I admit you're very pretty, but why would I do something so foolish?"

She shrugged then. "Human men do it all the time. We're flattered, of course, but the drowning part seems rather self-defeating."

"It's your song. Mermaid songs drive fishermen and sailors to their doom. Everyone knows that. Since my mother was a mermaid, maybe it doesn't work on me." He hastened to add, when he saw just a little fire in her eyes, "I mean it was a very beautiful song. I just didn't feel inclined to kill myself over it."

She shrugged her small shoulders. "I'm not especially inclined to harm anyone. But I'm not going to stop singing."

"Even if people die?"

"Now and then our folk get tangled in your nets. Are you going to stop fishing?" she said.

"Fishing is how we live!"

"And singing is how *we* live. It's a peculiarity of our kind that we can't sing under water like the whales do, though our singing does carry under the waves; it's how we bedazzle the fish so that we can catch them. They're faster than we are. Or did you think we ate human flesh?"

"There were rumors," Makan said frankly. "But Mother never seemed inclined." He had to admit that the mermaid had a point about the singing, if what she said was true, and he rather believed it was.

"Please let me go. I've been out of the water a long time and I've used almost all of my breath singing."

"You still haven't answered my question—have you seen my mother? Do you know of her? Her name is Aserea."

The mermaid frowned. "It's a very large ocean and my people are very scattered. I'm sorry."

Makan sighed and released the mermaid's wrists. "Forgive me. I just miss her, that's all. I wanted to know that she's all right."

The mermaid looked suspicious. "You're actually letting me go?"

"I said I would."

She blushed slightly. "I know, but . . . ."

Makan just shrugged. "I'm sorry if I frightened you and I certainly don't blame you for doubting me. If our roles had been reversed I'd probably still be trying to bite you."

The mermaid smiled then. "If our roles had been reversed that would have been wise, but then when you looked into my eyes you would not see in me what I see in you. Farewell."

Makan thought of asking her to explain what she'd just said, but didn't wish to delay her longer. "May I ask your name before you go?"

"May I ask yours?" she returned.

"Makan. Mind my nets, as I'll be using them here later."

"Gaena. Warning taken."

"Pleased to meet you," Makan said, but Gaena had already dived into the sea, the splash of her leaving lost in the crash of waves against the island.

That evening Goblec the tavern keeper sent for Makan to come fetch his father, and Makan walked straight into the village and came back stooped over, the burden of his drunken father heavy on his back. He propped Jal against the wall of his room long enough to get the older man's boots off, then put him to bed.

Jal opened an eye. "What're you doin' at the tavern?"

"We're not at the tavern. We're home now. Go to sleep."

"I don't 'member walking home."

"You didn't. I carried you."

A faint smile from his father. "There's a good son."

"No more," Makan said. "You're done now. All right?"

Jal just yawned. "How was the fishing off Snakepit?"

"Good. I got a late start, but still managed to fill the boat. I was the first, so it fetched a good price."

"Why were you late?"

Makan thought about not telling his father, but didn't see much point. "There was a mermaid at Snakepit Island . . ." Jal was struggling to sit up, but Makan pressed him down gently. "It wasn't Mother. And I didn't fall in love with her, don't worry."

Jal looked relieved. "At least she didn't sing. Could have lost you, boy."

"She *was* singing. It didn't bother me. I mean, it was pleasant enough, but it didn't bother me."

"Then you're the first."

Makan shrugged. "I've got mer-blood in me, remember? We figure that's why."

"We? You *talked* to her?!" This time Jal did sit up, despite Makan's best efforts.

"Of course. I wanted to know about Mother. Gaena didn't know anything, though."

"Gaena. Heavens above . . . " Jal's manic energy seemed to desert him and his head fell back on the pillow. "You're either the bravest man I know or the stupidest."

Man. It was the first time his father had called him that. Not "young man," just "man." Makan wasn't entirely sure his father had meant that as a compliment.

"If you want to grieve for Mother still," Makan said. "Find a way other than Master Goblec's wares. We can't afford it and I'm not going to carry you home every night. You're heavy."

"Whatever you say, Son," Jal said, and drifted off to sleep.

⬦

The next day Jal drydocked the new boat he and Makan had spent so much time building together and began repairs on his former work boat, which he re-christened "Aserea." Considering the condition of the old hulk, Makan thought it rather an insult to his mother's memory even as he offered his help. This offer was cheerfully refused.

"You've got your own fishing to do. Since you're to inherit the *Windhorse* I don't want to add any more wear and tear to it; this old boat will be quite good enough for me in my declining years."

Makan sighed. "If you're in decline, then I'm a halibut. And I like the boat I'm using now. Stop this nonsense and take out the *Windhorse*."

Which was true enough. Makan had built his work boat himself, and while not as stable in rough seas as a larger craft, it was more than large enough for one person and all the fish he could manage. Jal insisted, however, and nothing else was said on the subject of mermaids or boats or, to be accurate, much of anything for the next several days as Jal made the old boat seaworthy.

The yellowhead were still schooling off the shores of Snakepit Island and both Makan and the once again sober Jal cast their nets alongside most of the rest of the fisherfolk of the village as long as the catch was good. Then, as suddenly as they had appeared, the fish vanished and the impromptu fishing fleet dispersed to wherever gossip or instinct took them. Some went east to the Turtle Isles. Others turned south to work the coast.

Makan lingered for a little while off Snakepit as he pondered what to do. He had just decided to sail north when he noticed a sinuous figure ride high up the cliffside on the ocean swell and then pull itself out of the water and climb up onto the ledge as nimbly as a snake. It was only when the figure turned and beckoned to him that he realized it was Gaena. He waved back and made his way to the island where the mermaid waited for him on the cliff.

"There are elders of our folk who have met nearly everyone, at one time or another. One knew your mother."

"You asked for me? That was very kind of you."

Gaena blushed slightly. "Well, it was no great difficulty. And it seemed important to you. I didn't learn very much, I'm afraid. Only that she had disappeared from our ken for some years; those who knew her suspected she'd died. Then she returned recently, only to vanish again."

"Vanish?" Makan felt a faint welling of hope. "You mean she might be returning?"

Gaena shook her head. "I mean she left this part of the ocean. She told her friend that she was going but not where. I gather that she said she never planned to return. I'm sorry."

Makan sighed and released the last of his stubborn hope like a butterfly that didn't wish to be free. "It's all right. I'm done being angry at her. She was wise to leave as long as there was the chance, even very slight, that she would meet my father again."

"Would that have been so terrible?"

"I don't know what it would have done to her," Makan said. "As for Father, I think it would have destroyed him."

Gaena seemed to consider this. "Sit down," she said, finally. "My neck's getting sore looking up at you."

"Oh, sorry." Makan found a flat place on the cliff's edge beside her and sat down. Gaena gave him an odd look.

"You actually did it. That's very trusting. It's not wise to be so trusting. You hardly know me."

Makan looked down at the sea, and the rocks, and conceded that, if Gaena wished him harm, this was the perfect spot to arrange it. "No, but I knew my mother."

"I'm not your mother," Gaena said primly.

"No, and I never saw my Mother in her true mermaid form, but I have to think she would have looked a lot like you. It's not just the tail, and not just the face, though she was beautiful, too."

Gaena rested her chin on her arms. "You shouldn't throw those words around so casually," she said. "Words have power. I hear that this word, spoken often enough, will make a human woman fall in love with you."

"I don't think I've ever made someone fall in love with me," Makan said. "And certainly not on purpose. Odd thing, though, but I think it is the women who don't really believe that they are beautiful are the ones who like to hear it the most. I wonder why, if they consider it a lie?"

"Very few women really believe that they're beautiful, deep down. Even the ones who know better," Gaena said. "So it's a nice sort of lie. No matter. Your flattery does not move me."

"It wasn't flattery," Makan said, frowning. "It was the truth."

She shrugged. "You believe in your own lie. All the more effective."

Makan scowled at Gaena for several long moments before it finally sank in that she was teasing him. He blushed.

"That was unkind," he said.

"Perhaps a little," she agreed. "I'm still mad at you about the song."

"Because I didn't die?"

"I said I didn't want to harm anyone and I meant it, and our songs are for the purpose I stated and no other. That doesn't mean that we're not a little pleased when human men risk death to reach us; I said as much before. Who wouldn't be?" She must have noticed the shocked look Makan gave her and she continued, defiant. "You seem to appreciate the truth, so I'm telling it. While the mirror and the comb legend is overblown, that doesn't mean we're without vanity."

Makan thought of many things to say, and thought better of each one until he was finally left with the one thing he did say: "We can meet here every three days and I can tell you how beautiful you are and how well you sing. Would that make up for it?"

"I don't know," Gaena said, looking thoughtful. "Perhaps we should try it for a while and see."

***

Several weeks later, instead of setting out at his usual early time, Makan's father was waiting for him at the docks. "You're going out today," Jal said.

Makan shrugged. "Aren't you? The weather is good."

"I mean you're going to Snakepit Island. Oh, yes. I know about that. Lokan passes there on his way west and he's seen you three times or more."

Makan shrugged again. "So? What business is that of his?"

"Or of yours?" Jal asked pointedly. "The fishing is poor there now and will be at least until fall. Or have you developed a sudden fondness for snakes?"

"I'm going to meet Gaena," Makan said. "I assume that's what you weren't asking me." He hadn't realized he was going to say it before he did, but he didn't regret the words once spoken.

"You're a fool," Jal said.

"Perhaps," Makan agreed.

"Perhaps? You know how this will end!"

Makan shook his head. "That's the thing, Father—I don't know how this will end. I don't know what this *is*, yet. I'm sorry, Father. I know you mean well and have my interests at heart, but whatever happens between myself and Gaena is something we're going to have to sort out for ourselves."

Makan braced himself for a fight, but there wasn't one. His father had simply sighed, called him a fool again, and mentioned that it wasn't Makan's fault, really, since the condition seemed to run in the family. He did ask that Makan pick up a length of rope that the chandler had set aside for him. Then Jal untied the *Aserea* from her moorings and sailed out of the small bay. After he'd run his father's errand, Makan followed.

It was a beautiful, clear day, with nothing but blue sky and a few wispy clouds visible. Makan steered toward Snakepit on a favorable wind. As he approached the island he saw another craft on the same course.

It was the *Aserea*.

"What is he . . . "

Gaena was singing. Her voice carried clearly over the water and, frankly, Makan didn't think she'd ever sounded better.

"Bloody hell!"

Makan's boat practically skipped across the water, but the *Aserea* was too far ahead. He'd never reach it in time. He shouted at his father to change course, but of course he didn't. He shouted at Gaena to stop singing, not certain if she would hear him or heed if she did. Jal was not half-mer; he was simply human, and Gaena's song would be irresistible.

Father's going to die. And there isn't a damn thing I can do about it.

The realization left him numb for a moment but quickly led to panic. He thought of trying to steer in front of his father's boat, but the *Aserea* was too far ahead. Perhaps he could get close enough to catch his father's boat from behind with a grapple . . . and then what? Have the *Aserea* pull him onto the rocks too?

If I drop my anchor as soon as the grapple hits . . .

Makan didn't really think it would work, but he had to try. He got the grapple ready. He was closing on the *Aserea*. Just a little more . . .

In the rush he almost didn't notice that Gaena had stopped singing. Now Makan could see his father clearly in the stern, his hand firm on the tiller. "Father! Turn starboard!" he shouted, almost giddy with relief. Without Gaena's song, there was still time—

The *Aserea* did not change course, and Makan never did get close enough to use the grapple. He threw it anyway, but missed the stern of his father's boat by several yards. In another few moments the *Aserea* broke its back on the rocks. Makan would have followed, but his grapple snagged on something and his own boat shuddered to a halt so quickly that Makan was thrown overboard just a few feet from the rocks. When he broke the surface again he saw the *Aserea* slipping beneath the waves and no sign of his father. The only other thing he saw was Gaena's lithe form, diving from the cliff into the sea before the waves pushed him against a rock and the world went dark.

⟨⟩

Makan regained consciousness to find Gaena leaning over him. "Not drowned?" she asked.

"No. Al—almost," he said. He spat out seawater and coughed. Gaena pounded his back until the fit passed.

"Oh, no. Father . . . !"

"He's right here," the mermaid said. "I don't think he's drowned, either. I pulled you both up but he hit his head too and he's not awake yet."

They lay side by side on top of the low cliff. All Makan could think at first was that Gaena was indeed much stronger than she looked. He turned to his father and confirmed that, yes, Jal was breathing. Makan slapped the older man's wrist until he opened his eyes.

"Makan?"

"I'm here, Father."

The older man coughed a few times and tried to sit up. "You saw . . . Your mermaid almost killed me!"

"I did see. She's not 'my' mermaid and she saved both our lives, you liar. You owe her an apology. We both owe her thanks."

"Liar? How dare you speak to your father that way!"

"How? Easily, when I consider what you just tried to do!"

Jal looked away. "I meant to try one more time to talk some sense into you, and then I got pulled in when she started singing, that's all."

Makan turned to Gaena. "Is that true?"

"I suppose," the mermaid said. "Once he set sail for my island, he must have heard me then."

Makan nodded. "Meaning he was too far away to hear your song until he deliberately steered toward the island. Father, you had plenty of time to reach the island before I did. You were waiting on me!"

Jal turned beet red, but Makan already knew it was the truth. Jal growled, "And what if I did? I had to show you what she is!"

"I know what she is, Father. So do you."

Gaena looked from one human male to the other, the frown on her face deepening by the moment. "It's rude to talk about someone in front of them, you know," she said.

"I'm sorry, Gaena. I think Father meant to kill himself and use your song as an excuse to do it."

"I meant to go look for your Mother," Makan said. "Even though I knew it was useless. Then I found out about you and this . . . person, and thought of a better way of throwing my life away. I figured at least this way maybe my death would bring you to your senses."

Makan shook his head. "You're no martyr, Father. This is about your pain, not mine."

"I didn't want you to make the same mistake." There were tears in the older man's eyes.

"Mistake? Father, look at me and tell the truth. If you had it to do all over again, when you found Mother helpless on the beach. Knowing now what you didn't know then? What would you do?"

"I—"

"What would you do?" Makan repeated, relentless.

Jal closed his eyes. "I'd have done the exact same thing. Heaven help me, but I am a fool."

"Why? Because you refuse to give up the happiest time of your life? If that's a fool I'll take a dozen. Why would you deny me a chance at what you had, even if, yes, it was only for a while?"

Jal looked like someone had punched him in the face. He finally put his face down in his hands. "I never meant . . . ."

"I know."

"Can you forgive me?"

"I'll think about it." Makan then turned to Gaena. "Gaena, do you love me?"

"Love you? I'm not even sure I like you at the moment. Between you and this crazy old man, I may never get any fish."

"I'll be sure to bring you some. Now answer my question."

She looked at him. "Suppose I say 'yes.' What then?"

"I don't know."

"Yes, you do. So does your father, and so do I. That's why I'm not going to say it. Neither are you. Promise?"

"I can't do that."

"I know," she said, and reached up and kissed him. It was a kiss that felt at once too brief and yet endless, and for a moment they both felt what the promise meant, and that word was loneliness. Gaena turned and dived headlong into the sea.

"I'll be here tomorrow," Makan said softly, but the sea made no answer.

A GARDEN IN HELL

"Tradition says there are anywhere from two to one hundred and thirty-six separate Hells, all of which are an illusion. Which is rather sad, considering the number of souls in torment there."

—**Dai Shi Johnson**

"This isn't happening, you know," the demon said to Hiroi just before the demon stabbed him. Hiroi didn't really mind. This was, after all, Hell. It was supposed to hurt. Hiroi screamed when the red-faced demon pulled the jagged blade out, since that hurt even more. In a moment the blood dried and the wound closed and it was time to do it all again. How long had he suffered? Hiroi wasn't certain. Besides, it was really difficult to concentrate when the lower half of one's body was on fire. Hiroi looked down at his burning limbs wistfully.

"I suppose this isn't real, either?" Hiroi asked.

Despite his calm, Hiroi's thoughts were racing. He didn't remember the demon ever speaking to him before. Hiroi forced himself to look at his tormentor. The demon was about eight feet tall, bright red with stubby yellow horns on its massive forehead, and it carried a club of iron which, oddly enough, it never used.

"No, but it is very depressing despite that," the demon said, sitting for a moment on broken stone and resting from its work of torment. "You hardly notice your punishments now. I do this for your own good, you know."

"It hardly seems like a favor when you run that great rusting blade through my chest."

"Another error," the demon said, and stabbed him again.

For some time after that Hiroi rather lost interest in the conversation, though later the demon's words would return to trouble him, even more than the fire or the jagged blade.

I do this for your own good.

It was nonsense, of course. The demon was toying with him with the same spirit and enthusiasm it used to drive its knife into him, that's all.

"Why are you telling me this? To what end? My karma brings me to Hell. There is no good or bad, it just is . . . to the extent that anything can be said to be. You don't exist, demon, but neither do I. My suffering may be an illusion but it feels real. If all must be illusion, then what one feels is all that matters; it is pointless to try to change anything."

"I'm telling you this because you need to hear it. As for the rest, all is not illusion," the demon said. "Who gave you such a notion?"

"Besides the holy writings? You did."

The demon shook his head, looking disgusted. "I said that *this* wasn't happening. I said that *I* wasn't real, and that's so. I didn't say that nothing was real."

"The scriptures—"

The demon waved one massively clawed hand in dismissal. "Yes, yes, I know all the words. 'Life is an illusion.' Hell is an illusion. Yet if *all* is illusion, then someone must be suffering that illusion. The only spirit great enough to contain all illusion is the Buddha. The Buddha has no illusions by definition. You see the contradiction?"

"Well . . . yes," Hiroi looked thoughtful, or at least as thoughtful as one could look with their nether regions on fire. "But if that's true, if my internal essence is real but you aren't and neither is Hell, then why can't I put an end to this torment?"

"Foolish question. It is your own need for correction that creates the Hell in which you now suffer in the first place. I'll go away when you don't need me anymore."

"In order to find the end, it would help to know where to start."

The demon sighed deeply. "I'm only a projection of your own necessity, but I can tell you this much: If you really want Hell to end, find out what, besides yourself, is real here. Pierce that much of the illusion on your own and maybe you will find the way out."

⊰━⊱

Nothing changed for some time. It was all very well for the demon to say that he should find what was real, but where was he to look? As far as the eye could see in all directions was nothing but smoking waste and desolation. What was the point of wandering anyway? Hiroi had tried to escape his tormentor, a few times in the early years, but that had never worked. Wherever he went, there was the demon, like his shadow. Which, if the demon was correct about its nature, made perfect sense. So where could he go now?

As was becoming his habit, he asked the demon this question, who merely shrugged. "Look anywhere you like. When your punishment is due I will find you, have no concern."

Hiroi sighed. "I wasn't concerned, believe me."

He walked away from that place then. That place which had been witness to his torment for years almost past counting. This wasn't like before, when he ran, frantic and fearful, through the wastes of Hell. This time he was not running. He was searching, though truth be told he hadn't the first clue of what he was searching for.

How will I know what is real when I see it?

The problem was that, illusion or not, *everything* looked real, smelled real, felt real. The black sand, the poisonous smokes and vapors, the bare, dead trees and brambles, the jagged rocks. Even the demon, whose objective existence the creature itself denied, always looked very real, and his blade certainly felt real enough. The flames burning him looked and felt real, though he had grown accustomed enough to them to function. Which, Hiroi belatedly realized, was about the same time the demon and its long knife had appeared in the first place. Hiroi just shrugged, guessing that, before then, the creature had been content to let him burn.

Or, perhaps, I was content to burn?

61

Hiroi realized as he walked that Hell was, not surprisingly, rather black. The trees were not only dead but burnt to charcoal from the heat. The dirt under his feet was closer in consistency to sand and that, too, was black. All this was more or less what he was used to, but Hiroi was trying to pay attention as he walked, on the theory that, if there was anything in Hell that he hadn't already seen, paying attention was the best way to spot it. As for the sand, Hiroi thought he'd seen black sand before, and had a sudden image of an ocean, but in another moment the memory seemed to blow away on the hot wind.

Hiroi soon learned that he was wrong when he thought himself and his demon were the only creatures in Hell. As he walked he encountered other sinners paired with their demons, but they took no notice of him. Hiroi, for his part, studied them as thoroughly as discretion allowed. The only real difference he noted had to do with where the sinner was burning. Some people's hands were burning. Others' eye sockets were flaming holes and yes, there were some like Hiroi who were burning from the waist down.

Punished for different things, I suppose.

He did wonder a bit that anyone could get used to burning eyes, but the sinners in question seemed to go about their suffering more or less oblivious to the pain, just as he did. All in all, there didn't seem anything unusual about any of that and, after a while, he tended to avoid them.

Hiroi kept walking. He walked for so long, in fact, that he was beginning to wonder why he hadn't seen his demon yet. Surely it was time for his next stabbing.

Delay means anticipation, and there's where fear comes in. Perhaps this is a new torture.

Hiroi was growing tired of walking across hot sand when he came to a valley. He stood on the edge of one of the surrounding ridges, looking down. For the most part it didn't look much different from the rest of Hell. There were a very few blackened trees, but mostly black rocks, and what looked like the same black sand as everywhere else.

Yet there *were* differences. The sand was fairly flat at the bottom of the valley; doubtless there was some lee there from the blasting hot wind everywhere else that whipped the sand into dunes and troughs that made walking difficult. The landscape of the valley wasn't just a little different—it was familiar. Again, it made him think of water, even though there was no water there. Try as he might, Hiroi could not grasp why that should be.

Perhaps a better look would help.

Hiroi trudged down the slope toward the valley's floor, where the heat was merely stifling rather than the blast furnace roar he was used to. Plus, once he reached the valley floor, the walking was much easier. He wouldn't go so far as to call the valley *better* so far as overall hellishness was concerned but it was definitely different. He stopped near a large round stone half buried in the sand and looked around. The more he looked the more convinced he was that he had seen something similar before. Yet the familiarity wasn't in the valley as much as it was in the arrangement of rocks and sand on the valley floor, shielded as it was from the high winds elsewhere. There was a hint of serenity about it that seemed so out of place there and yet was, somehow, appropriate. Yet he still didn't understand why it reminded him of the ocean.

Where have I seen this before?

The position of the larger rocks in front of him seemed familiar as well, but . . . wrong, somehow. He didn't know what was wrong with the arrangement of rocks and sand and debris, only that it wasn't quite *right*. Perhaps if he made a few changes? Hiroi smiled at the idea of changing Hell to suit him but, then again, why not? He decided to start with the stone beside him. It was very large and hard to move. Worse, of course, was that it was also very hot. He gasped, startled by the pain into dropping the stone. Hiroi blew on his blistered fingers, ruefully.

You'd think I'd be used to pain by now.

Granted, he wasn't as used to pain in his hands specifically as he was to pain elsewhere, and no doubt that was what startled him.

Hiroi shrugged. Nothing for it; he would simply have to get used to a new form of pain. He reached for the stone again.

"Would you mind telling me what you are doing?"

Hiroi looked up. A demon sat on top of heap of stones about twenty feet high, looking down on him. The demon's head and hands were all that he could see; the rest of the creature was covered with fine silks and brocades fit for a prince. The face and hands were a rich green. Hiroi frowned. "Who are you?"

"I am your demon," said the demon.

Hiroi shook his head. "My demon is red."

"Your demon *was* red," the demon corrected firmly. "For one who has no objective reality, changing appearance is child's play. Now I will be green."

"So why change?" Hiroi asked, but the demon just shrugged.

"Why does one do anything? Because one chooses. There are rationales and excuses and theories, but they all come down to this in the end."

Hiroi shrugged in turn. "That explains nothing and everything, including why I choose to move this stone." He took another grip on the rock. This time he was prepared for the burn and he did not drop his burden. He shifted it quickly and not very far, no more than three feet from its former position, then set it down again. The stone still formed a very rough triangle with two other large stones in the vicinity; all he had done was to change the angles slightly. He frowned.

That's closer . . .

To what? He did not know, but he could not shake the feeling of familiarity. If anything, with this one slight change that feeling had gotten much stronger.

"I didn't ask 'why,' " the demon said finally. "I asked *what*. What is the point of moving those stones? You have a purpose; I can tell."

Hiroi shrugged. "There's something about the arrangement of stones here; it seemed close to something I'd seen before. I thought perhaps, with adjustments, this might jog my memory."

"You really don't remember much of your life, do you?"

Hiroi studied the stones. "A few scattered bits, and an image or two. The ocean. A woman's face. Someone I knew, I think."

The demon considered this. "Clearly I am negligent in my duties."

"How so?"

"This is Hell. You're being punished. Where does the pointless arrangement of rocks in sand enter into this?"

Hiroi shrugged again. "If what you said before is true and you are simply a manifestation of my own need for correction, how can you do anything at all except exactly what you *should* be doing? And if *that* is so, then it follows that I am doing exactly what *I* should be doing, including taking that walk and arranging stones in sand. For whatever reason."

The demon raised an eyebrow. "That is an interesting point. Let us both assume for the moment that your argument has some validity. That still doesn't tell either of us what the true purpose of this activity is, or what end it will serve."

Hiroi sighed. "True enough."

"No matter. I have sorted it out. You could do the same, if you follow your premise to its natural conclusion."

"How so?"

"I am an illusion, your punishment is an illusion. What follows from this?"

Hiroi looked around. "Hell is also an illusion—we talked about this before. The fact this isn't real doesn't matter so long as it hurts and I can't make it go away."

The demon laughed at him. It was several moments before the creature could compose itself enough to speak again. "Oh, Hiroi. You're the *only* one who can make it go away. The Buddha himself cannot help you if you will not. Or do you expect the Goddess of Mercy herself, Kuan Shi Yin, to float down from the clouds and rescue you? No? Then you'll have to do it yourself."

"I don't know how."

"Then you are not ready. I will return when you are prepared to suffer in earnest."

Hiroi just stared at the creature. "I'm on fire. If this isn't suffering, I'd like to know what is."

"Good, because you will."

The demon left him then. It was only much later that Hiroi realized the creature had not stabbed him. Not even once.

———◆———

Hiroi wasn't certain how long it took to get the arrangement of stones correct, but he finally managed. He was sure of it. The stones matched perfectly with the image in his mind. Yet despite that, something wasn't right. Or rather, Hiroi realized, something was *missing*. He clambered up on the nearby hill of stones that the demon had used earlier and peered down at his handiwork.

Hiroi had first arranged the stones to his satisfaction and then set about removing all the other smaller stones and debris from the area. Now the three stones sat by themselves on a wide flat expanse of sand about thirty yards from the rocky hill. The image was evocative and, yes, captured that sense of familiarity that he had tried so hard to qualify since his first discovery of the valley. Yet it was still incomplete.

What's missing?

He tried beating his head against the rocks for a while as if that might jar the memory loose, but it did nothing except to start his head bleeding and make him dizzy. He tried to climb down from his perch and ended up tumbling down the slope, smashing his head and limbs against what seemed like every single stone in the pile before he finally came to rest, battered and bleeding, on the hot sand.

"That must have hurt. It seems you hardly need me at all when it comes to pain," said a familiar voice.

Hiroi opened his eyes. The green-faced demon sat on the top of the hill that he himself had just, somewhat hastily, descended. The effort of seeing was too much; he closed his eyes again.

"If that's true," Hiroi said when he got his breath back, "then why are you here?"

"To see if you're ready for your real punishment."

"My pain is great enough, I assure you."

"Don't assure me. I only do what I must, remember? The question is, will you do what you must? After all this time, I still don't think you grasp the implications of your situation here."

"I'm still dizzy from the fall and not inclined to debate you or solve riddles. Say what you mean."

"Hell is an illusion. Whose? Yours. So what else does that imply about Hell?"

"That everything in Hell is a projection of my need for punishment, including the other sinners. We talked about this, too. Frankly, I'm not convinced. Why would anyone do this to themselves?"

"Who else in all the universe cares about you so much?" the demon asked.

Hiroi frowned. "Well . . . that is a point. Yet if everything here is just an extension of myself . . . "

The demon smiled, showing very pointed teeth. Hiroi tried to remember if the creature had always had such teeth. He supposed so, though he wouldn't have sworn to it.

"You're beginning to understand, I believe. If everything here is an extension of yourself, then it follows everything you need for self knowledge is also here. Including your memory."

Hiroi's eyes opened again, and this time they stayed that way. "Where is it?"

"Weren't you paying attention? All around you, of course."

"All I see are stones."

"You remember the first stone you picked up? Touch it again. You needn't move it, just touch it."

"I touched that stone a thousand times!"

"As a stone," replied the demon, calmly. "Because that's all it was. Touch it now as a memory. That's all you need to do."

It was some time before Hiroi could move but, when he was able to crawl again, he drug himself over the hot sand to the first stone and placed his hand against it.

"Oh," he said, and that was all.

"What is it?" the demon asked, leering at him.

Hot tears were streaming down Hiroi's face. "Tofuku-ji. The rock garden at the temple, arranged to resemble . . . I thought I was remembering the ocean. I only got part of it . . . "

"Just three stones," the demon said, nodding. "Yet there was so much more, wasn't there? The way the small stones were raked to flow around the larger stones like the ocean around islands. Well, I don't suppose you can be blamed. The small pebbles were white, and all you have is black sand, some gravel and grit. No pebbles."

"It was so beautiful," Hiroi said. "How could I forget so much beauty?"

"Perhaps because you needed to forget. You can forget again, if you want. I recommend it. The memory of beauty lost is too painful, Hiroi. Even for Hell."

"Don't tell me what is too painful," he said, blinking through the tears.

The demon raised an eyebrow. "Oh? Is there a point to your meddling with the stones now? Knowing you will never recapture the beauty that inspired them? What you do will never be more than a crude mockery. Better to forget and get back to your slated punishment. It's less painful."

Hiroi's hands balled into fists. "I won't!"

The demon sighed. "Suit yourself. Embrace the torment, for all I care. Though I should point out there's a great deal more where that came from."

The demon went away again. First it was there, and then it wasn't. Hiroi slowly forced himself to his feet, though he was sure several bones were cracked. No matter; they would heal. The memory would not. He would not let it. He reached for another stone.

When the last stone was in place Hiroi turned his attention to the sand. He could not hope to duplicate either the texture or the color of the small white pebbles at Tofuku-ji; he resolved to work with what he had.

I need a rake.

There wasn't one to be had, of course. Hiroi walked some distance away to where one of the blackened trees had long since fallen and lay half-buried in the sand. It took some effort, but he managed to break off a branch that forked in just the right place. He then broke off shorter branches and used a piece of fractured obsidian to cut them to length and sharpen one end to form tines. Carving the baked dry wood was like carving stone, and he cut his hands as often as not, but whenever the damage was too great he simply waited to heal and then got back to work. Attaching the tines to the rake frame was even trickier, and he finally got around that by weaving strands of his own hair into twine to tie the tines onto the frame. When he was done he had a crude but very serviceable rake.

Hiroi immediately went to rake the sand. This went a little slower than he'd hoped since, beneath the surface, there were even more buried stones waiting to snag the tines of his rake. He spent more time digging for and removing these obstructions, at least a first, than he spent raking. Yet in time the sand around his garden stones was properly prepared and he got to work in earnest. Now and again the green-faced demon reappeared in its same perch atop the hill of stones and watched him work, but it didn't say anything. It seemed thoughtful, or at least that was the best interpretation Hiroi could make of the expression on the creature's tusked and fanged visage. For his own part, Hiroi was grateful to be able to work uninterrupted.

Finally the day came when he was finished, or at least Hiroi realized that he had done all he could do. He had not created a perfect replica of the garden at Tofuku-ji; that had not been possible from the start. And yet his creation was not without some beauty of its own. The black sand flowed in rivulets around the stones, which sat like islands in a dark sea. The feeling of motion and scale were both present, if imperfectly. Hiroi climbed the stone hill himself again to get the full effect.

"Is that the best you could do?" the demon, suddenly again manifest, asked.

"Yes," Hiroi said. "I believe it is."

The demon nodded. "Pity. It's not like the original at all."

"It is what it is," Hiroi said. "I rather like it."

"A feeling of accomplishment after hard work. Illusory. Ultimately pointless."

"No, that's not it," Hiroi said.

"Then what is?"

"I remember beauty. I can create it . . . in my own way. I feel—"

"Alive?" the creature asked, grinning.

"You mock me, demon."

"Certainly, and why not? You're dead, Hiroi. Rake the sand of all the Hells that ever were or will be and that fact does not change. You seek to connect again with the living world, and you cannot. Nor should you. Beauty is an illusion, and the lust for it doubly so. You made that mistake often enough. Will you repeat your error in Hell itself?"

"I did? You mean . . . I loved? Is this why I am burning now?"

The demon sighed gustily. "This your manifestation of error and therefore your Hell. You tell me."

"I can't. I don't remember any of it. And why is loving someone wrong?"

"Something about it was, or you wouldn't be here. And if you really want to remember, I promise it will cause you more pain than the memory of that silly rock garden. Still, you do have a choice, Hiroi, if I do not."

"I've chosen. Tell me how to remember."

"All you have to do is touch the second stone."

Hiroi had no doubt which of the first three stones the demon meant; it was the second one he'd adjusted in his first struggle to remember. "But in order to do that I would have to disturb the garden. I worked for such a long time."

"Yes. And to remember is to undo all you have done. Which is more important? To remember why you're here or to preserve a garden in Hell?"

"How can I know until it's too late?"

"Obviously you cannot. Hell is like that. But then, so is life."

Hiroi considered. "Well . . . I can always re-rake the sand."

He walked carefully over to the second stone and touched it. "Oh," he said, and that was all.

"Who was she?" the demon asked.

"Her name was Michiko," Hiroi said. "I lusted after her with thought both pure and impure. That's why I'm burning now. Interesting, I suppose, but it doesn't change anything."

"What do you remember?" the demon asked.

Hiroi just frowned. "I just told you."

"Her name? You already knew that you loved. Now you have a name and, one presumes, a face. Is that it?"

"Isn't that enough? Now I know why I burn here."

The demon laughed at him. "Hiroi, you don't know anything, and the worst of that is *why* you don't know anything. If that is the best you can do, then you will burn for a very long time and the Goddess of Mercy will never appear to fetch you from this place."

"Assuming she's not an illusion as well. If you really want to help, then do so! Help me. And don't say that you 'already are helping' or anything so uselessly cryptic."

The demon nodded. "Fair enough. I will help you by lessening your ignorance the slightest bit. I will tell you where you are."

"I am in Hell!"

"Yes, but which one?"

That stopped him. Hiroi was familiar with the concept of multiple Hells, appropriate to the sin of the sinner. Yet in his self-absorption he had never connected that to his own hell. It seemed more than enough to suffer.

"Where . . . where am I?"

"You are in the Hell reserved for inappropriate love. I've heard it called the Fire Jar Hell, but that seems rather plain considering the delicate irony of your plight."

"Delicate irony? My lust brought me here and keeps me here, and that seems straightforward enough. Where is the irony in this?"

"The irony is in what you still refuse to understand. You remember Michiko. You remember your lust. What, Hiroi, are you forgetting?'

"I-I don't know."

"Yes, you do. Somewhere inside that confusion you call a mind, you know very well."

"You're wrong!"

"Then prove it."

"How?"

The demon grinned again. If anything his teeth seemed longer and sharper now. "I'll tell you. First, remake your garden."

"I see. And then touch the third stone?"

"Yes."

"What if I just touch the stone now? I've already gotten footprints through the garden. Why fix it only to wreck it again?"

The demon shrugged. "Why seek an answer you don't want to hear?"

Hiroi sighed and reached for the rake.

Remaking the garden wasn't so easy as he thought it would be. There were more buried stones to clear away. Hiroi would have sworn by any power you'd care to name that he had gotten them all yet there they were, just beneath the surface of the hot sand, waiting to snarl the rake. The tines finally broke once and then again. He had replaced the tines three times and the handle twice before he was done, but once again the garden was complete, beautiful, and serene. Hiroi could almost smell the water of the ocean in the graceful spirals and swirls in the raked sand. The garden was nearly perfect. Better, even, than before. Hiroi leaned on his newly-made rake and admired the view.

I can leave it now. I don't have to know. The demon lied to torture me, that's all. I won't learn anything by touching the third stone, except that I'm a fool.

"Correct," said the demon. "You are a fool."

Hiroi looked up at the pile of stones beyond his garden and, sure enough, the green-faced demon perched there, smiling at him. "It's impolite to intrude on another's thoughts, demon."

"I am your thoughts, Hiroi. So. You've chosen to stay in Hell? Is that your wish?"

"I have no choice!"

"Of course you do. If you had no choice there would be no need for Hell, yours or anyone else's. Touch the stone, Hiroi."

"No."

"Then I will."

The demon got to its feet and slowly descended the pile of rock.

"What are you doing?"

"I thought I made that clear," the demon said. "I'm going to touch the stone. I'm going to take your most precious memory and lock it safely away so you need never be troubled by it again, you need never change, never know any existence other than Hell. In time you will forget what little has returned to you. Perhaps even your name, and Hell will seem Paradise because you know no other. That is what you want, isn't it?"

"You'll wreck my garden!"

"A small detail. You can make it again."

"No, I can't. It wouldn't be the same."

"It's always the same."

"I said no!"

Hiroi stepped between the demon and the garden and the demon grinned wider, though Hiroi had hardly thought this possible. "I must serve your wishes, Hiroi, even if you do not know them. That is my function here and I am capable of no other. Move aside."

"I will stop you—"

The demon swatted him aside. Hiroi scrabbled back from where he fell and threw his arms around the demon's knees. "I won't let you!"

"Why not?" the demon asked. "A garden in Hell is worthless."

"A garden in Hell is still a garden!"

The demon looked amused. "You do have a history of wanting the wrong things. Don't bother to deny it. Otherwise you would not be here."

The demon took one step and broke Hiroi's grip, as well as his right wrist. Hiroi grimly held on with his left hand as the demon dragged him toward the garden.

"Wait," Hiroi said.

The demon stopped. "'Wait' is not the same as 'stop,'" he said. "Why should I wait? You're not going to change, you're not going to learn, by your own choice. Best to have it done with for good and all and make Hell your home for eternity."

"Before you touch the stone, I want to know something," Hiroi said. "All this time you've claimed that this Hell is my own creation and all here serve my purpose, true?"

"True," said the demon.

"Lies," said Hiroi. "And I will prove it now."

The demon raised an eyebrow. "Oh? How will you do this?"

"Simple. If you are a manifestation of my will, then you know everything I know, correct?"

"I know more than you know, apparently."

Hiroi's grip faltered and he lay gasping on the hot black sand. "Your knowledge may or may not be greater and right now that's beside the point. It must be at least equal."

"So?"

"If you are what you say you are, you can tell me the name of Michiko's mother."

"Easily done: it's Yoritomo no Kiyuko."

Hiroi smiled. "Liar."

The demon frowned. "I assure you, that is her name."

"I'm sure it is. Only I never knew Michiko's mother's name! You didn't lie about her name, but everything else! You're nothing of me! This Hell is not my own! Admit it, you're real! Admit it!" He lay on his back, laughing in triumph.

The demon just smiled. "Look where we are, Hiroi."

Hiroi blinked back tears of laughter and looked. They were within the garden, Hiroi's outstretched left hand just inches away from the third stone.

"Oops," the demon said.

"Damn you! Now I'll have to do it all again!"

"I suppose so," the demon said. "Though it's already served its purpose—it got my attention. You don't need to make it again."

"I will do it," Hiroi said. "As long as it takes. You wrecked my garden but you haven't beaten me. I've beaten *you*." He was laughing again.

"I was never the one you needed to beat, Hiroi," the demon said. "Touch the stone."

"No." Hiroi was gasping for air now he was laughing so hard.

"The garden is wrecked. There's no reason not to. Unless, of course, there is a reason?"

"Because you want me to! And . . . and you're not me. The red-faced demon told me to search for the one real thing in this place, and all along it was him . . . well, you. You don't want what I want. 'Who else cares so much about you' indeed! No one!"

"Then defeat me one more time, Hiroi. Prove me wrong. Touch the stone."

Hiroi placed his hand on the third stone, and stopped laughing immediately. "Michiko . . . "

"I thought you already remembered her. Or was, perhaps, your memory incomplete? What do you know now that you did not know a moment ago?"

It was a long time before Hiroi could speak again. "Michiko did not love me," he said.

The demon nodded. "Your obsession was Michiko, but her obsession was love, and her idea of the perfect man. Which you were not. Yet because it served your purpose, you fed that obsession, pretended to be that something you were not. In the end she killed herself. That is your guilt, isn't it?"

It would have been easy enough to accept the demon's answer, but Hiroi truly remembered now, and fooling himself was not quite so simple as that. He finally took a deep breath and shook his head. "No. My guilt was far worse. I understood what she wanted . . . and then I forgot. I fell in love with her, but my love was never what she needed. Deep down I knew that."

"What did she need, Hiroi?"

"She needed someone to pull her away from the path she chose, not someone to lead her further down and feed her delusions. I died having failed her. That's the real reason I'm on fire now. That's why I'm burning . . . "

"Twice in one day, Hiroi. That's something of a record for you."

"Twice I . . . ? Twice what?"

"Twice you were right. You are right about why you burn. And yes, I admit it—I am real, at least in part. Though it wasn't your cleverness that found me out. You already knew and had known for some time; you just weren't ready to admit it, as with Michiko. Still . . . all things in their time."

Hiroi closed his eyes. "What is my punishment to be now? Have you thought of something better?"

"Much," the demon said cheerfully. "I'm throwing you out of Hell."

Hiroi sat up. For a moment he felt a shot of pain as he braced himself with his broken wrist, but in a moment the pain was gone as his wrist healed itself. "What are you talking about? That's beyond your power!"

"You want to stay? Perhaps tend your garden?"

Hiroi looked at the garden. Try as he might, he could no longer see the garden. It was just rocks on sand, and nothing more. "No," he said. "I'm done with the garden."

"Then Hell is done with you. Come with me."

The demon held out its hand. Hiroi hesitated.

"Michiko. Did . . . did she ever find what she needed?"

"The answer is 'no.' She's still trapped, still searching from rebirth to rebirth, over and over."

"Then how can I leave Hell? My failure remains, and no 'Goddess of Mercy' has come to fetch me."

"You can't leave Hell. Hell has left you."

Hiroi looked around. The black sand was gone. The fire was gone. Hiroi stood with the demon on a vast expanse of nothing. "Whatever Enlightenment is, I'm sure it's not this," he said.

"Certainly not," the demon said. "You're just ready for the next turn of the wheel, your next chance to put things right. Give Hell credit that it did that much for you and trust the rest to patience, Hiroi. Even a great fire cannot burn a forest all at once."

"When I return to the living world can . . . can I help Michiko?"

"Perhaps. If you can find her. Perhaps she will find *you*, when the time is right. Perhaps she already has, many times before."

"What if I fail again?"

The demon smiled. "Then Hell is waiting," it said. "Whenever you need it."

Hiroi took far more comfort in that fact than he thought perhaps he should. Yet before he forgot almost everything and his slate was wiped clean, Hiroi wished, for a moment, he had thought to ask the demon's name. It was a failure of courtesy, since the demon was real, after all. It must have had a name . . .

Just for an instant and, perhaps, for the first time in his life or death, Hiroi managed to see through the illusion, and what he saw was that the demon was not an "it."

It was a "she."

Oh, of course. How stupid of—

Hiroi forgot everything, save what really mattered.

THE TWA CORBIES, REVISITED

"In behint yon auld fail dyke, I wot there lies a new-slain knight; And naebody kens that he lies there, But his hawk, his hound, and lady fair."

—Traditional Ballad

Prince Malthan considered the tableau before him with more than professional interest. The knight's name was—that is to say it had been—Sir Gillan. He died bravely, which was no less than you'd expect for a knight errant bent on doing brave and dangerous deeds. Now his body lay in the grass by an ancient oak. His opponent, likewise departed, had left his own mortal coil some distance away. Dogs had been at it, possibly because his foe's armor was much more damaged than Sir Gillan's and therefore his body easier to reach. Sir Gillan hadn't been touched. Yet.

"I wager it was a lucky blow," Malthan said.

Malthan's friend Gurgash peered out from his side of the oak. Like Malthan, his eyes were large and dark, his teeth long and sharp. Like Malthan, he was a young ghoul. Handsome, as their kind went. And, also like Malthan, the sun hurt his eyes. No matter, it had been a slow week for death and the two were hungry. Hunger overruled the sun.

The two corbies who had arrived some time later croaked a protest from the branches of the oak above. Gurgash spared them one sour glance. "Oh, get off. Times are hard," he said, in the common language that even corbies understood. The two corbies did understand but merely glared back, not approaching but not leaving either. There was always the chance of leavings and corbies knew even more than ghouls about patience.

It was pure chance that Malthan and Gurgash had stumbled onto the feast; wars had been unusually scarce of late. The knights were all scattered around the land, searching for cups and whatnot. Human deaths had thus been reduced to isolated affairs, mostly old age and disease.

Lean times for the Kingdom of the Ghouls.

The noise of the duel had drawn the two ghouls just in time to witness the end. Malthan knew the knight's name solely from the way his Lady had wailed that name over his prostrate form until her servants had forcibly packed her away, claimed the two combatant's horses, and rode off. The ghouls had waited for a long time after to make sure they would not soon return; humans weren't supposed to know about them.

Gurgash glanced at Sir Gillan's body. "I wonder why they left the armor? I gather humans rather value it."

Looking at Sir Gillan's silvered plate edged in gold, Malthan rather valued it himself. "I suppose they were in a hurry. Something about reaching some castle before nightfall. Doubtless they'll return for it in the morning, or send someone."

"Another reason to get down to business," Gurgash said. "I do wish they had taken the time to remove it. It's rather in the way."

"Here, let me . . . "

Gurgash stared at his friend as the young ghoul set to work on the straps and fastenings. Malthan had the armor neatly stripped and set aside in just a few minutes. The hose and padded gambeson took even less time. Gurgash frowned. "How did you know how to do that?"

Malthan looked almost embarrassed. "Haven't you seen a tomb effigy before? They're pretty much accurate as to the specifics of armor."

Gurgash nodded. "And if I'd seen one a thousand times I wouldn't know how all the buckles and straps worked. You've been paying attention to the things, haven't you?"

Malthan just shrugged, and looked away. "What if I have?"

Gurgash shook his head. "I have known you all my life, Malthan, but I do not understand you. What is this interest in humans? Other than as meat for our bellies, I mean."

Malthan looked down at Sir Gillan's corpse. "I don't know. It just seems a shame, really."

In truth the blond, ringleted Sir Gillan could have posed for a statue even in his current state. His opponent's dying blow that slew the knight may indeed have been sheer luck—bad, for Sir Gillan—it had barely pierced the mail at his neck but pierce it had, and too close to an artery. Sir Gillan's padded gambeson was soaked with blood, although the armor itself was almost spotless.

"I know," Gurgash said. "By rights this meat should age properly for a week or so, but if we carry it back to the necropolis we won't get any at all."

"That's not what I meant," Malthan said.

Gurgash looked up from Sir Gillan's arm, which he had just begun to gnaw. "I know. I was being polite and not mentioning that. I was hoping you'd do the same. Are you going to eat or not?"

Malthan sighed, then reluctantly reached out for the gobbet Gurgash offered. He was awfully hungry.

Later, when Gurgash was sleeping off his meal peacefully in the shelter of a nearby cave, Malthan slipped back out into the welcoming darkness and made his way back to the oak. Some nocturnal creatures with bright red eyes had found the remnants of the corpse and were busy scavenging what meat Malthan and Gurgash had left. Malthan paid them no heed. He very carefully gathered up the pieces of Sir Gillan's armor and crept away. It was only near morning when he rejoined his friend, still fast asleep, in the cave.

<hr />

For several moments, Gurgash just stared. "What, by all the Cold Stones of Caldun, are you doing?!"

Malthan, for a moment, could only look as guilty as he felt for several long moments, then thought of something. "Reconnoitering."

Malthan lay under the bushes on a high hill, overlooking the drilling fields of a local guard tower. Two men-at-arms took turns swinging blunted swords at each other; further away a score of archers practiced on a straw opponent.

Gurgash crouched beside his friend. "Malthan, when did you develop the delusion that you're talking to a fool?"

Malthan sighed. "All right, I was spying on the humans. So?"

Gurgash shrugged. "It rather depends on *why* you were spying on them. A sensible ghoul might be looking for signs of impending conflict. We compete with the vultures and corbies more effectively if we find a battlefield first."

Malthan turned his attention back to the practice, particularly the shield-work of the smaller man. *He's quite good.* "Yes," was all he said.

"But it's not why you're watching them, is it?"

Malthan thought about it. "I don't know," he said.

Gurgash nodded. "That's truth, if I've ever heard such. You're frightening me, My Prince."

Malthan groaned. 'My Prince' could only mean one thing. "Father wants me, doesn't he?"

"Yes. As the only son of the King of the Ghouls, you have duties."

"Meaning that carrion has been found and he wants me to help back up his claim to First Portion. That's what being 'King of the Ghouls' really means: the most vicious and brutal of the lot!"

Gurgash sighed. "I wager it means something similar among the humans. Shall we go?"

Malthan hesitated. "You're not going to tell him where you found me, are you?"

Gurgash shuddered. "Certainly not."

Malthan followed Gurgash away from the hilltop, but his thoughts were elsewhere. There would probably be a fight coming back at the Necropolis. Shield technique wouldn't be much use to him there, but some of the footwork looked interesting; he'd have to try it.

Malthan blinked, realizing they were passing under the oak where

Sir Gillan had died. The two corbies glared down at them from the limbs as if they had never left, though Malthan doubted there was so much as a scrap of Sir Gillan left now; even the bones were gone. Malthan wondered if the knight's lady had come to claim them; more likely wild animals and dogs had carried them away. Still, one could dream.

⸺◆⸺

Malthan stood at the entrance to his father's tomb, watching the sunrise. The bones of the original owners lay quietly in their stone coffins, or arrayed tastefully in their niches on each wall; there hadn't been anything left of them to concern a hungry ghoul in some time. At the far side of the mausoleum Malthan could see the patch of blackness that served as a doorway for the tomb's current owners. Across the hilly necropolis rose other tombs and barrows apparently left just as they were when the village in the valley below had been abandoned years before.

Below the surface, of course, things were very different. Others of his kind lay claim to the ground below, sleeping snuggled into the buried vaults and tombs, making their way like moles through the earth. Malthan should have been asleep, too. Foraging had improved slightly due to a nearby border dispute; now there was nothing to concern a proper ghoul during daylight hours but rest and dreams of charnel houses yet untapped.

Malthan wasn't the least bit sleepy.

The underground ways were narrow and, at the moment, hard to pass without disturbing the sleepers. Malthan looked carefully about and then slipped out into the morning sun. He carried his offering in a small cloth bag.

He ran upright and not bent close to the earth in the shambling gait common among the ghouls. It wasn't such an unusual thing, he told himself once more. There was nothing shameful in walking and running upright when he had a mind to; any ghoul could. Yet

82

with so much time spent underground it wasn't a skill many of his kind practiced often. Malthan had, as well as other skills even less appreciated among ghoul kind.

Malthan was outside the Necropolis proper now, standing at the gaping hole that had once been the doorway to the village church. Looters had smashed it in years ago, once fear of the plague had subsided somewhat. Inside the church it was dark and quiet, even after sunrise. A prime location, forbidden even to the King of the Ghouls. But then, kings among the ghouls were a late addition. The Ancient had been around much, much longer.

"Honored one, I must speak with you."

"Honor among the ghouls? What a notion."

What had at first appeared to be a greasy bundle of rags near the vestry stirred, and a pair of yellowed eyes opened in the gloom. The Ancient wasn't asleep, any more than Malthan was. He didn't sleep at all, if the stories were true. Malthan doubted that; surely the Ancient slept but not, it was clear, very much. His face was ugly even by ghoul standards, scarred and wrinkled. Most of his nose was gone but he still had all of his teeth.

Malthan held out his bundle. "I've brought a gift."

"Food? Yes, of course. What else has value?"

"Your wisdom, Ancient," Malthan said, and the withered ghoul laughed at him.

"Your manners are terrible. That is to say, they are excellent. Which in a ghoul *is* terrible. You are confused, young one."

"I know." Malthan tossed the bag at the Ancient's head.

The Ancient snatched it out the air, faster than Malthan would have thought possible. "Better. Or at least appropriate." He sniffed the aroma of decay appreciatively, then ripped the cloth aside to reveal the prize.

"A whole arm, by the Cold Stones . . . " The Ancient took an experimental bite and chewed, then closed his eyes in contentment as he swallowed. "Aged to perfection. You must want something very badly."

"I want to know what it means to be a ghoul."

The Ancient looked up from his meal. "As opposed to what? You are a ghoul. You eat decaying flesh. That is our way, now."

"Now? You mean we have not always done so?"

The Ancient grunted. "Of course not. We used to be human."

For several long moments Malthan just stared. "What . . . what did you say?"

"You're not deaf, nor am I inclined to waste my breath repeating things I've already said. I've more respect for my time than that."

Malthan shook his head. "Pardon, Ancient. I was just surprised."

"A capacity for surprise is a human trait. We still share it, for all that we are not human now."

"But what happened?"

"Time and circumstance. Take for example, this village where we now reside. Suppose not all had died? What would the survivors have eaten, with the food supplies spoiled and everyone too weakened to hunt or forage?"

"That would have been a great sin in their eyes . . . or so I am given to understand," Malthan added hastily. "But it would have made them cannibals, not ghouls."

"As long as the meat was fresh," the Ancient conceded. "But does it remain that way? No it does not. Hunger compels, even as the corpse ripens. Now imagine what those who survived were forced to do. Now imagine how their tastes must change to allow that survival. Fewer still by now, I would think. Now they no longer tolerate rotted flesh; they crave it. See the difference?"

Malthan nodded, reluctantly.

The Ancient yawned, and continued. "It didn't happen all at once, but there have been plagues enough over the years. Many years, many centuries. Our kind has been around for a very long time. Never so many of us to outstrip supply, or to be that easy to find. Our rarity has served us well, just as the fecundity of the humans serves them . . . and by extension, us. We kept human speech because it was useful. We kept memory, since experience teaches us what we need to know, just as I teach you. The rest . . . " The Ancient dismissed it with a wave of his taloned hand.

"This is why cannibalism is a sin among the ghouls, as well, isn't it? One of our few."

The Ancient smiled then. "Thus demonstrating the value of memory, even among the ghouls. Yes, to eat another ghoul, even one dead for a week, is a shameful thing. Mostly because we know better than most where such things may lead."

"The humans fascinate me, Ancient," Malthan said. He hurried the words out; it sounded like a confession.

The Ancient wasn't impressed. "Not terribly unusual. I went through such a time myself, long ago. It should pass."

"But . . . what if I cannot be content as a ghoul?"

"Then you are going to be very unhappy. You're a ghoul, young one. Your face marks you. Your strength—remarkable even by our standards, I'm told—marks you. If that weren't enough, your *scent* marks you. You can not be human again, if that's what you're thinking. Now go away; I hunger and the scent of your gift is making me giddy."

Malthan almost smiled at the thought of the Ancient being giddy about anything, but he could not quite bring himself to do it.

⚊⬧⚊

Malthan made his preparations as best he could. He went off into the woods alone; he told no one, not even Gurgash. For five days he bathed in a cold water stream morning and evening and, though the taste and texture disgusted him, ate nothing but apples and berries. He couldn't keep the fruit down the first few times, but after the second day it got easier. He let nature do its work and by the fifth day he was of the opinion that he didn't smell too much like carrion, or at least he didn't smell the same. On the other hand his breath, despite the change of diet, was slower to give up that mark of ghouldom. Malthan started chewing wild mint on the fourth day and, by the fifth, realized it was probably as good as it was going to get.

Malthan took Sir Gillan's armor from its hiding place and laid it out on the oiled cloth he'd kept it wrapped in. There was very little rust, he noted with satisfaction, and the straps on the few pieces of plate were still supple. He started with the washed but still blood-stained gambeson and worked his way outward to the mailshirt.

I'm beginning to see why knights have servants.

It was a bit tricky, but he did manage the small breastplate and elbow and knee guards without assistance. He had seen what were apparently more prosperous knights with even heavier, more complete plate than Sir Gillan had worn, and Malthan wondered how they ever managed. He thought perhaps it had something to do with the fact that they were always on horseback, and didn't have to carry it all.

Malthan had no mount, and wasn't likely to get one; Ghouls were not noted for their horsemanship. Still, it amused Malthan to think he might one day learn. As a last touch he put on the surcoat and belted on his sword. He studied the effect in a nearby pool.

This will never work.

Oh, the armor fit well enough, chain mail being rather forgiving and Sir Gillan being no small man to start with. The surcoat wouldn't give Malthan away, since Sir Gillan had followed the current custom of knight-errants and wore a blank surcoat and carried a blank shield, so there was nothing to identify Malthan as someone he was not and possibly bring unwanted attention and questions. No, the problem was—and as he knew it would be—his face. There was just no getting past the fact that a ghoul in human armor was still nothing but a ghoul.

Unless . . .

There was one piece of armor left, one that Sir Gillan hadn't even put on until the time came for his final battle. Malthan unwrapped Sir Gillan's helm. It was a heavy thing of thick steel, but it covered the entire face, leaving only slits for the eyes and a series of holes around the mouth area. Malthan lowed the helmet onto his head, buckled the strap, and gazed back into the pool.

For a second he thought Sir Gillan had come back to life. With the helmet on, it was impossible to tell the size of Malthan's eyes, the pointed teeth, the squat nose. It was the perfect disguise and much more comfortable than the humans apparently found it, else why not wear it all the time? Malthan rather liked it, but then he was used to tight, confined places with bad air. Wearing Sir Gillan's helmet was almost like coming home. As a bonus, the eye slits cut down on the sun's glare.

Malthan smiled. *Now what?*

The sensible thing, Malthan knew, would be to take the armor off, bury it in a deep hole, and go hunting carrion with Gurgash. Malthan of did no such thing. He walked off into the woods, whistling as well as his long teeth allowed.

⊰⊱

"You shall not pass!"

The person speaking to Malthan was a human knight dressed in bright green trappings and standing on the far side of a rather nondescript stone bridge along the woodland path.

Malthan stopped, more from surprise than anything else. "Why not?" He started to add, "Is it because I'm a ghoul?" but he managed to stop himself.

The knight drew himself up to his full height, which was only a little shorter than Malthan himself. "I have sworn that I shall let none pass this bridge unless they first defeat me in combat."

Malthan thought about this for a moment. "Why?" he asked. It was more than strange. Malthan had considered himself something of a student of human behavior, and was a little chagrined to be baffled so early on.

The knight just stared for a moment. "Are you simple, Sirrah? A true knight would have accepted my challenge on the spot."

Challenge. That was something Malthan understood. "Well," Malthan said, "I am a true knight, so I of course accept. You startled me, that's all. I didn't expect to find another knight in these woods."

"We are not very thick on the ground here," the knight conceded. "I've met only one other such in a fortnight."

"Did you challenge him, too?" Malthan asked.

"Of course I did!" The stranger nodded at a nearby tree, where hung a rather nice set of armor. Malthan sniffed the air but it was clear there was no body in it, just empty armor. Malthan wasn't sure what this meant, but now his caution had overcome his curiosity, and he didn't ask. The stranger's suspicions were nearly aroused as it was.

"As challenged, you have your choice of weapons." The knight looked Malthan up and down, and sniffed. "I assume it will not be a passage of lances. What happened to your mount?"

"Died, poor beast." Malthan said, quickly. "Sword and shield will have to do." In truth, those were the only weapons Malthan had.

"So be it."

The stranger took up his own shield, magnificently painted with a green phoenix on a silver background, and drew his sword. He took a stance at the center of the bridge and waited. Malthan drew his own sword and, his mind full of the things he had seen on the human's practice field, went to meet him.

The fight got off to a slow start. The stranger seemed to be testing him at first. Throwing blows with little force behind them, quick but not very dangerous. Malthan was quick with the shield; the weight of it was next to nothing, so far as Malthan was concerned. He had studied the way the men-at-arms used it to counter blows and knew roughly what to do, though he knew it could not be so simple as it seemed at first.

He's testing to see what I will do. What if I don't do anything?

Malthan had his answer soon enough. The timing of the stranger's attacks changed, his stance changed; he seemed to lean back slightly so as to present a less upright target, and his sword blows became more forceful. Plus, where before there had been single blows, now they were coming swift combinations, and it was all Malthan could do to keep himself covered. Soon the stranger aimed a high blow that forced Malthan to raise his shield, blinding him for just an instant, and the stranger immediately changed direction on the blow and brought the sword edge down. Malthan stepped back instinctively but was still stung by the stranger's sword tip across his thigh. A few moments later the stranger did it again.

That hurt!

Malthan glanced down. The mail across his thigh was torn in two places, and a patch of blood had appeared. Malthan thought it was perhaps time to give the stranger something to occupy him *other* than the best way to kill Malthan. The ghoul knight snapped a blow right at the stranger's head. He countered easily but the force of it sent him staggering back a step.

"Well struck, Sir," said the stranger, grudgingly.

"And you," Malthan answer, trying to find the politeness that the Ancient had so recently accused him of. He realized that a little time watching a fight was not the same as being *in* one. He knew how to fight as a ghoul would, indeed he was very good at it, but he was unsure how to apply that here. Malthan was at a disadvantage, and the next glancing blow, this time on his arm, just emphasized this.

The stranger's blows were painful, and Malthan had seen enough of battles to know what a really well-landed blow would do to flesh, even tough ghoul flesh. His breath came a little faster but, even though Malthan knew he should be at least a little afraid, he was not. He had a more immediate concern.

This is silly. He's going to ruin Sir Gillan's armor at this rate.

The stranger pressed closer, seeking an ending and Malthan, feeling the pressure, reacted. He punched his shield hard against the stranger's, thinking only to push him away and give himself some space. Malthan was a little surprised when the stranger was lifted bodily off the ground to fly through the air and land several paces beyond the bridge, flat on his back. He didn't move for several moments, clearly stunned, and when he did move it was a vain attempt to rise. Malthan reddened slightly, unseen behind his visor, worried perhaps that he'd violated some unwritten rule of combat, until he remembered.

I've seen them use the shield to strike before. It's not against the rules.

Actually, as he thought about it, in a skirmish very little seemed against the rules. This was a more formal combat, though, and Malthan still had to worry. He thought perhaps he should apologize.

"Are you hurt, Sir?" he asked. The stranger just twitched, gasping hard for breath. Malthan sighed and stepped over the bridge. His opponent was clearly going to need a hand up.

Apparently his opponent misunderstood his intent, since he immediately released his sword, up till now still gripped tightly, and spread his hands, gasping, "I yield, Sir."

Malthan stopped. "That means I'm not supposed to kill you, yes?"

The stranger just stared at him for several long moments, and Malthan added. "Of course it does. A poor jest. I accept your . . . your yielding."

He reached down and grasped the stranger's hand, pulling him upright. For a moment he had to hold him there, until the stranger managed to find his breath and his footing again.

"Well . . . well fought, Sir. I haven't met my match in some time."

The knight reached up, unbuckled the strap on his helmet and pulled it off. He took several deep breaths while Malthan studied him impassively. The stranger was certainly no Sir Gillan: his teeth were crooked and his hair was dark and unruly. Yet he did have the advantage of still being alive.

The man frowned. "Why don't you remove your helmet? I'd like to see the face of the man who bested me."

"Ummm . . . I cannot."

"Cannot? Why is that? Have you taken a vow?"

Malthan latched onto the straw the man had given him. "Yes, that's it exactly. I've taken a vow . . . " Malthan thought quickly, then added, "not to show my face to any human being . . . until I've returned home after doing deeds worthy of renown."

The stranger nodded approvingly. "A worthy vow indeed. May I not at least know your name?"

"Certainly. It's Mal—" Malthan stopped himself. He wasn't sure how well ghoulish names mixed with human and quickly thought of another. "Malthus," he said finally. "Malthus of Darktomb . . . it's rather far from here; you wouldn't have heard of it."

"I wager I might, if it produces more like you. I'm Sir Dald of Westshire." The knight held out his hand and Malthan grasped it, carefully, so as not to break any bones.

Sir Dald started to remove his armor. "As the victor, you now have the spoils. My armor and mount belongs to you, as I do not have the means to ransom it just yet."

"Thank you, but I have all the armor I need just now, and no way to carry it."

"You'll have my horse," Dald said, frowning.

Malthan didn't really want the beast, but couldn't think of a polite way to decline and decided to change the subject. He nodded at the empty armor hanging from the tree. "Who was the knight you bested? I wager it was a fine fight."

Dald smiled. "And so it was; it was a near thing I admit. Still, I did rather hate to send the poor fellow off without his armor, and his lady now devoid of proper protection."

Malthan blinked. "You mean you took their things and sent them off into the woods alone?"

"Certainly not," said Sir Dald, a little affronted. "I let the lady keep her mount, of course. Having bested her champion, I would have offered to escort her myself, save for my vow."

"You couldn't leave the bridge. I understand," said Malthan, though in truth he wasn't sure if he did understand. It was the knight's silly vow to hold the bridge that had put the lady in peril in the first place. It occurred to Malthan that this 'honor' business that knights were so fond of was not as simple thing as it appeared. "I'll make a deal with you: give me the mount and armor you took from the lady's knight, and you may keep your own."

"Well . . . as you have bested me I don't see how I can refuse you. But why that horse and armor and not my own? Mine is better."

"I'm sure of that," Malthan said, though the armor seemed identical and, except for coloring and size, one horse looked pretty much like another to him. "But it's a whim of mine. And, since you did win this horse and armor in combat and they were thus yours, you could say I'm taking your armor and horse now. Isn't that what the custom dictates?"

Sir Dald couldn't see any flaw in that logic, so he helped Malthan bundle up the spare armor and secured it to the unknown knight's big dun warhorse. Dald waited expectantly when all was done, holding the reins, and after a moment Malthan had the horrible feeling that he knew what was expected.

He assumes I'm going to ride that thing.

Malthan felt a moment's panic which he quickly suppressed. He reached out for the reins, not knowing what else to do, and the horse shied away. Dald may have been fooled, but clearly the horse was not. The beast knew what Malthan was and was plainly terrified. Fortunately Dald had a good grip on the reins and the horse didn't bolt. Malthan quickly reached out and took the reins and pulled the horse's head forward. He appeared to be soothing the beast as he stroked its neck, but in reality he just wanted to lean close to whisper a few words of the common tongue in the beast's ear.

"Behave yourself or I'll break every bone in your worthless carcass."

All animals understood the common tongue—as did all ghouls, who were beasts themselves by all practical definition—but very few spoke it. Horses, being rather stupid creatures, were not among that number. Yet they did understand it well enough, and after hearing what Malthan said the beast appeared much more docile, and Sir Dald nodded approval. "You do have a way with horses."

So it seemed. The beast didn't so much as twitch as Malthan slowly mounted. He'd seen the process numerous times; he even managed to pick the correct side. When he was safely in the saddle he bid Sir Dald goodbye.

92

"And to you, Sir Knight. May you find the great adventure you desire."

Just then Malthan considered figuring out the mechanics of horsemanship to be a great deed, or at least one far beyond his ken, but fortunately the horse seemed to understand what was expected of it. It broke into a brisk walk and continued down the only trail. Sir Dald and the contested bridge were soon far out of sight. As soon as Malthan felt it prudent, he dismounted.

"I'm just going to return you to your owner," he said to the shivering animal. "Run away and the wolves in this wood will get you, and if they don't, *I* will. Do we understand one another?" The horse nodded once and made no attempt to flee, even after Malthan tied the reins loosely to the saddle. It just followed a few paces behind Malthan, looking downcast, as the young ghoul followed the forest path.

Malthan kept to the trail partly because he knew the humans would, but mostly because his own senses told him it was the correct way. A ghoul's sense of smell was almost as fine-tuned as a hound's, useful for tracking its dinner, and in the tangle of scents along the trail two spoors stood out. One smelled of sweat and just a hint of blood; doubtless Sir Dald's defeated challenger. The other scent was . . . strange. Like flowers but clearly attached to a person, and Malthan started wondering what the owner looked like. Malthan had seen human women before, of course, but usually not at their best and certainly not smelling of lilacs. The scent was intriguing and made him want to sneeze all at the same time.

Malthan snapped out of his reverie; there was a new scent, a familiar scent, on the trail now, and it was very strong.

"Hello, Malthan," said Gurgash. "Do you have any idea how silly you look?"

His friend was leaning against an oak tree in plain sight. He looked at Malthan with expressions ranging from bewilderment, consternation, and amusement. Malthan wondered if such a vigorous workout was tiring for Gurgash's facial muscles; ghouls weren't given to emotionalism as a rule.

"Silly? In this armor I look just like a human; indeed, I passed for one just now!"

Gurgash sighed deeply. "I know, and that's what I meant. You've been too preoccupied to even notice, but I've been watching you for the last few days and following you for the past several hours. I'm trying to understand what you think you're doing. I even, after much struggle, worked out a sensible theory; would you care to hear it?"

"If you'd care to tell me."

"Knights challenge each other all the time; they kill each other as often as not. Disguised as a human knight, you could do the same . . . and make carrion for us, your father's subjects. *There's* a noble cause, a worthy cause, and so brilliant in concept I was quite awestruck. But what did you do? You defeated a human and let him live! So much for my theory."

"Gurgash . . . " Malthan's voice trailed off.

"Gurgash, what? Weren't you going to explain? *Can* you explain? I hope so, because I would really like to know the answer."

"So would I," Malthan said, finally.

Gurgash just closed his eyes. "Malthan, take that silly armor off and come with me now. There's something dead in the woods; let's go find it together and forget all this human nonsense."

"I can't, Gurgash. I'm not human; I know that and you know that. But I've never been happy as a ghoul. Maybe this will make me appreciate my ghouldom; I don't know. I'm still working that bit out, but I had to try . . . well, something. Anything."

"What makes you think you can be more than what you are?" Gurgash sighed. "When you come to your senses, I'll be around." Gurgash slipped off into the trees. Malthan watched him go, feeling sad for no reason he could think of. Then he remembered something Gurgash had said.

There is something dead in the woods.

Malthan hurried down the trail.

It was the lady's champion. Malthan had no doubt of it, for all that he asked and the dun warhorse's nod confirmed it; the man was his former master. His gambeson still bore the traces of his armor's straps, and the scent of the trail was still on him. The smell was changing, though. Blood now, but soon it would speak of nothing but death and decay.

What happened?

There were wolves about; Malthan smelled them. He was in danger now himself; the enmity between ghouls and wolves was longstanding, but he knew they would not attack until their numbers were better. Now and then he caught glimpses of movement in the trees and knew they had been drawn by the scent of blood, but only after the fact. The man hadn't been killed by wolves or any other animal.

The body lay half sitting, half reclining against an elm no more than six paces from the trail, the limbs composed, the hands folded on the corpse's lap. A small dagger lay nearby. Malthan read the signs and came to only one conclusion.

He killed himself.

Such a notion was hard to get a grasp on; Malthan had heard rumors of humans and suicide but it was almost beyond comprehension. What reason for departing this life early, with no promise of another? Ghouls didn't live very long as a rule, the Ancient notwithstanding. As for despair, well, among ghouls it was pretty much a missing emotion. In his own curious longings Malthan almost thought he could grasp the idea of it, but the stark reality as shown in one man's dead body was nothing short of bewildering.

Not knowing what else to do, Malthan actually considered burying the body, but the notion was so ridiculous that he almost laughed.

Gurgash would truly know I'd lost my mind then.

The horse could smell the wolves loitering nearby also and it jerked hard on the reins, its eyes rolling white with terror.

"Don't worry," Malthan said. "We're leaving. Wolves don't like ghouls either."

The beast didn't seem very reassured, but it followed Malthan's lead willingly enough. Soon he heard the sound of the wolves closing in. It had been hard times for them, too, and if they preferred fresh kills they would not disdain carrion if available. Which was the main reason wolves and ghouls didn't get along; time and again they became competitors.

Malthan knew that the easy meal came first but that the wolves could be after the Lady herself soon enough. Malthan still couldn't explain to himself why he cared, but he forced himself to hurry. The horse seemed grateful for the extra speed. Malthan rather thought the horse would be more content to gallop, if Malthan would care to ride him again, but when danger threatened Malthan felt much more secure moving on his own two good legs.

⎯⎯◈⎯⎯

The trail was much fresher now, yet the sun was an hour lower in the sky before a commotion ahead on the trail told Malthan he had found his quarry.

"They were moving quickly, horse," Malthan said. "But I think someone has caught them first."

Malthan found them in a small clearing; they huddled together on the far side, while an old man stood trembling but defiantly in front, waving a cudgel at the band of men approaching them. The men were ragged but well-armed, with a variety of edged weapons clearly salvaged or liberated from former owners.

Brigands.

Another hazard of the woods. Malthan didn't blame them for it, especially. It was all about survival at heart, and a ghoul understood survival. It occurred to Malthan that his quest was about the things he *didn't* understand, but there was no time to think about that now. Malthan dropped the reins after giving the warhorse a quick reminder about the wolves waiting nearby, then positioned his shield and drew his sword.

"Stop, knaves!"

Malthan wasn't sure if the challenge didn't sound as silly to the bandits as it did to himself, but it had the desired effect. As one they turned their attention away from the travelers to Malthan, then they turned to look at each other as if doing a quick count. The answer came back at something like seven to one, which seemed to reassure them. They grinned, advancing, while one remained behind, apparently to make sure their prey didn't escape in the meantime.

"I'll have his sword," said a husky fellow at the head of the pack, and Malthan shrugged and gave it to him in a vicious overhand chop. The fellow blocked in plenty of time with his own blade, but it didn't seem to matter. Malthan's blow struck sparks as it pushed the fellow's own blade deep back into his skull, and with the return stroke Malthan sent the man's body sprawling to the ground, where it twitched for several moments before finally going still.

The others, not quite realizing what had just happened, pressed ahead. One struck at Malthan's knees, another rushed forward to stab with a short lance. Malthan took the first blow on his shield, and cut off the head of the lance with his sword, shearing through the iron strapping holding the point in place. In short order the pieces of the next two attackers joined those of their leader on the ground.

I think I'm getting the knack of this!

Malthan knew he was fortunate that none of the brigands seemed to have the skill of Sir Dald. Still, three down in just over as many seconds wasn't a bad accounting. The other three paused, and the fourth one guarding the travelers could only stare in consternation for a long moment.

"Bloody he—" He didn't finish. The old man used the distraction to swing his cudgel hard against the brigand's bare skull and he went down without finishing his comment. That seemed to decide the matter; the survivors took to their heels and vanished into the forest. Malthan heard the noise of them for some time, but it was clear they were leaving the area in a hurry. Malthan, the immediate danger past, finally took a good hard luck at what he had done.

Gurgash would think this well done, but somehow I do not. The flush of victory was fading fast. Malthan felt a little ill, and cursed himself for a weakling.

The knot of travelers slowly unraveled as Malthan stood there, catching his breath, and Malthan finally was able to make out more detail. There were two older women in blue and white dresses, and a small boy wearing a tunic likewise of blue and white, evidently a page of some sort, but they got no more a cursory glance, for Malthan finally saw who they had been trying to shield.

Even a ghoul would call her beautiful.

Her hair was black and long, gathered in a single braid down her back; her skin paler than any female ghoul Malthan had ever seen. True, she was far too delicate by ghoul standards. Her nose was too small and her teeth were too small and well, she was just too small. Such a child born to a ghoul wouldn't survive past its first Feeding; the other pups would tear the carcass away and she'd starve if she wasn't killed outright. Human ways were clearly different, because she was here now, cared for and protected.

Didn't you just do the same?

Malthan wasn't sure where the thought came from, but there it was, and it was true, for all that he didn't understand the reason. There didn't seem to be a reason; so far Malthan had just done what he thought a human knight would do, and so far it had worked. Yet did he really understand humans that well? Especially when some of Sir Dald's actions concerning the lady and her champion still didn't make sense to him. Perhaps now he could find out.

Malthan bowed in the Lady's general direction. "I'm glad you are unhurt."

She stepped forward boldly. "Thanks to you, kind Sir. I'm Lady Jessyn of Westford."

Malthan bowed again. "Malthus of Darktomb . . . It's a land far from here."

"However ominous your name, you must be thirsty after such work. If you'll remove your helmet my servants will be glad to bring you a goblet."

Malthan quickly repeated the story of his "vow" to Lady Jessyn, who listened without interruption and then gave a wistful smile. "It is a knight's nature to do such things, for all that they often seem to be very inconvenient for very little advantage . . . " She looked away, and reddened just a bit. "I must apologize. Being the mistress of my own domain I tend to say what I think; my ladies assure me it's not known as a virtue."

Malthan, who also thought the whole "oath for this and that" business rather silly, hastened to assure her that he was not insulted. She smiled at him. Malthan thought it was a fine smile, if not the sort he was used to. Ghoul women had fangs and looked rather different when they smiled. It always looked like—and usually was—a threat. Lady Jessyn's smile did not look that way at all.

"If you have Sir Palan's armor, then you must have defeated Sir Dald at the bridge. My thanks; that one needed taking down a peg or two. Pray, can you tell me if you saw a young man alone in the woods? Sir Palan had gone seeking shelter for us."

"Protector . . . " muttered the old man standing nearby, and he spit on the ground.

Lady Jessyn glared at him and he looked away, chastened. "Mol, it's true he was defeated, but he did his best." She turned back to Malthan. "Did you see him? A young man, yellow hair?"

Malthan didn't know what to say, so he told the simple truth. "Lady, I am sorry to tell you that he is dead."

"Oh." That was all she said. Malthan was a little puzzled at first; his beliefs about human feelings led him to think there might be more to it. Then he noticed that Lady Jessyn was swaying just slightly, like a willow in a gentle wind. Her two ladies-in-waiting picked up on the clues a little quicker. In a moment they were at her side, steadying her.

To her credit, Lady Jessyn recovered quickly. After a few moments she gently disentangled herself and her two women stepped back. "I must crave your pardon again. Palan's loss . . . I wasn't prepared."

Malthan didn't tell what he knew about the suicide. For some reason the words sounded wrong even as he thought them. "He—he was beset by wolves before I found him, and died bravely I'm sure. I regret I was unable to help. Did . . . did you love him?" Malthan regretted the words as soon as they were spoken. One of the ladies-in-waiting gasped and the other two servants stared at him as if he'd suddenly sprouted a tail. "Now I must ask your pardon," Malthan said. "The question was ill-considered."

Nonetheless Lady Jessyn, who neither gasped nor stared, did seem to be considering it.

"Love? No. He was a sweet fool and deserved better of life than his destiny proved. He had no more business with arms and armor than I do, yet his birth and his pride would allow no other course; he offered me aid when I needed it and did his best for me. I did not love him but I do mourn him, Sir Malthus."

Malthan spoke his next words straight from the heart, though it surprised him a little to think that a ghoul might have one. "If he strived to be more than he was," Malthan said, "no one should fault him for that."

She smiled at him then, though there were tears in her eyes. "Nor do I . . . I'm afraid our ordeal has left me quite exhausted, Sir Malthus, and night is coming. Please accept our hospitality, such as our camp can afford. I must rest soon."

Malthan nodded. "Gladly accepted, but I'd advise making camp somewhere else. Those brigands doubtless had friends who will return. We'd best not be here."

No one disputed that. The servants broke camp and fetched the Lady's palfrey. Malthan, seeing no other way out of it, had a quick chat with the dun warhorse—out of earshot of the others—and rode beside her until the scene of the fight and the bodies of the brigands were as far behind as daylight permitted. He was careful to stay far enough way just in case his breath or personal aroma was still an issue. He didn't know what Lady Jessyn thought of it all, but he himself found the conversation they had on the way entirely fascinating.

Malthan bathed in a nearby stream that night, in part out of worry about the smell but also in an attempt to shake off the effects of the wine. Though Malthan would not remove his helmet in the humans' company he had taken a goblet with him on Lady Jessyn's insistence. She apologized that it was poor travel fare, and watered at that, but Malthan found the effects more than a little disconcerting.   ·

Why are the stars moving?

Malthan closed his eyes. The world didn't spin quite so much then.

"Shouldn't you be keeping watch, or something?"

Malthan opened one eye. Gurgash kneeled down on the bank of the stream, eyeing the armor with distaste and the bathing with something more like morbid fascination.

"I spoke to a raven, and few night creatures; no one will approach the camp without my knowing . . . oh, do stop swaying like that."

"I'm not swaying! *You* are." Gurgash picked up the goblet, sniffed it. "Did this do that to you?"

"I think so. I know a little of the stuff purifies water. Apparently that water is more pure than most."

Gurgash sniffed. "Purify? What rubbish."

"Still, it is the custom among them."

"You're not 'them.' " Gurgash said. "For all that you're copying outward appearance better than I expected."

Malthan smiled. "Was that something like a compliment?"

Gurgash growled low. "Don't be daft . . . or any more daft, that is. I couldn't bear it."

"Why are you following me?" Malthan asked.

Gurgash looked suspicious. "What do you mean?"

"It was a simple question. You've been keeping close to me on this journey. Is it simple curiosity? Could it be you care what happens to me?"

Gurgash drew himself up to his full height. "Don't be stupid! Maybe you've forgotten what it means to be a ghoul?"

Malthan shook his head. "Not in the least. You are my friend, and you and I both understand that friendship among ghouls simply means that we won't try to tear each other's heads off over a piece of carrion, and that we can hunt together, and that's pretty much all it means. Don't you agree?"

"Yes," Gurgash said grudgingly. "So?"

"So why are you following me, Gurgash?"

"In the vain hope that you'll come to your senses so we can hunt together again. You . . . you're good at hunting, when you set your mind to it."

Maybe it was the wine, but Malthan couldn't help smiling. Coming from a ghoul, Gurgash's admission was little short of an outburst of affection. "I like hunting with you, too, Gurgash."

"Then come home, you fool! You've made a few bodies. If we bring them back before the wolves get them the women will come to *us* for meat in a day or two."

"They're not too large. Take a couple back yourself, and have fun. I'm not finished."

"By the Cold Stones, when *will* you be finished?!"

"When I understand what I'm looking for. When I find it."

Malthan still didn't know what it, was and thought his chances of understanding the whole mess were even less, but he still needed a reason to justify what he was doing, and a poor one was better than nothing. Gurgash just shook his head, and disappeared once more into the woods. Malthan watched him go.

I wish I could explain, Gurgash. Friendship among ghouls is functional, useful. Friendship among humans seems to get them killed, and yet they still crave it. Maybe there's something I could understand as a human that I don't as a ghoul.

Malthan couldn't be human, but he could act like one and, perhaps, learn to think like one. He wasn't sure what this might accomplish, if anything, but he just knew that he wasn't done. Not yet.

Malthan hid the armor and himself in a hollow tree, and settled in for the night.

The old man named Mol was heating something over a fire the next morning. Some sort of porridge. There were oats involved, so far as Malthan could tell. The ladies were getting dressed in a small tent nearby; Malthan could hear and smell them.

"Breakfast, Sir Malthus?" Mol asked, but Malthan politely declined. He'd found a few wild blueberries and was in fact very hungry, but the oat mash appealed even less than the wild fruit and nuts he'd been subsisting on for the last day or so. It was at once more decayed than what he had been eating, yet not nearly decayed enough. Malthan felt his stomach rumble.

I don't know how much longer I can do this . . .

It took Malthan a moment to realize that Mol was speaking to him. "Your pardon, but I didn't catch all of that."

Mol sighed. "I *said* that I'd like to know what happened to Sir Palan."

"The wolves . . . "

"Was a very nice story. I want the truth. Don't worry, Sir Malthus. It's just the two of us; the ladies won't be with us for a moment. I know the wolves are vicious in these woods, but an attack in broad daylight?"

Malthan met the old man's eyes for several long moments. Neither looked away. Malthan finally sighed. "It's true that I found him too late. He killed himself in the woods. I didn't think I should tell Lady Jessyn that. Was I wrong?"

Mol grunted. "He told us he was going back to Sir Dald, to beg, plead, or indenture himself for the return of the armor and a chance to redeem himself. I guess he couldn't bring himself to do it. Wrong? No, it was kind of you. No reason to tarnish the poor lad's memory."

"He's dead and can no longer suffer. How he's remembered is important?"

Mol just looked at him for a moment. "You're a strange one. Wouldn't we all like to be remembered well?"

It was a new thought for a ghoul. Malthan thought about it for a moment, and it gave rise to another thought.

Something about a legacy, if that was the right word. Memory. Ghouls understood memory; it was one of the few things ghouls and humans had in common. This was a new use for memory, in Malthan's experience. He needed to think about it some more, but he also needed to know more.

Malthan knew he was treading on dangerous ground, but he knew the ladies would not stay in their tent much longer and he might not get another chance. "Of-of course, but remember I'm from a distant country, and our customs may be different. I have to ask you something that's been troubling me, Sir Mol."

Mol laughed. "First, I'm no 'sir,' nor ever desired to be. I've been around that lot enough to see what's entailed and want no part of it, even if my birth allowed. Second, there's something troubling about you, Sir Malthus; I think there's more to you than we know and that worries me."

Malthan felt a chill, but Mol held up his hand. "Do not concern yourself with an old man's fretting. For the service you've done both to my lady and to that feckless boy Sir Palan, you've shown yourself to be a good man, whatever else you may be. If there's a question I can answer for you, I will."

Malthan took a slow breath, let it out. "Sir Dald's vow was to contest that bridge. By taking Sir Palan's armor he put Lady Jessyn's party at risk. Isn't it also a knight's duty to protect the weak?"

Mol smiled, showing missing teeth. "It may be different in your land, but here it's the sort of contradiction knights are always making for themselves. Sir Dald's honor demanded that he challenge Sir Palan, and take his armor when he won. To let Palan keep his armor would be an insult to the boy, which Sir Dald did not intend. That this also put Lady Jessyn at risk was a breach of Sir Dald's chivalry. He had to make a choice, since he could not serve both honor and chivalry. He chose honor."

"I see," Malthan said, though he wasn't quite sure that he did. "So his chivalry came up short. He failed to uphold his ideals."

Mol shrugged. "As did Sir Palan when he chose to let the prospect of losing his own honor by begging move him to take his own life and leave Lady Jessyn with no protector at all . . . save me and my poor cudgel. Some battles are impossible to win. Is it so different in your country?"

When put like that, Malthan had to admit that, no, it wasn't so very different at all.

Lady Jessyn joined them soon after with her attendants, and Malthan stood up because it seemed the thing to do. She greeted him warmly. "I'm glad you're still among our company, but I fear we have not been honest with you."

"If so, I think I could find it in myself to forgive you," said Malthan dryly. *I've lied to her, in effect, and that's it for honor. Maybe I'll do better with chivalry alone to worry about.*

Lady Jessyn smiled, but it faded quickly. "The truth is that I have no claim on you, save for what charity you choose to show. I must reach the castle beyond Stonebrier Bridge, and there is a very powerful man who will try to prevent it. It's not just for myself I must ask, but for all those who dwell under my protection—"

Malthan raised a hand, and she fell silent for a moment, then sighed in resignation. "It's of course your right to refuse, nor can I blame you."

"You misunderstand me, Lady. I'm not refusing; in fact I accept heartily. I'm merely trying to save you the trouble of the explanation. There are always reasons for what must be done. One either chooses to do them or does not."

Lady Jessyn looked at him intently. "I must warn you that I have not the means to pay you for your trouble; we have little more than what we carry with us."

Malthan shrugged. "Should I be rewarded for doing what is right?"

Lady Jessyn smiled then, blushing slightly. Malthan thought the effect rather sweet.

"I am ashamed of myself," she said. "I'm afraid I was searching for conditions when perhaps there were none."

Malthan thought about the situation a little more. "I do have one small condition," Malthan admitted, "and only one. After this adventure I will have to return to my own country. All I ask is that, whatever happens, when that time comes you remember me fondly. Will you do that for me?"

"It seems so little," she said.

"It's everything," Malthan said. "Will you promise me?"

"I will, Sir Malthus. I do swear it."

"Then let's be gone. I would not want to keep the foe waiting."

⊰⊱

His name was Lord Ergas of Stonebrier. Malthan knew that because the fellow announced it very loudly as he blocked passage on the bridge. Malthan sighed. Bridges again. What was it about knights and bridges? He dismounted, much to the warhorse's relief, and sized up his opponent.

Lord Ergas was a big fellow, clad all in black. Malthan rather liked the color; he considered it quite fetching. Which could not be said for Lord Ergas himself, or what Malthan could see of his face through the raised visor.

He'd make a better ghoul than some true ones.

"You're in our way," Malthan said.

Lord Ergas just stared at him for a moment. "Where is Sir Palan?"

"Dead, I'm afraid. You'll have to deal with me instead."

Lady Jessyn stood some distance away, but apparently heard the exchange clearly. "How did your know Sir Palan was my escort, Lord Ergas?" She said the man's name like one describing a particularly vile substance that needed to be scraped off her shoe.

He laughed, and the sound rather reminded Malthan of the way his own father laughed when he'd scored a particularly fine piece of carrion. "How? Good lady, I arranged it. I spoke the praises of that young fool to the skies. My brother was quite impressed, and so commanded that the little whelp be the one to fetch you. I knew he would be no difficulty for me. So now I must kill this fellow instead. So be it. Either way, you will marry *me*, Lady, and not my brother. Once my lands are joined to yours, even my brother will bow to me."

"He will not and I will not," Lady Jessyn said. "Though you kill me."

Malthan frowned. "Lord Ergas, you have no chivalry in you at all, do you?"

Lord Ergas, startled, turned his attention back to Malthan. "How dare you speak thus to me, you cur! You're a knight of the hedges at best, and not worthy of my sword."

Lord Ergas raised that sword, and brought it down suddenly, striking at nothing. Malthan heard the twang of bowstrings, then felt two white hot brands of fire in his side. He glanced down, saw the feathered ends of two arrows protruding from his side. They did sting, but in a moment the pain settled down to a gentle numbness. Malthan didn't bother to dodge, or even to move. Mos and the Lady Jessyn's servants covered her with their own bodies.

"Fear not," Lord Ergas said. "I wouldn't harm my bride on her wedding day."

"You'll harm no one," Malthan said. "I'm going to kill you."

Lord Ergas frowned. "He still stands?" He raised his sword again, brought it down. Nothing happened. He did it again with the same result.

"Your archers seem to have deserted you," Malthan said. "No matter, when I said you had no chivalry, it was not an insult, merely a fact."

Lord Ergas spurred his horse forward, waving his sword high. "I'll cut that impertinent tongue out myself!"

For all his talk, Lord Ergas did not swing his sword at Malthan but rather charged directly at him, obviously intending to merely ride him down. Malthan found his legs a bit slow to respond, and Lord Ergas' mount crashed into him. Malthan flew several paces to the side and fell hard. The arrow shafts brought a new wave of pain. Malthan knew full well that, save for his ghoulish constitution, he would be dead already. He sighed, finally admitting to himself that there were times when being a ghoul was not altogether a bad thing.

Lord Ergas dismounted, advancing on the fallen Malthan with his sword held high. "And thus it ends."

"Yes," Malthan said clearly. "But not how you think."

Lord Ergas froze, disbelieving, as Malthan got back on his feet. Malthan knew he was hurt, but he knew too what strength remained in him.

"I said you had no chivalry, and it is true," he repeated. "Now I say you have no honor as well." Malthan's voice rose to a peak of triumph. "And *that* is also true! That I am a prince in my own country matters not, Lord Ergas. What matters is that, poor wretch that I may be, I am still a better knight than you!"

Malthan drew his sword, and as Lord Ergas both frantically and futilely signaled his archers once last time, Malthan proved the truth of every word he said.

"I don't suppose," Gurgash said, from his perch atop Lord Ergas's mutilated body, "that it occurred to them to send you a physician?"

Evening was falling. Malthan lay, still in armor, stretched out on the road on the near side of the bridge. "It will take them a while to reach their destination even without Lord Ergas to trouble them." He winced, then. While it was true that their diet and constitution made ghouls very hard to kill, they felt pain as well as any human. "Did you see, Gurgash?"

"I more than saw, Prince. I helped. Those two archers, for instance. I dealt with them . . . although a bit late."

"My thanks for that. A few more arrows might have done for me, but I meant Lady Jessyn. Did you see?"

Gurgash sighed. "Ah, yes. Quite a scene, with her crying and wailing, and her servants pulling her away because they simply *had* to be going before dark. She would have ripped your helmet off if that old man hadn't stopped her."

Malthan smiled. "Mos. I think he suspected something. No matter. They thought I was dead already. I made them think so. Besides, what would have happened if they had remained to loosen my armor? They would have known the wrong truth."

Gurgash came close and, after a bit of fumbling, removed Malthan's helmet. "Wrong truth? What wrong truth? The truth is you were born a ghoul and remain a ghoul. You found no magic to make you human!"

Malthan smiled then. "You're wrong, Gurgash. Now the truth is what Lady Jessyn will remember all her days, and all those who saw, and all who hear the story, that an unknown knight named Sir Malthus fought and died bravely with perfect chivalry. Those tales will live, Gurgash, as will I. I may be a mystery, but I'll be a human one. That is the truth, Gurgash. I *made* it the truth."

Gurgash just stared at him. "Malthan . . . "

He was interrupted by a rush of wings and then a squawk from the oak tree nearby. Two carrion corbies had landed in the high branches and looked down, impassive. In the distance were the silhouettes of vultures beginning their circle, outlined against the sky.

"They've come for Lord Ergas, but he's ours."

Malthan smiled. "No. They've come for me."

Gurgash stared, disbelieving. "Crows and buzzards do not eat ghouls, any more than we eat our own!"

Malthan smiled. "Exactly."

Gurgash sighed. "Fine, so you think you fooled the world. Did you fool yourself, too?"

"If I had," Malthan said sadly, "you'd be drooling over the prospect of my flesh even now."

Gurgash just looked disgusted and reached down to take hold of the arrow shafts. "Yet the ghoul in you asserts itself, meaning you'll survive what would kill a human twice over, though this is still going to hurt for a while." He yanked the arrows out with one vicious motion. Malthan winced again, but otherwise made no sound. Gurgash helped him to stand.

"Good thing those were war arrows instead of the broadheads they use for hunting. Even a ghoul couldn't survive being bled out like a stag." Gurgash looked his friend up and down. "So your little adventure comes to an end and you're a little worse for wear, but that's all. What was the point, my Prince? I mean, really?"

Malthan didn't answer right away. He just gazed at the two disappointed-looking carrion birds in the tree above. He finally answered with a question of his own. "Do vultures, in dreams, remember what it was to be eagles?"

Gurgash frowned. "I don't know."

"I do," Malthan said. "Let's go home."

LORD GOJI'S WEDDING

The training of young monks at Hanaman-ji in Kyoto was rigorous, and the old monk in charge of their training sometimes used blows to reinforce the lessons, and sometimes he used stories. The young monks were generally in agreement that storytelling was the harsher method of the two: the sting of a blow would fade in an hour or so, but a story could have them puzzling for days on end with no real understanding in sight. So it was with some trepidation that fine spring evening when the young monks noticed the gruff old man looking especially thoughtful.

This was always a bad sign.

Two of the more optimistic monks were already seated *zazen* and made a decent show of being in deep meditation when the old monk entered the training hall. Perhaps they thought to escape their fate, but the older boys knew better. They simply waited.

And waited.

The old monk stood in the doorway, looking at them for a long time. "You're young," he said.

Normally when he said such a thing it was clearly meant to imply that "You don't know anything, so be quiet and listen." Not this time. The old monk said it as if reminding himself of something he'd almost forgotten.

"Cushion," he said after a while, and the two closest acolytes scrambled to bring it to him. He kneeled down there on the floor and made himself comfortable. One of the two "meditating" monks let out a gentle snore and the other sighed, opened his eyes, and punched his companion awake. The old monk finally started speaking.

"Long ago in a place not very far from here, there was a young scholar of good family. His name was Goji. He took his religious training at the local temple and was so moved by the piety of the monks and the purity of what he was taught there that he was actively considering a life in the temple. All that changed when he fell in love."

Several of the youngsters visibly relaxed. Clearly this was going to be one of those "sins and distractions of the world" fables. So long as they could sort out the story type and extract the lesson the old monk expected, they knew there would be no problem. The old monk just smiled a wistful smile.

"Now, in that same temple there was a most worthy monk. Most worthy indeed. He knew quite a few things, and was always telling what he knew, for he believed that sharing knowledge was the act of an enlightened being."

The old monk fell silent again, and one of the younger monks was moved to ask. "Was he an enlightened being, Master?"

"It was said of him," the old monk replied. "He never said it of himself. Weigh that in the scales, for what it may be worth."

The young monks just looked at each other, and after a moment the old monk continued his story. "He was invited to the wedding, of course, as one of Lord Goji's favorite teachers. It was summer, and the monk was taking the breeze on the *engawa* when the bride's wedding party arrived. It was his karma that he would be the first to greet them, or perhaps it was everyone's karma present, for it happened just that way."

"What happened then, Master?"

"He greeted them, of course. It would have been rude to do otherwise. Since the girl was of noble family she was escorted by five *samurai* and several maids, plus servants bearing her sedan chair, and all in summer clothes and colors. The bride herself was wearing a *shiromuku* of such pure whiteness that she seemed made of snow. She was veiled, as is the custom."

He paused again, and again one of the younger monks asked a question. "Master, I have sometimes wondered . . . in China a bride wears red, or so I am told, for the color is considered lucky. Why does a bride in our country wear white, the color of death?"

The old monk shrugged. "Perhaps because both marriage and death are transformations. Also, among old samurai families it was an indication that the bride came to them in the same spirit that blank *washu* comes to the calligrapher. As the paper takes the ink, so would she accept the family colors and *mon* of her groom. In the old days I believe the wedding costume was actually taken and dyed appropriately after the wedding was done. However, dye would not be enough to let this bride become part of Goji's family. No, that was not possible."

"Why, master?"

"She was a fox. For that matter, so were her attendants."

The young monks gasped in such perfect unison that perhaps the old monk wondered, for a moment, why they could not chant the Lotus or Diamond Sutras with the same precision. Or perhaps he thought nothing of the sort.

"She was of ancient and noble family, as I said. But she was not human."

"How did the teacher know?" asked another.

The old monk shrugged. "He couldn't fail to notice. Years of practiced meditation and discipline had given him the ability to pierce many of the illusions of this world. Not all, perhaps, but many. When he saw the wedding party, he knew what they were, even as he greeted them. Foxes, every one."

"The young lord had been cruelly deceived," said the oldest boy.

"Perhaps," said the old man.

"I don't understand," said the oldest boy. "You said she was a fox."

"I did and she was. As for your not understanding, well, listen to what happened then. You still won't understand, but you'll know more. So, as I said, she was a fox. The teacher requested a moment alone with the lady to bestow his blessing. As he was a respected guest, her retainers withdrew to a discreet distance, though the bride of course remained veiled in her chair. He approached her with every outward sign of respect and he whispered the following words to her: I know what you are, Lady. Leave now and never return, or your beloved will know, too."

"How do you know exactly what was said, Master?" asked the youngest monk. The oldest boy punched him then, but the old monk just smiled.

"It's a story, young one. How can I not know what I have decided the words should be?"

The youngest monk blushed furiously even as he rubbed his sore arm. Still, he must have assumed that his embarrassment couldn't get any worse, since he asked another question. "You are saying, then, that this story isn't true?"

"No, I am not saying that."

Now the oldest boy frowned. "You're saying it *is* true?"

"I'm not saying that either. Now be silent and let me finish."

The young monks subsided though they looked, if anything, more confused than before. If the old monk noticed he didn't show it. "The lady made a small sound, rather faint. A bit of breath, perhaps, no more. Behind them there was the whisper of sliding screens. A servant had informed Lord Goji of his bride's arrival and the young man was on his way. The monk spoke to the bride again, saying: "I see what you are and I will not allow you to deceive my pupil, for whatever your designs might be they cannot be to his advantage. You are a fox, and no human girl at all. Begone while you can."

There might have been no more questions then, but once more the old monk fell silent. One might think he had forgotten that he was telling a story at all, or perhaps the words had slipped away from him. He seemed puzzled, almost, looking off into nothing as if whatever was missing now might, perhaps, be there instead.

"Master, wasn't the teacher afraid of being cursed? I've heard that foxes sometimes do that."

The old monk grunted. "Why should he fear, he who saw with such excellent clarity? How could he fail to see, or speak what he knew? What heed of curses when there might, at the end of the day, be a profaned wedding instead?"

"What happened then?"

"The lady lifted her veil and the monk could see her beauty, despite the fact that he knew it was illusion, and she said: 'I know what I am, good monk. Yet I love Lord Goji and mean no harm to him. If you can truly see what I am, then you can tell if I speak the truth.' The monk, of course, said that this did not matter."

"Master . . . did it matter? What would you have done?" asked the youngest.

"What would I have done?" The question seemed to confuse the old monk for a moment. Then he shook his head. "It is useless to speak of what might have been done. What matters is what *was* done. The monk's spiritual power was great. So great that, when Lord Goji came out to greet his new bride, he saw what his teacher saw—a fox. She smiled at Lord Goji, and she said: 'I would have made you happy.' Then she reverted to her true form, she and all her attendants, and they fled from Lord Goji's house. They were never seen again."

"What happened to Lord Goji?" asked the oldest boy.

"He searched for her, for a time."

"Why? To punish the fox for deceiving him?"

"To find her," the old monk said. "As to his purpose, who can say? I'm not sure even he knew. Yet, before he began his search, he said this much to his teacher: Master, I was happy."

"That sounds rather ungrateful," said the youngest.

The old monk shrugged. "I suppose. However, I don't think he ever found her. In time Lord Goji returned, shaved his head, and joined the temple. He became a fine monk, one of many more fine, pious monks just like him."

The old man rose slowly and carefully off of his cushion and started toward the door. The young monks watched him, frowning as one. Finally the oldest could stand it no longer. "Master, is that the end of the story?"

"It is," the old monk said, not even pausing.

"But master," the oldest persisted. "What does it mean?"

"Meaning is an illusion too," said the old monk. "but if you insist, I'll tell you—It means that I was a fool."

The arguments started before he was even through the door. Some monks insisted that their own teacher was the wise teacher in the story. Others insisted just as loudly that he must be Lord Goji himself. Others said it was just a made-up story, similar to the tale of Madame White Snake told in China and the old monk was simply trying to confuse them again. "There are many such stories," they insisted. "This one is only a little different." "Yes, but . . . " someone else would say, and everyone was off again. The discussions went on for days.

The old monk listened, as he always did, but would answer no more questions. He never spoke of the matter again.

THE FEATHER CLOAK

This is one version of a very old story. The difference is that this version is true. Unlike all the others, which are also true.

Long before the reign of the Emperor Sanjo, there was a mountain monk named Hakuryo. Hakuryo was not a very good monk, as those things were measured. He never could meditate properly, and the deeper meanings of the sacred scriptures always eluded him. In his favor, he was both pious and sincere, which were virtues not universally present even in the Great Monasteries of the country like Hiea-zan or Todaii-ji. He also had a remarkable talent for solitude. In fact, of all Hakuryo's skills, being alone was probably what he did best. Yet that solitude did little to enhance his meditations.

Still, being a sincere and pious fellow, he continued to try. One day he was sitting in silent attempted meditation on a mountainside near the sea at Miwo when he heard the music of female laughter.

Ah, he thought, *at last I must be near the truth. There is no one here for miles. This must be some evil spirit come to test me!*

Hakuryo kept his eyes tightly shut and tried to push all thoughts aside, even that last one, but it was difficult. And evil spirit? Was he so worthy of being tested? This was exciting stuff to a rustic ascetic such as Hakuryo. He considered chanting, but was afraid that this would make the evil spirit think that he was afraid. He was not afraid.

The laughter did not stop. If anything, it became louder, more animated. Finally Hakuryo could stand it no longer and he opened first his right eye, then his left. Before him stretched the same quiet valley, the beauty of which had prompted him to choose that very spot for meditation. Beside him gurgled a small but energetic mountain stream, which flowed on down the mountainside to gather in a large quiet pool.

In that pool were now three young maidens of indescribable beauty. The laughed and splashed each other as their long black hair streamed out behind them in the clear water like separate dark rivers, all apparently oblivious to his presence. Hakuryo quickly shut his eyes again, but it was no use.

He remembered the stories of the Buddha, who was tempted by all the pleasures of the earth and yet was not dissuaded from his path. He remembered the stories he heard growing up, of *tanuki* and mountain goblins, of foxes and ghosts who would wear such disguises, to distract the righteous.

"It clearly has worked," Hakuryo said finally, "for I am surely distracted."

Hakuryo tried not to dwell on his failure. It had not been the first and, he was sadly certain, would not be the last. As he watched the young women bathing in the pool below him, he wondered if he had really been close to the truth, or was merely privy to some strange, yet esthetically pleasing, coincidence.

These girls did not seem to have much in common with the fishermen's and farmer's daughters with which he was, if only from about the same distance, familiar. Nor was it simply that they were beautiful, though they were. It was rather that the effect their beauty was having on him was not the sort that as a young man, monk or not, he was also familiar with. Rather, he felt nothing, save awe and wonder.

"Clearly I am in the presence of something I do not understand. If I cannot meditate upon it, then I must examine it."

Hakuryo rose slowly; sitting in meditation usually made his legs fall asleep and this time had been no exception. He waited for the pins and needs feeling below his knees to fade enough that he dared to move again, then he crept down the hillside as silently as he could.

Getting closer did little to change his initial impressions: there were indeed three lovely young maidens bathing in the pool, and as he approached they did not suddenly turn into animal spirits to vex him or *oni* to devour him.

Hakuryo saw three brilliant white cloaks of an odd texture draped carefully over the low limb of an ancient *hinoki* that grew by the pool. He got close enough to examine them without being seen, and realized that he was looking at the legendary *hagoromo*, flying cloaks created for the *tennin*, and thus these were no human girls at all but creatures of heaven. Hakuryo realized all this just before he brushed against another low branch of that same tree. The fine, soft fronds tickled his nose and he sneezed.

In that moment the maidens' laughter turned to shrieks. Before he could even react, two of the maidens had rushed, naked, onto the shore to seize their cloaks. For an instant Hakuryo was frozen in place as they wrapped the cloaks about their nakedness and began to rise into the air like kites.

Incredible.

The third young maiden had been farther from the shore than the other two, daring her companions to swim as far as she. Hakuryo's astonishment did not stop him from rushing forward and seizing, before the third young maiden could return and retrieve it, the remaining cloak.

For a few moments he could only stare at her and hold his prize as the first two of maidens continued to ascend and were soon lost to sight among the clouds. It was a little while before he could turn his attention, at least for a moment, to the cloak he held. The texture was even more soft than the finest silk; the entire cloak was made of fine, downy feathers whiter than snow.

The third maiden stood in the water, glaring at Hakuryo. "Sir monk, that *hagoromo* belongs to me. Please give it back."

Her voice was neither pleading nor commanding, but rather as if she calmly stated a fact and expected that fact to be acted upon. For his part, Hakuryo had thought the maiden was beautiful from a distance, but up close he realized what an inadequate word that really was for such a person. Her hair was long and blacker than obsidian, her skin white and unblemished as new snow. Her gaze made him distinctly uncomfortable, as if he were the one who stood naked, there on the shore.

"Who are you?"

"I am a *tennin*, as you must know by now. My name is not for one such as you to demand."

On the one hand, Hakuryo vaguely wondered if he should feel insulted. On the other, he was so carried away by excitement that he did not care. Hakuryo found himself staring again. A *tennin* was a member of the Heavenly Court. He was in the actual presence of a Celestial Maiden. It was a preposterous claim for anyone to make, and yet Hakuryo did not doubt the girl's word for a moment. If nothing else, he had the evidence of her now-vanished companions, the sight of her own exquisite person, and the wondrous cloak that he still held in his hands.

Hands, which he realized, were not the cleanest. He thought of taking a ritual bath, but that also did not seem appropriate. Yet, it seemed that he had little to fear in that regard. His hands left no sign upon the cloak, no mark or stain, as if it was quite beyond his power to affect the robe in any way at all.

"But . . . if I return your robe, you will fly away," Hakuryo said.

She just frowned. "Of course."

Hakuryo was a little taken aback. He had rather expected her to deny it, or to make promises, or plead. Anything but what she had said, which was that, once he returned her robe, she would leave and he would never see her again.

"No," he said. "I cannot do that. Here."

Hakuryo did not give the maiden her cloak of feathers, but he did remove his own outer robe and hand it to her so that she could cover herself. She accepted it reluctantly, and her nose crinkled.

"While I do appreciate the covering since I am wet and a bit chilled, are you really going to claim that this is a fair exchange?" she asked.

I really should have bathed more frequently, Hakuryo thought, but ritual impurity had always seemed so much less of a concern when he was alone. "No, but I need to think, *tennin-sama*, and that is very difficult to do with a naked woman so close to me."

"I am not a woman," she said, frowning again. "I am a *tennin*. Did you not understand?"

Again, Hakuryo heard the truth in her words. Yet by all appearance she was indeed a woman and, now that he had been in her presence for a bit, those aspects of her form were beginning to make themselves more familiarly known to him. "Well. You are female, at least. As a monk, I should not be even this close to you."

"As a monk, you should not be taking what does not belong to you."

Her words stung him, more so because he knew that she was right. And yet he still did not want to surrender the cloak. He tried to change the subject.

"If you are a creature of Heaven, what are you doing in the mortal world?"

"As a monk, you should know that even such an exalted place as the Court of Heaven is but one more step on the final journey. It does one good, from time to time, to remind oneself of how far one has come, rather than simply wondering how far one has to go," she said. "And this quiet pool was a pleasant respite on such a hot day. Now give me my cloak."

"I cannot," he said.

"Why? Without it I am trapped where I do not belong. Of what possible use is my cloak to one such as yourself?"

"I could use it to fly to the heavens!" he said, seizing an inspiration.

"In which case we will *both* be where we do not belong. You were sent to the world of your birth for a reason, monk, even as I was. Even if you have no regard for me, why would you deprive yourself of what you were sent here to learn?"

Hakuryo could not question the theological accuracy of what she had just said, since he never really understood such esoteric points in the first place. He tried to think of something else. "I can take this robe to the temple where I was trained," he said. "It would be revered as a national treasure!"

She sighed. "Perhaps. Bringing both yourself and your temple great acclaim within the world of men. Is that what you want?"

Hakuryo frowned. "Many men would think this more than sufficient reason to keep your wondrous cloak."

"True, but that is not what I asked. Must I repeat myself?"

Hakuryo thought about it, and then released his breath in a great gusting sigh. Not that he would have minded such things, but he rather considered them beside the point, even if he could not quite articulate what the point, as such, was. "No," he said finally. "That is not what I want."

"Then give me my cloak."

"If I do, you will leave. I don't want you to leave," he said. "I want you to stay."

The *tennin* was silent for a time. Then, "Why?"

Hakuryo thought about it, and gave an honest answer. "I do not know."

She looked at him then with something like pity. "You do not desire me as a man does a woman, yet I think you would try to make a wife of me, for want of an alternative."

Hakuryo blushed, as that was precisely where his thoughts had gone. "Would that be so terrible?" he asked.

"Yes, but more for you than for me. In embracing me, you would only make of me a creature of the earth, no different than yourself. Many men would find this reason and reward enough, but not you, monk. You could never escape the knowledge of exactly what you had done to me. You would go mad."

"I do not think it wise," Hakuryo said, "to insult one who holds such power over you."

The maiden looked at him then, and her eyes were sad. "I am a *tennin*. I do not insult you. I merely tell you the truth."

"All my life," Hakuryo said, "I have been searching for you. For what you are, for what you mean to this existence. How can I let you go now that I have found you?"

"What have you found?" she asked.

"Why . . . the heavens! All embodied in you. So close I can possess them, touch them . . . "

She sighed. "You can touch me, but that's not the same thing. Did it never occur to you that you've been looking for the wrong thing?"

"Wrong . . . ? I seek Enlightenment!"

"And you think it can be found in either me or a feather cloak? You are an idiot."

"I . . . ? How dare you!"

"Tell the truth? Because I am a tennin, and can do nothing else, and I tell you truly that I am not what you seek," the maiden said. "The gods are on the same journey as you, monk. In time, yes, even we will die and the heavens pass away to make room for what comes next. There is nothing I am, nothing I have, nothing about me that will take you one step closer to where you wish to be."

"Still," Hakuryo said slowly, "now and then it does one no harm to remind oneself how far one has to go, not how far they have come."

She smiled at him, then. "Fair enough. So. Does holding my cloak and gazing at me tell you anything you did not already know?"

Hakuryo found the presence of mind to actually think about the Celestial Maiden's question. The first thing that occurred to him was that the answer was "no." He had always believed that one such as she existed, and from there it was no stretch at all to include the *hagoromo*. It wasn't a question of belief, and never had been; faith had never been a problem. It was a question of understanding. He knew that he still did not understand. He wanted to.

"Yes," Hakuryo said, finally. "It tells me that I cannot hold either of you and so must let you go. Still, may I ask something of you first?"

"What is it?"

"I have heard that the Celestial Maidens dance to hold the moon in its course and to honor its changes. I would think that any mortal who witnesses this dance would have an understanding far beyond that of other men. Is this so?"

"No. It's true there are many dances," the tennin said. "Including the Dance of the Fifteen Phases. And many reasons to dance. Some bring joy, but none of them bring understanding. They are what they are."

"I would still like very much to see it."

"Why?" she asked one more time.

Hakuryo thought about it. "Because I believe you when you say I cannot touch what you are. That is really what I want to do, and yet I cannot, no matter how I might wish the truth was different."

"That does not explain why you wish to see me dance."

"I may not be able to capture what you are, but I can experience it, embodied in your dance. I can make that experience part of what I am."

"You will not be able to contain it," she said. "Any more than you can capture the divine in one *tennin* or a thousand feather cloaks."

"I do not wish to contain the dance, no more than I really want to tie you to the earth," Hakuryo said. "You are right; that would debase you and destroy me. That is not what I want."

"Then what do you want? Do you really know?"

"Yes," he said, "I do not want to possess you; I want to experience what you are. My meditations fail me in this, so if it is true that experience is what changes one, then, at least once in my life, I want to experience the divine. That is what I ask of you in exchange for your wondrous cloak."

She smiled then. "Perhaps you are not such a fool after all."

"I thought you always spoke truly," Hakuryo said.

"I do," she said, "which is not the same as saying that that I'm never wrong. Very well, I will dance for you. But I will need my cloak to do so."

"How do I know you will not fly away as soon as I give it to you?"

"Deception is for the hearts of men, monk. It has no place in the heavens. I did not insult you. I ask that you grant me the same courtesy."

Hakuryo accepted her reprimand as a just one and felt shame. He humbly and carefully handed the robe to the maiden. He was tempted to try to touch her, but he did not. He merely watched as she removed his old cloak and donned her celestial robe.

"Now you may watch me," she said, and she walked to a place where the shore was flat and open to the sky.

As always, the Celestial Maiden had told the truth. What Hakuryo saw then he could not contain, nor grasp, nor fully describe, nor even truly remember, save that once, just once, he had seen an angel dancing, and it was enough. After a time that might have been moments or an eternity, the *tennin's* delicate feet lifted from the coarse earth and she rose, still dancing, and was lost from sight in the sky.

Hakuryo stood there for a long time, now alone on the mountainside. He tried to meditate on what had happened to him; old habits were hard to break. Yet after a while, and also for the first time in his life, Hakuryo was aware of being alone. Or rather, being *separated* from the life of the world. This world. His home. He decided that being alone was not such a grand or desirable thing as he had once thought.

In a story less true than this one, perhaps it would be said that Hakuryo focused his meditations on the meaning of his encounter with the Celestial Maiden and achieved Enlightenment, becoming a great priest and teacher, later to be copied in wood or stone and called a saint. As I said before, this is not one of those stories.

Instead, what happened next was that Hakuryo crossed the mountain and went down to the sea, where he cast off his monk's robes to become a simple fisherman. That is why, in many tellings Other than this one, he is a fisherman from the start and not a monk at all, but that actually came later.

Hakuryo never did learn to meditate in the properly prescribed manner, nor did he ever have a statue. He did learn to throw his nets and to haul them in with the same attention whether they were full or empty, and to understand and appreciate the eternity between one breath and the next, and the dance of sunlight on the ocean. And yes, in time and despite himself, people were drawn to him and he became both a great priest and teacher, though he never wore the robes of either priest or monk again.

There was only one thing that interrupted Hakuryo's peace for the rest of his days, and it was simply this: whenever a crane flew by, whether it was a flock or simply one lone bird, Hakuryo would stop

SKIN DEEP

The hardest part of Ceren's day was simply deciding what skin to put on in the morning. Making an informed decision required that she have a clear view of her entire day, and who other than a prisoner in a dungeon or a stone statue on a pedestal had that particular luxury?

Ceren went into her Gran's store-room where the skins were kept. She still thought of the store-room as her grandmother's, just as the small cottage in the woods and the one sheep and a milk goat in the pen out back belonged to her Gran as well. Ceren still felt as if she was just borrowing the lot, even though she had been on her own for two full seasons of the sixteen she had lived. Yet she still felt like a usurper, even though she herself had buried her grandmother under the cedar tree and there were no other relatives to make a claim. She especially felt that way about the skins, since Gran herself hadn't owned those, at least to Ceren's way of thinking. Borrowed, one and all.

They lay on a series of broad, flat shelves in the store-room, covered with muslin to keep the dust off, neatly arranged just as a carpenter would organize his tools, all close to hand and suited for the purpose. Here was the one her Gran had always called the Oaf—not very bright, but large and strong and useful when there were large loads to be shifted or firewood to cut. There was the Tinker—slight and small, but very clever with his hands and good at making and mending. On the next highest shelf was the Soldier. Ceren had only worn him once, when the Red Company had been hired to raid the northern borders and all the farmers kept their axes and haying forks near to hand. She didn't like wearing him. He had seen horrible things, done as much, and the shell remembered, and thus so did she. She wore him for two days, but by the third she decided she'd rather take her chances with the raiders. The Soldier was for imminent threats and no other.

The skin on the highest shelf she had never worn at all. Never even seen it without its translucent covering of muslin, though now that Gran was gone there was nothing to prevent her. That skin frightened Ceren even more than The Soldier did. Gran had told her that at most she would wear the skin once or twice in her life, that she would know why when the time came. Otherwise, best not to look at it or think about it too much. Ceren didn't understand what her Gran was talking about, and that frightened her most of all because the old woman had flatly refused to explain or even mention the matter again. But there lay the skin on its high shelf. Sleeping, supposedly. That's what they all were supposed to do when not needed, but Ceren wasn't so sure about this one. It wasn't sleeping, she was certain. It was waiting for the day when Ceren would be compelled to put it on and become someone else, someone she had never been before.

It'll be worse than the Soldier, she thought. *Has to be, for Gran to be so leery of it.*

The day her grandmother had spoken of was not here yet, since Ceren felt no compulsion to find the stepstool and reach the mysterious skin on the high shelf. Today was a work day, and so today there was no guessing to be done. Ceren slipped out of her thin shift and hung it on a peg. Then she slipped the muslin coverlet off of the Oaf. She had need of his strength this fine morning. She could have even used that strength to get the skin of its shelf in the first place, but for the moment she had to make do with what she had. She used both hands and finally pulled it down.

Like cowhide, the skin was heavier than it looked. Unlike cowhide, it still bore an uncanny resemblance to the person who had once owned it, only with empty eye-sockets now and a face and form much flatter than originally made, or so Ceren imagined. Gran never said where any particular skin came from; Ceren wasn't sure that the old woman even knew.

"They once belonged to someone else. Now they belong to us, our rightful property. I also came into a wash basin, a hammer, a saw and a fine, sharp chisel when my own mam died, and I didn't ask where they came from. Your mam would have got them, had she lived, but she wouldn't wonder about those things and neither should you."

Ceren had changed the subject then because her Gran had that little glow in her good eye that told anyone with sense that they were messing around in a place that shouldn't be messed around in. Ceren, whatever her faults, had sense.

It took all of her strength, but Ceren managed to hold up the skin she as breathed softly on that special spot on the back of its neck that Gran had showed her. The skin split open, crown to crack, and Ceren stepped into it like she'd step into a dancing gown—if she'd had such a thing or a maid or friend to lace up the back when she was done.

Next came the uncomfortable part. Ceren always tried not to think about it too much, but she didn't believe she would ever get used to it, even if she lived to be as old as Gran did before she died. First Ceren was aware of being in what felt like a leather cloak way too large for her. That feeling lasted for only a moment before the cloak felt as if it was shrinking in on her, but she knew it must have been herself getting . . . well, *stretchy*, since the Oaf was a big man, and soon so was she. Her small breasts flattened as if someone was pushing them, her torso thickened, her legs got longer and then there was this clumsy, uncomfortable *thing* between them. She felt her new mouth and eyes slip into place. When it was all over, she felt a mile high, and for the first dizzying seconds she was afraid that she might fall. Now she could clearly see the covering of muslin over the topmost skin on its shelf. She looked away, closed her eyes.

The uncomfortable part wasn't quite over; there was one final bit when Ceren was no longer completely Ceren. There was someone else present in her head, someone else's thoughts and memories to contend with. Fortunately the Oaf hadn't been particularly keen on thought, and so there wasn't as much to deal with.

The Soldier hadn't been quite so easy. Ceren tried not to remember.

"Time to go to work," she said aloud in a voice much lower than her own, and the part of her that wasn't Ceren at all but now served her understood.

She was never sure how much of what followed was her direction or The Oaf's understanding. Ceren knew the job that needed doing—a dead tree had fallen across the spring-fed brook that brought water to her animals and had diverted most of it into a nearby gully. That tree would have to be cleared, but while Ceren rightly thought of the axe and the saw, it was the Oaf who added the iron bar from her meager store of tools and set off toward the spring, whistling a tune that Ceren did not know, nor would it have mattered much if she *did* know, as she had never had the knack of whistling. Ceren was content to listen as she—or rather *they*—set out on the path to the head of the spring.

Ceren's small cottage nestled into the base of a high ridge in the foothills of the Pinetop Mountains. The artesian spring gave clear cold water year round, or at least it did before the tree dammed up the brook. Now the brook was down to a trickle, and the goat especially had been eyeing her reprovingly for the last two mornings as she milked it.

The Oaf had been right about the iron bar. It was a large old tree, more dried-out than rotten. Even with her new strength, it took Ceren a good bit of the morning with the axe and saw and then a bit more of that same morning with the iron bar and a large rock for a fulcrum to shift the tree trunk out of the brook. She moved a few stones to reinforce the banks and then it was finally done. The brook flowed freely again.

The Oaf cupped his calloused hands and drank from the small pool that formed beneath the spring. Ceren knew he wanted to sit down on a section of the removed log and rest, but Ceren noticed a plume of smoke from the other side of the ridge and gave in to curiosity. The ridge was steep, but spindly oak saplings and a few older trees grew along most of the slope, and she made her borrowed body climb up to the top using the trees for handholds.

My own skin is better suited for this climb, she thought, but The Oaf, though not nearly so nimble as Ceren's own lithe frame, finally managed to scramble to the top.

Someone was clearing a field along the north-south road in the next valley. Ceren recognized the signs: a section of woodland with its trees cut, waste fires for the wood that couldn't be reused, a pair of oxen to help pull the stumps. She counted three men working and one woman. The farmhouse was already well under way. Ceren sighed. She wasn't happy about other people being so close; her family's distrust of any and all others was bred deep. Yet most of the land along the road this far from the village of Endby was unclaimed, the farm did not infringe on her own holdings, and at least they were on the *other* side of the ridge, so she wouldn't even have to see them if she didn't want to.

Ceren had just started to turn away to make the climb back down before she noticed one lone figure making its way down the road. It was difficult at the distance, but Ceren was fairly sure that he was one of the men from the new homestead.

Doubtless headed toward the village on some errand or other.

Ceren watched for a while just to be sure and soon realized the wisdom of caution. The ridge sloped downward farther east just before it met the road. To her considerable surprise, when the man passed the treeline he did not continue on the road but rather stepped off onto the path leading to her own cottage. She swore softly, though through the Oaf's lips it came out rather more loud than she intended. Ceren hurried her borrowed form back down the ridge to the path from the spring, but despite her hurry, the stranger was no more than ten paces from her when she emerged into the clearing.

"Hullo there," said the stranger.

Ceren got her first good look at the man. He was wearing his work clothes, old but well-mended. He was young, with fair hair escaping from the cloth he'd tied around his head against the sun, and skin tanned from a life spent mainly outside. She judged him not more than a year or so older than she herself. Well-formed, or at least to the extent that Ceren could tell about such things. There weren't that many young men in the village to compare to, most were away on the surrounding farms, and those who were present always looked at her askance when she went into town, if they looked at her at all. It used to upset her, but Ceren's grandmother had been completely untroubled by this.

"Of course they look away. You're a witch, girl, the daughter of a witch and the granddaughter of a witch, the same as me. They're afraid of you, and if you know what's what, you'll make sure they stay that way."

The memory passed in a flash, and for a moment Ceren didn't know what to do. The stranger just looked at her then repeated, "Hullo? Can you hear me?"

Ceren spoke through her borrowed mouth and tried to keep her tone under control. The Oaf had a tendency to bellow like a bull if not held in check. "Hello. I'm sorry I was . . . thinking about something. What do you want?"

"I'm looking for the Wise Woman of Endby. I was told she lived here. Is this your home, then?"

"The Wise Woman is dead, and of course this isn't my home. I just do some work for her granddaughter who lives here now," Ceren/Oaf said.

"So I was given to understand, but is her granddaughter not a . . . not of the trade?"

Ceren nearly smiled with her borrowed face in spite of herself. The stranger's phrasing was almost tactful. Obviously he wanted something. But what? She finally noticed the stained bandage on the young man's right forearm, mostly covered by the sleeve of his shirt. Obviously, he needed mending. That was something Ceren could do even without a borrowed skin.

"She is," Ceren said. "If you'll wait out here, I'll go fetch her."

By this point Ceren was used to her borrowed form, but she still almost banged her head on the cottage's low door when she went inside. She made her way quickly to the store-room and tapped the back of her neck three times with her left hand.

"Done with ye, off with ye!"

The skin split up the back again like the skin of a snake and sloughed off, leaving Ceren standing naked, dazed, and confused for several moments before she came fully to herself again. She quickly pulled her clothes back on and then took just as much time as she needed to arrange the Oaf back on his shelf and cover him with muslin until the next time he'd be needed.

When she emerged from the cottage, blinking in the sunlight, the young man, who had taken a seat on a stump, got to his feet. He had pulled the cloth from his head like a gentleman removing his cap in the presence of a lady. For a moment Ceren just stared at him, but she remembered her tongue soon enough.

"My hired man said I'm needed out here. I'm Ceren, Aydden Shinlock's grand-daughter. Who are you?"

"My name's Kinan Baleson. My family is working a new holding just beyond the ridge there," he said, pointing at the ridge where Ceren-oaf had stood just a short time before. "I need your help."

"That's as may be. What ails you?"

"It's this . . . ." he said, pulling back the sleeve covering the bandage on his right forearm.

Just as Ceren had surmised, he'd injured himself while clearing land at the new croft, slipped and gouged his arm on the teeth of a bow saw. "My Ma did what she knew to do, but she says it's getting poisoned. She said to give you this . . . " He held out a silver penny. "We don't have a lot of money, but if this isn't enough, we have eggs, and we'll have some mutton come fall."

"Unless the hurt is greater than I think, it'll do."

Ceren took the coin and then grasped his hand to hold the arm steady and immediately realized the young man was blushing and she almost did the same.

Why is he doing that? I'm no simpering village maid.

She concentrated on the arm to cover her own confusion and began to unwrap the bandage, but before she'd even begun she knew that Kinan's mother had the right of it. The drainage from the wound was a sickly yellow, but to her relief it had not yet gone green. If that had happened, the choice would have been his arm or his life.

"Should have come to me sooner," Ceren said, "with all proper respect to your mother."

"She tried to make me come yesterday," Kinan said gruffly, "but there's so much to do—"

"Which would be managed better with two arms than one," Ceren said, planting a single seed of fear the way her Gran had taught her. In this case Ceren could see the wisdom of it. Better a little fear in the present than a lifetime disadvantage. "Hold still now."

Kinan did as he was told. Ceren finished unwrapping the bandage and pulled it away to get a good look at the wound. The gash was about two inches long, but narrow and surprisingly clean-edged, considering what had made it. The cut started a hand's width past his wrist, almost neatly centered in the top of the forearm. A little deep but not a lot more than a scratch, relatively speaking. Yet the area around the cut had turned an angry shade of red, and yellowish pus continued to ooze from the wound.

"Sit down on that stump. I'll be back in a moment."

Ceren picked up her water bucket, went to the stream and pulled up a good measure of cold, clear water. Before she returned to Kinan, she went back into her cottage and brought out of her healer's box, a simple pine chest where her Gran had kept her more precious herbs and tools. While most everything else in her life felt borrowed, Ceren considered that this box belonged to *her*. She had earned it. Both by assisting her Gran in her healer's work for years and by being naturally good at that work. Ceren inherited the box, inherited in a way that didn't seem to apply to the rest of the things around her.

Especially the skins.

Ceren carefully washed out the gash as Kinan gritted his teeth, which Ceren judged he did more from anticipation than actual added pain. A wound of this sort had its own level of pain which nothing Ceren had done—yet—was going to change. Once the wound was cleaned out, she leaned close and sniffed it.

"I can't imagine it smells like posies," Kinan said, forcing a smile.

"I'm more interested in *what* it smells like, not how pleasant it is."

Ceren wondered for a moment why she was bothering to explain, since her Gran had been very adamant on the subject of secrets: "Best that no one knows how we do what we do. Little seems marvelous, once you know the secret." And it was important for reputation that all seem marvelous; Ceren saw the wisdom in that as well.

Even so, Ceren found it easy to talk to Kinan, she who barely had reason to speak three words in a fortnight. "My Gran taught me what scents to look for in a wound. A little like iron for blood, sickly-sweet for an inflamed cut like this one. Yet there's something . . . .ah. You said you cut yourself on a saw? Fine new saw or old, battered saw?"

He sighed. "Everything we have is old and battered, but serves well enough."

"Yes, this saw has served you pretty well indeed. There's something in there that smells more like iron than even blood does. Unless I miss my guess, your saw left a piece of itself behind and is poisoning the wound. That's why your arm isn't healing properly."

He frowned. "You're saying you can smell iron?"

"Of course. Can't you?"

"Not at all. That's amazing."

Ceren almost blushed again. *So much for Gran's ideas about secrets*, Ceren thought. *Or at least that one.*

Ceren reached into her box and pulled out a bronze razor, which she proceeded to polish on a leather strop. Kinan eyed the blade warily, and Ceren nodded. "Yes, this is going to hurt. Just so you know."

Kinan flinched as Ceren gently opened the edges of the wound with her thumbs. More pus appeared and she rinsed that away as well. She judged the direction the sawblade had cut from and looked closer. A black speck was wedged deep into the wound's upper end. Now that she had found the culprit, it only took a couple of cuts with the razor to free the piece of broken sawblade. Kinan grunted once but otherwise bore the pain well enough and kept still even when new blood started to flow. Ceren held the fragment up on the edge of her bloody razor for Kinan to see before flicking it away into the bushes.

She then washed the wound one more time and bound it again with a fresh strip of linen.

"Considering what you're likely to do with that arm, I really should stitch it," she said. "And it's going to bleed for a bit as things are. Let it, that'll help wash out the poison. If you'll be careful and wash the cut yourself at least once a day—clean, clear water, mind, not the muck from your stock pond—you should get to keep the arm."

"We have our own well now," Kinan said. "I'll heed what you say. I'm in your debt."

She shook her head. "You paid, so we're square. But mind what I said about washing."

Kinan thanked her again and left. Ceren watched him walk back down the path toward the road. After a moment she realized that she was, in fact, watching him long past the point where it was reasonable to do so. She sighed and then went to clean her razor in the cold stream.

===⟡===

That night Ceren dreamed that she walked hand in hand with Kinan through a golden field of barley, the grain ready to harvest. Yet no sooner had Kinan taken her in his arms than there stood his family: the brothers whom Ceren saw that day from the ridge, a mother and father with vague, misty faces.

"Stay away from that witch! She's evil!" they all said, speaking with one voice.

"There's nothing wrong with me!" Ceren said, but she didn't believe it. She knew there was. Those in the dream knew it too. Kinan turned his back on her and walked away with his family as the barley turned to briars and stones around a deep, still pool of water.

"You can't do it alone, you know. Your Gran knew. How do you think you got here?"

Ceren looked around, saw no one. "Where are you?"

"Look in the pond."

Ceren looked into the water but saw only her own reflection. It took her several moments to realize that it was not her reflection at all. Her hair was long, curly, and black, not the pale straw color it should have been. Her eyes were large and dark, her rosy-red lips perfectly formed. Ceren looked into the face of the most beautiful girl she had ever seen, and the sight was almost too painful to bear. "That's not me."

"No, but it could be. If you want."

When Ceren opened her eyes again, she had her own face once more, but the other girl's reflection stood beside her on the bank of the pool, wearing golden hoops in her ears and dressed like a gypsy princess. Ceren couldn't resist a sideways glance, but of course there was no one else there.

"Dreams lie," Ceren said. "My Gran told me that."

"This one is true enough and you know it. Even if Kinan was interested, what do you think his family would say if he came courting a witch?"

"He's not going to court me. I'd toss him out on his ear if he did. What a notion."

"Liar."

Ceren's hands balled into fists. "I just met him! He's not even that handsome."

The girl's laugh was almost like music. "What's that got to do with anything? He's young, he's strong, he has a touch of gentleness about him, despite his hard life. And he's not a fool. Are you?"

"Be quiet!"

The strange girl's reflection sighed, and ripples spread over the pond. "I never cared much for your Gran, but I will say this: she was always clear on what she wanted and never feared to go after it, too. So. She's dead and now you're the Mistress here. Tell me you don't want him. Make me believe you, and I'll go away."

"How do you know me? Who are you?"

"I've known you all your life, just as you know who I am."

Ceren did know. Just as she knew how she felt about Kinan and how strongly she tried not to feel anything at all.

"The topmost shelf. That's you."

"No, there is no one there. What remains is little more than a memory, but it is a memory that can serve you in this, as the memory of the Oaf and the Soldier and the Tinker cannot. What remains is merely a tool. Your Gran understood that. Use me, as she did."

"No!"

"Mark me—you will." The ripples faded along with her voice and reflection, but just before she awoke, Ceren gazed into the pool once last time and saw nothing at all.

For the next few months Ceren kept herself too busy to think about either Kinan or what lay on the topmost shelf. It was easy enough. There was always something that needed doing around her croft and a fairly steady stream of villagers and farmers from the surrounding countryside.

After her grandmother was cold and buried, Ceren had worried about whether the people who had come to her Gran would come to her now, she being little more than a girl and not the Wise Woman of Endby, who always wore her Gran's face so far as Ceren was concerned: ancient, bent, hook-nosed and glaring, while Ceren was none of those things except, now and then, glaring. But she needn't have worried. A Wise Woman was always needed where more than a few folk gathered, and as long as there was someone to fill the role, there were always people willing to let her. Ceren knew she would grow into the part, in time. Besides, "Wise Woman" was them being polite; she knew what they called her behind her back. Such rubbish had never bothered her grandmother. Ceren couldn't quite say the same.

One day it will seem perfectly natural, she thought, but the prospect didn't exactly fill her with joy. Fear and secrecy were the witch's stock in trade, just as her Gran had always said. She had no right to complain if other, less pleasant things came with them.

Ceren had just doled out the herb bundle that would rid a silly village girl of her "problem" when she heard an alarm bell clanging from the village itself. The girl mumbled her thanks and hurried away. Ceren looked south toward Endby but saw nothing out of the ordinary. When she looked back north it was a different story.

Smoke.

Not Kinan's home, she realized with more relief than she cared to admit; this was further west. Still, too close, to all of them. Ceren didn't hesitate. She didn't think of all the other things so much smoke in the sky might mean. She knew what the smoke meant, just as her Gran would have known. She went to the store-room and put on the Soldier, because it was the only thing she knew to do.

The face and form of the Soldier remembered, so Ceren did too. There was no time to worry about what she did not want to see; it was all there, just as she'd left it the last time she had worn his skin, but now there was too much else that needed remembering.

Too far from the Serpent Road for this to be the main body. Most likely foragers.

This was what the Soldier knew, and so Ceren knew it, too. After a moment's reflection, the Soldier took one long knife from the cutlery rack and placed it in his belt. Ceren had expected him to take the felling axe, but now she understood why he didn't—too long in the handle and heavy in the blade to swing accurately at anything other than a target that wasn't moving. A short, balanced hatchet would have been better for their purpose, but there was none.

The Soldier trotted up the path toward the ridge, not hurrying, saving their strength. They passed the spring and scrambled up the ridge, and from that height the flames to the west were easy to see. Neither Ceren nor the Soldier knew which farm lay to the west, but they both knew there was one, or had been. The foragers would be spreading out from the Serpent Road; it was likely that they didn't know the north road—little more than a cart path—or the village of Endby even existed, but it looked like one group was going to find it if they kept moving east.

How many?

That was a question that needed to be answered and quickly. From the ridge the Soldier simply noted that a group of farmers had arranged themselves at the western border of their field, armed with little more than pitchforks and clubs. Ceren noted that Kinan and his father and his two brothers were about to get themselves killed, and there was nothing she could do about it.

They mean to keep the raiders from burning the field! thought Ceren.

Foolish, thought the memory of the Soldier, *they'd be better served to save what they could and make for the village.* Ceren couldn't disagree, since she knew the same could be said for herself. Yet here she was. She tried not to dwell on that or why her first instinct had been to don the Soldier. She thought instead of how hard the Balesons had worked to get their farm going. And how hard it would have been for them to let it all be destroyed.

The Soldier's thoughts closed in after that, so Ceren didn't understand at first why they turned left along the ridge rather than descending to stand with Kinan's family, but she knew better than to interfere. He was in his element, just as she was not. The Soldier kept low and moved quickly, using the trees and bushes that grew thick on the ridge as cover. Soon they left the bramble hedge that marked the edge of the Baleson farm. About three bowshots from the boundary, the ridge curved away south. They peered out of the thicket at the bend. There was still no sign of the foragers.

"Maybe they've stopped."

The Soldier's thought was immediate and emphatic. *Not enough time. They're not finished.*

Ceren and the Soldier found a way to descend and, once they were on level ground again, slipped away quickly into the trees. Ceren realized that they were approaching the burning farmhouse by a circular route, keeping to the cover of the woods. They heard a woman scream—and then silence.

They found a vantage point and looked out in time to see a man tying the straps of his leather brigandine back into place. He was lightly armored otherwise, but well armed. A bow and quiver lay propped against a nearby railing. The body of a man and a child lay nearby. A woman lay on the ground at the raider's feet, unmoving, her clothing in disarray and even at their distance they could see the blood. It took Ceren a moment to realize that the sword that she'd thought stuck into the ground was actually pinning the woman's body to the earth. She felt her gorge rising, but the Soldier merely judged the distance and scanned the rest of the scene. The farmhouse was still burning well, though the flames were showing signs of having passed their peak. Another moment and the roof came crashing down in a shower of embers.

Unmounted auxillaries with one scout. We have a chance, thought the Soldier.

Kill him, she thought in her anger.

The Soldier remained cold as a winter stream. *Not yet.*

The memory contained in the Soldier forced her to look toward the east. She saw four more men armed and armored similarly to the one lagging behind, but only the straggler had a bow. For some reason this seemed to please the Soldier. The other four carried bundles over their shoulders, apparently the spoils of the farm.

"You said there was another farm this way," shouted one of them. "We need to hit it and then return before nightfall if we're to be ready to move at daybreak. We haven't got time for your dallying."

"I'm almost done," said the first. "but this baggage has befouled my good blade. I'll catch up when I've cleaned it."

One of them swore, but they didn't wait. The other four disappeared into the trees, heading toward Kinan's farm. Ceren still felt sick but now there an even greater sense of urgency.

Kill him!

Soon.

They kept out of sight. They didn't move until the man had carefully wiped his sword on the dead woman's torn dress and sheathed the blade, then reclaimed his bow and quiver. The Soldier moved quickly and quietly, keeping to the trees at the edge of the woods, Ceren little more than a spectator behind borrowed eyes.

The Soldier caught the scout from behind before he had taken six steps into the trees. The scout managed only a muffled grunt as the Soldier clamped his hand over the man's mouth and neatly slashed his throat. The raider's blood flowed over their arms, but the Soldier didn't release their grip until the man went limp. They took the sword and the bow and quiver, but that was all.

The armor?

No time.

Ceren felt a little foolish for asking the question in the first place, and the reason was part of why she so feared to wear the Soldier's skin—she was starting to think like the Soldier. Like he had to think to serve his function. She knew why they left the armor, just as she knew why they did not follow the raiders along the same path, even though it was the most direct route. They took their course a little to the right, to place themselves just south of where the raiders would have to pass the barrier. At this point Ceren wasn't certain if this was the Soldier's direction or hers, but she knew they did not want to place the farmers directly in front of the raiders, not when arrows were about to fly.

They found a gap in the bramble thicket bordering the field, but the raiders had already emerged and were a good thirty paces into the field, moving directly to where Kinan stood with his father and brothers. Their numbers were matched, but that was all. It was hay fork and club against sword and spear, the difference being that those who held the sword and spear knew how to use them for this particular form of work.

Kinan, his family. . . . They'll be slaughtered!

The first arrow was already nocked, but the Soldier did not draw. Not yet. Ceren again knew why, and she hated it. The raiders were still too close. Fire now and they'd probably get one of them, but then the three left would charge their position. The Soldier was waiting for advantage; a longer shot versus time to aim and fire. Ceren understood the tactical necessity, just as she understood that it might get one or more of Kinan's family killed. She let the Soldier wait until she could stand it no longer.

Now.

The closest raider went down screaming in pain with an arrow in his thigh. At first Ceren thought it was a bad shot, but then realized the Soldier had hit exactly what he aimed at. He wanted the raider incapacitated but calling attention to himself. The distraction worked. The raiders hesitated and turned toward their fallen companion. The Soldier's second arrow hit the next-closest raider high in the chest. He went down with barely more than a gasp.

This was the Soldier's purpose, and he was serving it well. Ceren felt the Soldier's satisfaction, and she felt sick as she realized that it wasn't just satisfaction that he felt. The Soldier was enjoying himself, and thus so was she, no matter how much she did not wish to, no matter how much she had wanted to see the raiders die.

Let them charge us now, Ceren thought, but it didn't work out that way. The raiders charged the farmers. Ceren didn't know if they meant to cut down Kinan's family or merely get *past* them to use them as cover, but now the odds were two to one in the farmers' favor. One farmer went down; Ceren couldn't tell who because the Soldier had already tossed the bow aside, and they ran full speed toward the fighting, borrowed sword drawn. The man on the ground made a feeble cut at him as he raced past, and the Soldier split the man's skull with barely a pause, but by the time they reached the farmers, it was all over. Kinan was down on the ground, a gash in his forehead.

Somehow Ceren knew it would be Kinan. She felt cold, almost numb at the sight of him.

The raiders were dead. The farmers were still furiously clubbing the bodies when Ceren in her Soldier skin reached them. The farmers eyed the Soldier warily.

"Who are you?" Kinan's father asked without lowering his club.

"The Wise Woman sent me," the Soldier said, sheathing the sword as he spoke. "She saw the smoke."

Ceren saw the look in the older man's eyes. Relief, certainly, but fear as well. One more debt. Ceren shook her head, and of course the Soldier did the same. "She figured they'd be at her steading next. Best to stop them here. What about the boy?"

They were all still breathing hard; Ceren wasn't even sure they'd noticed that Kinan was down, but then they were all clustering about him. Ceren shoved her way down to Kinan's side in her borrowed skin.

It was a glancing blow, and that was probably the only reason Kinan was still breathing. Even so, it was a nasty gash, Kinan was unconscious, and they could not rouse him.

"We should take him to the Wise Woman," one of the brothers said, but Ceren had the Soldier shake his head for her.

"No. Until we know how bad his hurt is you shouldn't move him any farther than needs must. Lift him gently and put him in his bed. Clean and bandage the cut, and I'll fetch the Wise Woman to you."

The father looked toward the barrier. "What if there are more of them?"

The Soldier shook his head without any help from Ceren. "Keep watch, but I doubt there will be. It was a foraging party. There's an army on a quick march south, and the king will have to deal with that if he can, but auxiliaries? It's likely no one will even miss these bastards."

The farmers looked doubtful, but they did as the Soldier directed. Ceren watched them carry Kinan off, then quickly turned back toward her own home.

She shed the Soldier's skin with relief, but she was nearly stumbling with exhaustion. Even so, she managed to carry her box of medicines up the road to Kinan's farm. It was his mother that greeted her this time.

Ceren had never met the woman before, but she could see Kinan in the older woman's eyes. Most of the rest of his looks he got from his father. She frowned when Ceren appeared, but she seemed to be puzzled, not disapproving.

"Kinan said you were young. I didn't realize how young."

"My Gran trained me well," Ceren said, a little defensively. "I can help him."

The woman shook her head. "That's not what I meant. You already have helped him, so I hope you can again. He hasn't moved since they brought him in. My name is Liea, by the way. Thank you for coming," she said, and sounded as if she meant it.

Ceren found herself blushing a little. She couldn't remember the last time anyone had said thank-you to her and seemed sincere rather than grudging. Except Kinan.

"I'm Ceren. I don't know if your son told you or not. . . . I trust no more raiders have been seen?"

The woman shook her head. "Not here, though we've heard rumors of attacks further south. The men are out burying the carcasses in a deep hole."

"Then maybe we won't see more of them again."

Liea shrugged. "Even if the army is beaten, likely some like them will come this way again, and likely be even more hungry and desperate in the bargain. We heard what they did to the steading west of us."

Ceren only hoped that they hadn't seen it as well, as she had. Liea took her to where Kinan had been put to bed. It wasn't a large room, and clearly he shared it with his brothers. Ceren found him lying pale and still under a quilt. His breathing was regular and strong; the head wound had stopped bleeding and she removed the bandage, noting with approval that it had been cleaned out properly, doubtless Liea's doing. Now it was easy to see that the cut had not gone clear through to the skull, though it hadn't missed by much. Still, Kinan's continued unconsciousness was not a good sign, and the longer it lasted, the worse the portents.

Liea stood nearby watching. Her eyes were moist and her lower lip trembled. Ceren believed she knew how the woman felt, at least a little. She took a needle and thread from her box and calmly proceeded to sew up the gash. She noted with approval that Liea turned away only once, on the first pass of the needle.

"These stitches will need to come out, but probably not before a fortnight. Just cut one side under the knot and pull. It'll sting him, but no more than that."

Liea looked as if she was ready to collapse where she stood. She put her hand against the lintel for support. "You . . . you think he will live?"

"The next few minutes should tell. Would you like to help me?"

Ceren mixed a pungent blend of herbs with a few drops of apple cider supplied by Liea. She then had the older woman hold Kinan's head while she soaked a bit of linen in the mixture and held it under Kinan's nose. "I'd try not to breathe for a few moments, if I were you."

While Ceren and Liea both held their breath, Kinan inhaled the scent at full strength. In a moment his eyelids fluttered and then his eyes opened wide and tears started to flow. He sat upright in the bed despite Liea's best efforts. "What is that damn stench?"

"Your salvation," Ceren said calmly. She took the rag and stuffed it in an earthenware bottle with a tight cork to seal it. After she closed the lid of the box the scent began to fade immediately. Liea already had her arms around her son, who didn't seem to understand what all the fuss was about.

"I'm fine, Ma. My head hurts, but that's all . . . Wait, what happened to—"

"Your father and your brothers are all fine, as are you. Mostly thanks to this young woman here," Liea said. "Ceren, I don't know where you found that man you sent to help us, but we are in your debt for that as well. I don't know how we can repay you."

Debt. Well, yes. That was how it worked. Gran had always said as much. You use your skills and make other people pay for them. It was no different from being a cobbler and a blacksmith. Except that it *was* different. A cobbler could make a gift of shoes or a blacksmith an ironwork, to a friend. What witch—yes, that was the word; Gran spoke it if no one else would—gave her skills away? Who would trust such a gift? Ceren's weariness caught up with her all at once. She rose with difficulty.

"Can we discuss that later? I think I need to go home. . . . "

Liea looked her up and down. "I think we both need to sit for a moment and have a taste of that hard cider first—without the herbs. Then I'll have Kyne or Beras make sure you get home safe."

━◆━

"She was worried about me. She was nice to me."

As Ceren lay in her Gran's bed trying to sleep, she examined the thought and wondered if what she thought was concern in Liea's eyes was something else.

Child, everyone acts nice and respectful when they want something or when they owe you, Gran said. *You think we wear a false skin? Feh. Everyone drops the mask as soon as they get what they want. You don't owe them courtesy or aught else.* Ceren remembered. She was still remembering when she finally fell asleep, and heard the voice again.

"Your Gran knew better."

"Go away," Ceren said.

"I can't. Neither can you. We're stuck here, each in our own way. Or do you still think Kinan or his family will welcome you with open arms? Fool, if you want Kinan, you'll have to take him. Your Gran knew. Your Gran always got what she wanted. Or who she wanted."

That was a subject Ceren definitely did not want to hear about, but the message had already come through. "I collect what I need, but I take what I want, and that's what makes me a true witch. Is that it?"

"It's what your Gran taught you, and she taught you well. Don't deny what you are."

"What if I don't want to be like that?" Ceren heard faint laughter. "Then you 'be' alone and you 'be' nothing. Stop talking rubbish and use the right tool for the purpose. It'll get easier as time passes. You'll see. Your Gran did. Use me, as she did."

"If I'm a witch, then don't tell me what I must do!"

More laughter. Ceren remembered the sound of it in her head when she finally awoke, even more so than the sound arrows made when they struck human flesh and the image of what a man looked like split from crown to chin by a broadsword. The sun was streaming in from a dusty window. Ceren blinked. How long had she slept? The sun was already high and the morning half gone, at least, and she was famished. Ceren didn't bother to dress properly. First she visited the privy, then washed her face and hands in cold water from the stream. After that she stumbled to the larder and found some hard bread and cheese.

"What do you plan, then? A courtesy call on the boy's family?"

Ceren pinched herself just the once to verify that she wasn't dreaming, but she hadn't really thought so in the first place. Ceren addressed the person who was not there. "Haunting my dreams was bad enough. Are you going to talk to me while I'm awake too?"

"Someone needs to, but no. Your Gran said you would know when the time came, and this is how you know. It is time, Ceren. Put me on."

"Why?"

"So that you may achieve your heart's desire, of course."

Ceren closed her eyes briefly and then spoke to nothing again. "Very well."

The shelf was high. She needed a stool to stand on when she pulled down the long wrapped bundle that rested there. She barely glanced at it, but what she did see confirmed what she had long believed. In a moment the new skin was settling around her. She felt her legs lengthen, her small breasts swell and reshape as she surged up to meet fit the appearance she now wore.

As always, there was more to it than appearance. As with the Oaf, and the Soldier, and the Tinker, now she wore another person's memories. Only this time Ceren did not keep her own thoughts and memories tight and protected. She did not fight the new memories, as she tried to do with the Soldier. She took them as far as they would go, all the while she looked in the mirror.

She wasn't merely pretty. She had a face and form that would stop any man dead in his tracks. Ceren was now the reflection of the girl in the pond.

Didn't I tell you? The Girl sounded a bit smug. *You know what life was like for me. What it can be for you. All you need do is take what you want.*

Ceren nodded. "You're beyond beautiful. Was that why that man drowned you in the pond?"

She felt the laughter. She wondered if she was the one laughing, but the reflection looking back at her was sad and solemn. Her own reflection, somewhere hidden beneath a borrowed skin. *So you've seen that as well. Some men will destroy what they cannot possess, and I chose poorly. What of it? Neither Kinan nor his brothers are like that.*

"I know."

All you need do is show yourself to him as you are now, and he is yours.

Ceren shook her head. "No. I show your face to him and he is *yours*."

A frown now showing in the mirror that was none of Ceren. *It is the same thing, and he is your heart's desire!*

"No. I merely want him. I even think I like him. If there's more to the matter, then time alone will tell. You never understood my heart's desire. Maybe because it took me so long to understand it myself." She tapped the back of her neck three times. "Off with ye, done with ye!"

The skin split as it must, but it did not release her quickly or easily. The Girl was fighting her. Ceren thought she understood why. She pulled off one arm like a too-tight glove and then another, but the torso refused to budge.

"Does the servant question the mistress? Let me go."

You can't do it without me, without us! You're ugly, you're worthless. . . .

"Let me go," Ceren said calmly. "Or I'll cut you off." And just to show that she was serious, Ceren went to her herb box and took out the bronze razor. She had already started a new cut down the side when the skin finally relented. In a thrice Ceren had the Girl wrapped carefully back on her shelf.

The voice was still there, taunting her. *You'll be back. You need me to gain your heart's desire. If it's not Kinan, then another! You're plain at best, hideous at worst. You'll never achieve it on your own.*

Ceren almost giggled. "I didn't understand. All this time I thought the skins were tools and we the purpose. Now I know it's the other way around. I am the instrument, just as Gran was before me. You, the Oaf, the Tinker, the Soldier. . . . You who died ages ago, and yet still live through us. You are the purpose. We serve you."

You still do. And will.

"Why?"

Because only we can give you what you want.

Ceren shook hear head. "You still don't understand. You already have, at least in part."

What are you talking about?

"I've always felt like one living in a borrowed house, with borrowed strengths, borrowed skills, but I thought it was because of Gran. It wasn't. It was because of *you*."

Fool! The raiders will return or bandits or village boys too drunk to know who they're forcing! You will fall in love. A heavy tree will fall. You can't do this on your own. You need us.

"No," Ceren said. "I need to find out what belongs to me and what does not. You gave me that last part, but now I have to find the rest. That is my true heart's desire."

Ceren left the storeroom and latched it behind her. Then, upon consideration, she slowly and painfully pushed her Gran's heavy worktable to block the door.

Setting fire to her Gran's cottage was the easy part. Watching it burn was harder. Listening to the four voices screaming in her head was hardest of all, but she bore it. She heard the pounding from inside as the flames rose, tried not to think of what supposedly had no volition, no independent action, and yet still pounded against a blocked door. Ceren led her sheep and her goat to a grassy spot a safe distance away, where they grazed in apparent indifference as the cottage and pen alike burned.

Her Gran had never taught Ceren any prayers. She tried to imagine what a prayer must be like, and she said that one as the voices in her head rose into a combined scream of anguish that she could not shut out.

"Go to your rest, and take your memories with you."

She didn't think the prayer would work. Some of the memories were hers now, and she knew that was never going to change. She wasn't sure she wanted it to.

The roof finally collapsed, and just for a moment Ceren thought she saw four columns of ash and smoke rise separately from the fire to spiral away into the sky before all blended in flame and smoke as the embers rained down.

Kinan found her sitting there, on the stump, as the cottage smoldered. He looked a little pale, but he came down the path at a trot and was only a little out breath when he reached her. "We saw the smoke. Ceren, are you all right?"

She wondered if he really wanted to know. She wondered if now was the time to find out. "I should ask you the same. You shouldn't be out of bed," Ceren said, not looking at him. "My home burned down," she said, finally stating the obvious. "Such things happen."

"I'm sorry," Kinan said. "But I'm glad you're all right. Have you lost everything?"

She considered the question for a moment. "Once I would have thought so. Now I think I have lost very little." She looked at him. "I'm going to need a place to stay, but where can I go? I have a goat and a sheep and my medicines . . . I have skills. I'm not ugly, and I'm not useless!" That last part came out in a bit of a rush, and Ceren blinked to keep tears at bay. She only partly succeeded.

Kinan smiled then, though he sounded puzzled. "Who ever said you were?"

Ceren considered that for a moment too. "Nobody."

Kinan just sighed and held out his hand. "You'll stay with us, of course. We'll find room. Let's go talk to Ma; we'll come back for your animals later."

Ceren hesitated. "A witch in your house? What will your father say?"

Kinan didn't even blink. "My father is a wise man. He may grumble or he may not, but in the end he'll say what Ma says, and that's why we're going to her first. We owe you . . . I owe you."

Ceren decided she didn't mind hearing those words so much. Coming from Kinan, they didn't sound like an accusation. Besides, Ceren understood debts. They could start there; Ceren didn't mind. Just so long as they could start somewhere. She took Kinan's offered hand and he helped her to rise.

Kinan then carried Ceren's medicine box as he escorted her, understanding or not, down the road in search of her heart's desire.

BRILLIG

"'Twas brillig, and the slithy toves—"
Brillig brillig brillig!

That's one way to beat the poem. Start repeating words in a random selection. Breaks up the rhythm, you see. It's the rhythm that's dangerous. Don't ask me why but I know I'm right. The words may *seem* dangerous, mysterious, eldritch, and all that, but they're just stuff and nonsense. Learian. Charles Dodgson would know what I mean. I don't know if he realized what he had unleashed, but he did know about Edward Lear. This isn't Lear. It's Charles Dodgson, Lewis Carroll, and it's Jabberwocky. Lear is safe. At least, I've yet to find a demon in Lear, probably because I stopped reading him ages ago. Fear. Fear of Lear. Pity, as I do miss the Jumblies. Their heads are green, their hands are blue. They went to sea in a sieve, you know. Marvelous. Still, can't risk it. One demon is quite enough.

Jabberwocky.

Vorpal swords ultimately useless. The creature is always slain but it's never killed. Gallumph all you want with whatever head you think you've taken, but it's so. The Jabberwock always dies but Jabberwocky always lives, and the monster is merely part of it and not even the most important part at that.

Jabberwocky is going to destroy me, I know. I don't know when or even why, but I do know how. Sooner or later the arms weary, the walls are breached, the sentries sleep. The poem wants me to recite it. I won't. It can't make me. Not again. Third time is magic. Third time's the charm. After the third time the drowning man is seen no more.

"Twas brillig—"

Hah. Thought it would catch me napping. Not that easy, you serpent of scansion, you coil of gyres and gimbles. Slithy as a tove, I elude thee once more, mimsy and outgrabed. So what if the Jabberwock haunts my dreams? It can't hurt me any more than I can hurt it, for all that I carry its head back to my father every night. My father with the empty face. He doesn't hug me. I'm no beamish. There is no chortling. Just the blood-painted sword and the smiling head of the monster, and my Father's face that has neither mouth nor nose nor eyes. Father is symbolic but doesn't have much else to do. He doesn't need a face. The Jabberwock does, to mock me. There's an efficiency in dreams; probably has to do with not being real.

I keep coming back to my father's face. It's silly. I know who he is. I know what he looks like. I don't remember him at all, growing up. Strange if I did, since he wasn't there. But I've met him. He's a man. Nice enough in his way. Nothing special. The Father in my dreams has no face. Tenniel never drew the father's face. The son, yes, the Jabberwock, yes, even the borogoves, but the Father? Nothing. You think that's a coincidence? I don't, because there's no such thing. Tenniel knew.

I do remember the first time for the poem. Not for reading it; I read it for years, off and on, along with Dodgson's silly book. No, the first time I recited it aloud. I don't know why I did. Fresh out of college and starting my life. New job that I was just getting to know, new fiancee, ditto. Stressful, but good. Busy. Feeling fey. Loved the feel of the words off my tongue. Brillig. Slithy toves. Gyre and gimble. Frumious. Once I'd done it that first time, my only question was why I hadn't done it before. Reading is all well and good, but those words, those weird and wonderful words, they want to be spoken. Maybe they need to be spoken, I don't know.

That was the end of that job. My first. Oh, they *said* it had nothing to do with the poem. Bad fit. Not working out. Interests not congruent. Mysterious, potent, eldritch words, but not the poem. Doing my job while it was my job, learning my job while it was my job, but saying the words.

Oh, bandersnatch . . .

"Twas brillig, and the slithy toves did jump and frizzle, mom's a babe . . . "

Okay if you change the words a bit. Did I say that out loud? The rhythm, it wants me to forget, but I won't. The rhythm, that's what does it. Sets up the echoes in your head and they go to work. As I said, dangerous. Gotta be careful. The words want to be spoken only because the sounds want to be heard, so it's not the words. They don't mean anything, I know that, I said that. Have to be more careful. Musn't . . . well, clear enough what I musn't, and that's that.

The second time I said the poem, I lost the fiancee. In my defense I didn't understand before then. I didn't know. Thought the job was a fluke, my bad luck, and I still had Jenni. Then I didn't. The poem came out as a sort of song that day. I hadn't said it in months, not since the job. I was still looking. I still had Jenni. Everything was good. The poem took that away, and now I'm all that's left. I know what that means now, but not then. Then the words came out of me in a little song and Jenni told me there was someone else. That was it. Happens millions of times a day, all over the world. Someone else. Don't love you. Not sure I ever did. You're weird. That's when I knew. Once is a fluke, twice is a trend. Three times is history. Tried to tell her, make her see the words, hear the way I heard. She got frightened, ran from me. Ran. From me.

" . . . all mimsy were the borogoves, and the mome raths . . . "

Did something unnatural to a hedgehog. There. Further than I've gone in a while but not too far. See? You won't beat me. I can stop any time I want to. I can say the words but not all of them, and the spell or curse or mystic vibration never happens. Won't let it happen and you can't make me. I'm in charge, not you. Never you. And yes, I whistle past graveyards too. Why do you ask? Just to make music for the dead things there, you understand. You never know who or what might be listening. The poem taught me that.

"Oh, frabjous day! Caloo, callay! He throttled his bok choy."

Damn, don't know why I keep changing the words. Doesn't help. Once I even thought of referring to Jabberwocky as "The Carroll Poem" the way actors refer to "Macbeth" as "the Scottish Play" but that's just superstition. "Jabberwocky" is real. And when was the last time I got to that part? Can't remember. It doesn't want me to. Or I don't. It hurts not to feel the words. Like a junkie missing his smack. I'm shivering for lack of a word, a sound, a rhythm. Uffish thots. I knew I was having uffish thots, of course. Always do that at brillig. And after. That's when you put water on for tea or start broiling dinner. Tea and dinner are always good. Brillig time comes early, stays late. Welcome, brillig. Suppose they couldn't find any? It always happens. There's no tea here. Just brillig. And a pair of toves. Slithy. When the bandersnatch shows up, I'm leaving. Where? To nowhere because, well, there's nowhere to go. Nowhere to go where I am not, therefore nowhere Jabberwocky is not.

"Twas brillig and the slithy toves did gyre and gimble in the wabe. All mimsy were the borogoves, and the mome raths outgrabe."

That was just the beginning. That's all right. I can recite the beginning as many times as I want. It's just a coincidence that the beginning is the same as the end, like an ouroboros swallowing its tail. Always the beginning couplet, but never the end. How can I tell the difference? Because the ending couplet comes at the end, silly. So I didn't recite all of the poem, I didn't! It was the beginning.

I swear I didn't do it.

Don't look a me like that, Father. Don't look at me with no eyes. But he does, they all do, all those things that don't really exist. But most of all Father, symbolic, always missing, always present, shunned. Shun the frumious bandersnatch. I do beware, I do shun, all my life I have shunned . . . I did not say the words, not to the end, the real end. I went back to the beginning. I always go back to the beginning. Always. Nothing's changed! Start over, always start over, never end. Never.

Why can't I go back?

Father doesn't answer. He just smiles at me. It's impossible, you know. It's all impossible.

He has no face.

ON THE WHEEL

"The problem with the rat race: even if you win, you're still just a rat."

Robert Matthews knew that clichéd metaphor as well as anyone. What he did not know was who had called the metaphor down on their heads because, at precisely 9AM, everyone in the old established advertising firm of Hathcock and Dunn turned into a rat.

Specifically, a rat in some variation of a track suit, with numbers sewn on. Probably the only reason they weren't literally running a race was that the "race" element was recognized as figurative within the greater context of the metaphor. Recognized, Robert knew, by the self-aware metaphor itself. Still, this much of the metaphor had manifested literally—they were rats.

Without, it appeared, the loss of identify. Male or female as before, large or small as before, but a rat. Black rats, brown rats, white rats, piebald rats. Rats with bright eyes and a mischievous twist to the hips as they scurried, rats of dignified girth and ponderous squeaks, or rats like Robert himself: six feet from the tip of his whiskered nose to the base of his fine bald tail, which would have added another three feet to his overall length if he wasn't still walking upright. Annoyed as he was with the transformation, Robert regarded his reflection in the third floor men's room mirror and conceded that, as rats went, he was still a handsome devil.

Bud Jenkins came in. Robert knew it was Jenkins by his short stature and the thinning fur on his head.

"I guess it could have been worse," Bud said, examining his own whiskers in the mirror before heading toward the stalls. "Who's the idiot?"

"Don't know yet," Robert said. "You get the Hialeah campaign done?" Rats or no rats, there were deadlines to meet.

"Yeah, just in time." Jenkins disappeared into a cubicle and Robert heard running water followed by a flush. Jenkins emerged and paused to muss with what was left of the fur on his head. He hadn't washed his hands, but then he never washed his hands after using the john even before he was a rat.

Robert studied his own reflection in the mirror again and Jenkins shook his head. "Man, if I had your looks I'd be humping a different girl every night."

"Mary might object," Robert said.

Jenkins grunted. "Like Mary would still be around," Jenkins said. "I never should have settled for that bitch."

Robert remembered the incident. "You actually used that word to her face, as I recall. Is she still a Boston Terrier?"

"A literal bitch rather than a figurative one." Bud grinned. "Yeah. So?"

"Oh, nothing. But I think I'm going to ask for a raincheck on our golf date for Saturday," Robert said, realizing that Bud didn't have a clue as to the full implication of the change in his marital relationship. Mary was every bit as large as her husband and twice as vicious, so Robert's money was on the missus. He considered warning Bud, but the urge passed when he remembered that he was next in line for Bud's corner office.

"No problem. It's probably going to rain now anyway." Jenkins ambled out, followed soon after by Robert.

Outside, it was pretty much business as usual. Dolores Haidy was buffing her nails and, even though she was now a blondish rat, those nails looked neither less nor more like talons than they always had. Johanssen and Lewis were arguing politics through the walls of their cubicles, their only concession to ratness was that they would pause now and then to worry at a hole they were chewing through the cubicle wall so they could talk easier. Jane Perlicue and her cute young assistant were having a quickie. The only difference was that now they didn't bother to slip into the fourth floor maintenance closet, but rather were going at it on the floor of her office. With the door open.

Robert paused for the entertainment value, but left when that proved disappointing. He was feeling a growing sense of mission.

His natural inclination was to just accept the situation and move on. Since the Causality Rift of 2015, such physical manifestations of metaphor had been common. People learned to live with them in much the same way that the world back in the twentieth century had learned to live with the constant threat of nuclear annihilation. He had once watched a scientist who was involved in the quantum determination experiment indirectly responsible for the rift try to explain the nature of the phenomenon, but in the middle of his presentation the man had turned into a literal egg-head, thus demonstrating both the dangers of attracting a metaphor's attention and the consensual nature of reality as it had always existed. It was enough to know that metaphors were both parasitic and alive, and like all living things they had their own agenda and sought out suitable ecological niches to call home.

Like, currently, Hatchcock and Dunn, Inc.

Robert had no illusions about the aptness of the metaphor; he had always been cursed with an excessive degree of self-awareness, and was saved from a life of complete misery only by the counter-curse of complacency. He had made peace with his demons, literal and figurative, years ago. He was in his element at Hathcock and Dunn, and had no problem with that. Still, one thing to map one to one with the rat race image, quite another to be a literal rat.

There were disadvantages. For one thing, he really wasn't attracted to rats. Dolores, for example, in her current state did nothing at all for him nor, really, had watching Jane Perlicue with her lesbian gal pal. He found that fact worrisome. Plus, there was the problem of relating to their customers, most of whom weren't literal rats. Robert was sure their current existence as rodents would cast the firm in a bad light, and whatever else he might be, Robert was a company man. He simply had to find out who had attracted the metaphor's attention.

His first suspicion had been Jenkins, but their conversation in the men's room had made Robert realize that this was nonsense. Bud was about as self-aware as a turnip. Robert also considered himself as possible culprit, but the problem with that theory was that he recognized the truth of the metaphor without attaching any special significance to it. He was what he was, and that attitude was entirely too zen to generate the emotional content necessary to invoke a metaphor.

Someone had to be both self-aware enough to recognize the appropriateness of the metaphor, and yet unhappy enough to attract it, like a bleeding fish draws in sharks. Who could that be?

As Robert surveyed his colleagues, the answer to that question was not immediately apparent. Robert saw only rats, and the usual low-level despair that had nothing to do with self-awareness and everything to do with situational awareness. People were miserable because it made perfect *sense* to be miserable, and to keep as cheerful an attitude in the manifestation of that misery as possible. Yet someone was not doing his or her part, and Robert had to find out who that was.

Robert stopped by his office long enough to pick up a folder with some papers in it so it would look as if he had an objective, no matter where in the office he wandered. When he had covered all of the main office he proceeded to the elevator and then up to Executive Territory on the eighth floor.

The elevator doors opened on a hallway, with thick carpet and polished pseudo-mahogany doors in either direction that marked Hathcock and Dunn's upper echelon. There were no sounds from any of them. Not even so much as the squeak of an executive assistant sitting down on some rich old fart's lap; Robert now recalled that a "sales conference" for most of the eighth floor and reps from the firm's larger accounts has been arranged for the week at a golf resort in Bermuda. Robert felt a pang of jealousy but quickly squelched it. Better a rat than a green-eyed monster.

He started to leave, but a sliver of light down at the corner of the hallway caught his attention—one of the doors was slightly ajar.

Dunn, Jr. He isn't supposed to be here.

Probably he wasn't, and the office was just being cleaned. Still,

Robert thought he'd better make sure. He knocked on the door even as he pushed it open. "Hello? Mr. Dunn?"

No answer.

The executive assistant's office was empty. He tried the door to the inner sanctum and it opened easily on oiled hinges. The door to Dunn the Younger's private balcony was open and the draperies stirred in a slight breeze. A piece of paper on the CEO's desk did the same, held in place only by a heavy glass paperweight. Robert leaned over the desk and read what was written there.

It was a rather maudlin suicide note. Signed.

Robert stepped out onto the balcony. "Hello?"

Maxwell Dunn, Jr., a portly young rat with heavy black glasses, leaned against the railing as he looked out over the city. He didn't bother to look at Robert.

"Matthews. About time someone showed up. I could have jumped and not a damned soul would have even known. Typical."

"I read the note, sir. Why would you jump?"

"Why? Because I hate my life, Matthews. Just not enough, I guess. I couldn't go through with it. Do me a favor and tear up the note on your way out. So. What did you want?"

For a moment all Robert could do was stand there and blink. "Want . . . ? Oh, I was looking for Mr. Hathcock, but then I remembered they were all out at the sales meeting."

The younger Dunn nodded. "Yeah. I was supposed to be there, but couldn't bear the thought. See, my father met my mother on one of those things. She was a high-priced call girl. Rather like the ones Hathcock arranged for this outing. The whole notion feels too much like incest. Granted, my mother was a fox . . . or rather, she is now."

Robert sighed. "With all due respect, sir, why are you telling me this?"

He shrugged. "Because it doesn't matter. You don't matter. Hell, even I don't matter. The funny thing was, for a long time I thought that I did. I thought I had a say in my life. See, I never wanted this. I was a rich layabout, and I was good at it. I was happiest when I was most useless. I hate this firm."

"Then why did you join it, if I may ask?"

"Because my old man wanted to retire, and for that he needed a replacement to keep an eye on Hathcock. He's a thief, but then so is my father. He knew I'd do it, to protect my inheritance."

"You could have chosen something else."

"And cross my father? Don't talk rubbish. I don't know how to be poor. I do know how to be miserable, so here I am. It's a nice wheel, but it's just a wheel, and I'm the rat on it. Maybe I wish things could be different. They can't."

Oh, Robert knew that "things" could very well have been different. For instance, Dunn Junior could have just then manifested a literal rodent wheel and cage to match. Probably the only thing that saved him was that the rat metaphor had already taken hold in another version and the wheel would have been redundant.

"You're wrong, sir. You have the power. You can change this."

"How?"

"You say you can't sacrifice your wealth. Maybe you can give up something else. It's what we all have to do, sir, when we don't have everything—or no longer have. We give up something we want for something else we want."

Dunn Junior frowned. "I don't understand. For instance?"

"For instance, this." Robert took one long step, placed himself squarely behind Dunn Junior and shoved. "You give up your misery. Me, on the other hand," he said to the now empty space by the railing, "I just gave up a corner office. I hope the firm appreciates my sacrifice, as I'm sure it does yours."

The police asked a few questions while the ambulance removed Dunn, Junior's body, but the questions were pretty perfunctory. After all, the signed suicide note was solid and unambiguous as to the younger Dunn's intent. That evening Robert walked to the metro station past a row of giant sunflowers that used to be streetlamps. A mounted patrolman riding by was a literal pig. There was too much of a suggestion of nostalgia in those manifestations; they probably wouldn't last long. Even so, Robert thought the sunflowers were pretty.

It's not, he thought, *as if things are all bad.*

That night Robert looked into the mirror at a human-looking face again, and was content. After a dreamless and refreshing night's sleep, he returned to the office the next morning, and as he knew in his heart, everything was different. Again.

But nothing had changed.

SOFT AS SPIDER SILK

"His visions led him, his courage fed him. Bright was the blade of Julan, parting the silken chains binding his love."

—The Ballad of Julan the Lucky, Folio version.

Julan, called "The Lucky" by the legions of folk who deemed themselves less fortunate than he, had been many things in his time: soldier, hero, lover, husband, father. Now, in his seventy-fifth year, he was one thing only: impatient.

"He's late," Julan said.

Makan, his youngest, looked up from the adze he was sharpening. "Who is late, Father?"

"Death. And don't give me that look, Son; it's simple truth. How old am I?"

"Seventy-five . . . last August."

Julan sighed. "Wait right there."

Julan went inside the farmhouse where he had spent thirty-five years with Kalissa, his first and best love. The evidence of her was everywhere. Only now, instead of refusing to see it, he went looking for it. When he emerged into the sunlight he carried his dead wife's bronze mirror. "Come here, Son."

Makan dutifully laid the adze aside. He rose from the bench where he had been working and brushed the metal filings from his lap. Julan waited until Makan stood beside him and then held up the mirror to show their images, side by side.

Makan was over forty years younger than his father, yet it was very difficult to tell them apart. Their hair was the same shade of black, their faces no more or less lined than their time working in the sun over the years could account for.

"Well . . . you're well preserved, Father. Part of your famous luck."

Julan laughed. "I am *not* well-preserved; I'm not aging at all! There's not enough luck in the world to account for that."

"If that is so, then what are you going to do?"

Julan thought about it a little more, though in truth he had done little else for the past few days. "What I should have done at least five years ago. I'm going to die."

Makan turned pale. "You don't mean to harm yourself??"

Julan shrugged. "If I thought it might work . . . yet for all I know this enchantment—if such it is—would let me live yet with my throat cut or my vitals pierced, and then where would I be? No, Son, do not worry: First, I will find out who has done this to me and lift the curse. Then, as will doubtless be right and proper, I will die. Not before."

Julan did manage to die in one small regard: He left the farm and all chattel to his son by the expedient of selling the land to him for the sum of one silver penny, duly recorded in the shire clerk's great book. All Julan took with him was some food, a blanket, clothes, his good cloak and the plain soldier's sword he had worn in his younger days. He wasn't sure if a sword was the proper item to carry on a quest for Death, but Julan was a firm believer in keeping his options open.

"The farm is yours. Marry soon, and I hope you choose as well as I did. Know you have your father's love, always, but you will not see me again," was all he said.

Then Julan embraced his son for the last time and left his home and what had been his life, seeking his death long-delayed. He walked until the sun went down, in no particular direction. When night came he found a place beneath a tree and slept, and dreamed. There were no visions to guide him now, not as there had been before, but still, there in his dreams, he saw a familiar face. The Enchantress Widow. After fifty years he had never managed to forget her. There was a time he had wondered about that. Perhaps it was guilt at what he had done, no matter how necessary. Julan had never quite been able to puzzle it out.

The next morning he woke and repeated the journey from the day before. At night he dreamed, and again it was the Enchantress Widow who came to him. After the third day it was clear that he was traveling, but it wasn't so clear that he was getting somewhere.

The situation had been very different on his first quest. Then he had a clear-cut goal; the fortress of the Enchantress Widow where, a fevered vision told him, a beautiful young girl wrapped in spider's silk awaited a horrible fate. There was a helpful forest hermit who was more than he seemed to show him the way and even, as Julan now recalled, a talking squirrel or two. Yet he hadn't seen a single hermit's bower in the last three days, and no animals of any kind other than birds, and none of them had said so much as 'good morning.'

Julan sat down under an ancient oak to puzzle on the matter for a bit. "I suppose quests can't be the same at seventy-five as they were at twenty-five. I'll have to learn all over again. First I need a direction. I'm searching for my death, which has gone missing. Where should I look?"

He heard his dead wife's voice then, clear in his memory, and the words she said every time he had ever misplaced anything and asked, as men do, if she knew where it was. The answer was always the same: *Where did you see it last?*

It took Julan a little longer to remember where he had last seen his Death, but he finally managed.

⟞⬦⟝

> "Julan, Blessed of Astonei, smote the evil with his bright blade, pure as the Fires of Eternal Truth, bringing light to the foul pit of darkness"
>
> **—The Ballad of Julan the Lucky, Amatok Monastic Version, lines 2087-2088 inclusive.**

Julan reached the borders of the Abandoned Lands just as the summer heat was finally breaking. Or perhaps it just meant he'd walked far enough north to change climates. He wasn't sure, just as he wasn't sure now why this place was called 'The Abandoned Lands' in the first place. When he was young he'd assumed that the Enchantress Widow's evil had kept the place free of people and most other animals. Now, fifty years or more since Widow's demise, it looked pretty much the same as Julan remembered: bleak, rocky, and full of spiders.

Julan saw their webs wherever he looked: large garden-spider webs strung between dead tree limbs in a place that had never been a garden. Dull gray funnel webs in rocky crevices, vast tent webs that covered the tops of small trees and bushes. Curiously, the only actual spiders he saw where the brown wolf-spiders that foraged among the rocks and, so far as he knew, made no webs at all. He wondered for a moment what they ate, but the answer was obvious: other spiders. It's not as if there was much else.

Julan felt the weight of his pack and tried to judge. He had maybe enough food for three or four days. He hoped that would be enough. Seeking death was one thing. Eating spiders along the way was quite another.

The sun was setting. Julan found a bare expanse of flat rock relatively free of spiders to make camp. Sleeping on stone didn't appeal to him but the idea of sleeping under and among spiders' webs appealed even less. He built two campfires on either side of where he planned to sleep in the hope of keeping them away. Firewood was no problem, as there were almost more dead trees than the living sort. It seemed trees did not get very tall, or live very long, in the Abandoned Lands.

"Yet new trees grow, despite that. Even in this wretched place."
LIFE WANTS TO LIVE.

For a moment Julan thought that, perhaps, he was not so alone as he had thought. Yet he was pretty sure he had actually heard nothing; the voice had come in its own way.

Another memory.

Certainly, but which one? Kalissa, his wife? No. The voice was wrong. Yet it was familiar. Julan couldn't quite place it. He shrugged and piled more wood on the fire; he couldn't do anything about the hardness of his bed but the sun had sunk below the mountains and the air was growing colder by the moment. At least he had an answer for the cold.

The spiders were stirring. Julan had more or less expected that. What he hadn't expected was that they would be so large. These weren't the small wolf-spiders he'd noticed earlier. These were large, black, and hairless; their bodies shone in the firelight like obsidian. He saw their eyes reflected in the firelight, row on row of them.

Been awhile since they tasted the blood of a warm animal, I fancy.

Yet whatever brought them to him, curiosity or hunger, it didn't last long. One by one they moved off, going about their own business of the night, whatever it was. All save one. It sat about twenty feet away from the campfire, all eight of its eyes on him.

"You should go away too," Julan said aloud. "There's no meal for you here."

"I'm not hungry," said the spider, in a low, clicking voice.

Julan didn't say anything for a long time. The spider waited patiently. "It's been a long time since an animal spoke to me."

"No doubt it's been a long time since you did anything worthy of comment," said the spider.

Julan reddened slightly. "What do you know of that?"

The spider shrugged. At least it raised its body slightly in a gesture that seemed like a shrug. Julan had never seen one do that before, though he freely admitted he was no student of spider ways and just might not have noticed.

"Perhaps nothing," the spider said. "Why are you here?"

"I'm seeking something I lost. The last time I saw it was at the fortress of the Enchantress Widow many years ago."

"Something? That's rather vague."

"I know what I lost. Pardon me, but I didn't tell you since it's none of your business."

The spider seemed to consider. "Or perhaps you didn't tell me because you don't really know what it is."

"Listen . . . oww!"

Julan slapped at his left hand with his right. A small black spider, almost a copy in miniature of the one speaking to him, had crawled through the gap in the fires behind him and bitten him. It curled up and died as it fell into the flames.

"It's only a little poisoned. You won't die—in case you cared. Go to sleep. You'll find Widow's fortress when you awaken."

The spider turned and disappeared into the night before Julan could answer. Julan started to look through his pack for medicines for the bite, but was suddenly overcome with an incredible weariness that made him feel as if his body had turned to lead. Despite his best intention, he lay down between the flames and did exactly as the spider suggested.

⟺

"The maid was fair, fairer than fair, glowing skin
and golden hair, the Golden Prize of the spider's lair.
That's why he's 'Julan the Lucky.' "
        **—The Ballad of Julan the Lucky, cleaner bits of
        the version sung in the taverns near Borasur.**

When Julan awoke there was no trace of the bite on his hand. He flexed his fingers carefully, but felt nothing, no numbing nor soreness. The fires had long since burned down to ashes but there were no spiders nearby. Julan shrugged and rolled up his blanket. A pause for a little water and dried biscuit, then a quick answer to nature's call and he was on his way.

He hadn't gone more than the length of a bowshot when the world fell away, almost beneath his feet.

"I know this place."

He stood at the edge of what seemed to be a vast cliff, but a closer

169

look showed the edges circling away on either side of him to meet again in the distance. Julan stood on the edge of a great dark pit, and in the center of which the land rose again on a rocky spire and there was the Widow's fortress. There was a mist hovering down in the pit that partially obscure Julan's view, but he could see well enough to be sure. Not that he believed there were so many great dark pits, even in the Abandoned Lands, that he might mistake this one for another. He found the way down, a very precarious trail winding its way down along the rock face, starting between two upright stones exactly as he remembered.

Good thing I didn't bring a horse. I'd have to leave the poor beast for the spiders . . .

Julan started down. He found himself looking away from the rock wall and appreciating the view. This was different from before; as a young man Julan had been terrified of heights, and it had taken every ounce of courage he possessed to make his way down the narrow trail to the bottom. Now he found himself looking with eagerness out into the distance. Perhaps it was because he was no longer afraid to die. Or perhaps because there was something of great heights and distance that suggested things unknown and beyond oneself, vast cosmic realities that had nothing to do with him or cared one way or another how his quest played out. Fall, don't fall. Find what you seek or simply endure until the end of Time itself. All one to them.

"A strange thought for this early in such a fine morning," Julan mused.

"What is?"

The spider was back. Just as large as Julan remembered, maybe six feet from him, clinging to a long thin web attached somewhere high overhead.

"I thought I'd dreamed you," Julan said.

"Maybe you did. Maybe you are. So. What's so strange?"

"I was thinking of infinity, if you must know."

"A large subject," the spider conceded, "or rather, an endless one, which is not quite the same."

"Why are you following me? Are you hungry now?"

"Human flesh's value as a meal is over-rated. Your skin is too soft to fully contain my poison and thus liquefy your insides properly, as any decent insect can manage. Besides, if I wanted to eat you I'd have done it already."

"It might not be so easy as you think," Julan said.

The spider gave our a whistling sigh. "Your pride hasn't changed."

"Are you claiming you know me?"

"Of you, which is often the same. Julan the Lucky, also called Widowsbane, though the name is subject to misinterpretation. One would think you went about murdering helpless old women."

"I did kill one woman in my time," Julan said, "and she was anything but helpless. Yet I am not proud of it, as some think. I had no choice."

"Didn't you? That's good to know." The spider dropped to the trail behind Julan and followed along about seven paces behind him.

Julan hadn't gone more than a few feet when he couldn't stand it any more. "Stop following me!"

"How do you know I am following? I might simply be going in the same direction."

Julan inched his sword out of the scabbard, just enough so that the spider could see the shine on his steel. "I will not have a dangerous creature like you so close to my back. Either leave or I will kill you."

"Humans are as dangerous as my kind, if not more so, and you have had several close to you over the years. Some very close indeed, back and front too."

"Those I trusted. I do not trust you."

"Fair enough, but I still have my own business to attend. Say I go ahead of you. Will that be all right?"

Julan wanted to say it was not, but so far the creature had done nothing of a threatening nature and he had no real reason to object. Besides, what did he really have to fear? That the creature would kill him?

Julan sighed. "Very well."

The spider scurried ahead on its eight legs while Julan followed at his own pace. The spider never seemed to be either hurrying or slowing down, but always managed to keep pace and distance with Julan as he made his own way down the trail. It took a few hours, but Julan finally stepped away from the sheer rock wall onto relatively level ground. That is to say, the drop was now gradual rather than sheer, and he was able to pick his way carefully down the slope.

Every now and then he could see the spider ahead of him. Julan thought it a little strange that the spider should be going in the same direction but, since it had no eyes in the back of its head he fancied that it couldn't really know which way he was going and thus was truly on its own path. He considered what little he did know of spiders, and one was that they sense vibration with their feet. Perhaps the spider could tell which way Julan was going by the small jarrings of his footfalls, and adjusted its own path accordingly.

OR MAYBE THIS ISN'T ALL ABOUT YOU.

The voice again. Julan was sure it was no memory this time, but what it might be was still a mystery. *If I live long enough I may try to sort it out, for want of something better to do.*

Julan stopped to rest at a place he knew very well indeed. The pillars were still there. Two massive columns of rough black stone flanked the only direct path to the fortress. Beyond them, the land rose again sharply to where Widow's fortress sat in brooding shadow well below the lip of the pit. Now the fortress, so far as Julan could see, was in ruins. The narrow defile that led to the stone bridge that was, as best Julan recalled, the only way to reach the fortress short of climbing up the little mountain it sat on, was choked with stones and debris. And everywhere, as always, were the spiders' webs.

There had been one more web the last time Julan had been there, a massive one stretching from pillar to pillar and blocking the way forward. On that web had sat the Guardian, a massive spider probably ten times larger than the small one—if a spider the size of a deerhound could rightly be called small—that had been accompanying Julan on his quest.

Julan smiled. This was the place. He remembered. His Death had been there, at the moment he met the Guardian in combat. Julan had recognized it at once from the look in its cold black eyes although, as it occurred to him now, he had not quite looked into Death's face before the battle had been joined and he had no time to look or even think about what the intent in those eyes might mean for him. When it was over, and the Guardian lay in ragged pieces, its web destroyed, Death wasn't there. Julan had then proceeded to the fortress and, youth being what it was, had given no more thought to the matter.

"This is where I saw it last . . . "

"The thing you are missing?"

The spider sat atop the rightmost pillar, idly spinning a small ball of silken thread like an old woman at her knitting. "I thought you had your own business to attend," Julan said.

"This *is* my business," replied the spider. "And I am tending it. I have made a pilgrimage to the shrine of my ancestor, whom you knew as the Guardian."

Julan smiled. "Ah. You came here for revenge! Well, then, I am ready for you."

"Far too ready," the spider said, and it sighed. "I'm not here for revenge."

"I killed your ancestor! You said as much yourself."

The spider lowered its body briefly; probably the closest it could come to a nod. "Who would have eaten you, had matters gone differently. If she had not wished to risk death, she should have chosen softer prey. Revenge is not the way of spider-folk; we're as like to eat each other as not. Even for the visit I'll admit more curiosity than sentiment. Was the Guardian really as large as they say?"

"So large that the length of my arms twice over would not have marked her tip to tip. Her mandibles where like the horns of a black ox. I have not seen her like before or since."

"That is an interesting to know. So. I told you why I am here. Why are you here? It's only fair."

Julan sighed. "Not that it matters to you, but I'm seeking my Death."

The spider considered this. "Why all the bother? Couldn't you have just made one too many steps at the edge of the pit and settled the matter?"

Julan shrugged. "Perhaps, but I don't *know*. I've already lived well past my allotted span, in good health and sound of limb. You may not realize this, but among my kind I am very old. Three-score and fifteen; far too old to be as I am. Unless I've found my Death, and know it for what it is, how do I know I wouldn't just lie, broken and in pain, on the rocks near here while I waited to heal? And then be misshapen and in pain for centuries to come? I should have died already, and I have not. I need to know why."

"Do you? That's not quite the same thing as seeking Death."

Julan thought about it. "Well . . . it's rather unusual that a man's Death should go missing. I'll admit to a certain curiosity."

"Why should the dead be curious? You seem to think you are, for all practical purposes, dead. Life is about curiosity; I don't fancy the dead are curious about very much at all."

"Whatever the reason, I'm not dead yet."

"So you think you should be dead, but you don't actually prefer it? Or welcome it?"

Julan was a little irritated. "I can't change the order of the world! It doesn't matter what I want."

"When did a hero speak so? Are you so sure what is and is not the order of the world?"

Julan had no answer to that, so he kept silent. The spider finished spinning her ball of silk and attached it to the top of the pillar like an offering. Which, Julan thought, it probably was.

"What was she like?" the spider asked after a bit.

"She who? You mean the Guardian? Or Kalissa?"

The spider laughed. It sounded like a rain of pebbles down a hillside. "I know what the Guardian was like. *Everyone* knows what Kalissa was like. Fair as summer, bright as the sun. It's in all the songs. I want to know about Widow; her evil and foul nature is often described, but never the lady herself."

Julan remembered Widow well enough, from memory and dream alike. He remembered her pale skin, her dark eyes, her long white hair, shining and soft as spider's silk.

"She was very beautiful," Julan said because it was, he realized, no less than truth.

"Was she? You'd think at least one of the songs would have mentioned that."

"I'm not responsible for those infernal songs!"

The spider laughed again. "Well, not *directly*, I'll grant you. No matter, I've enjoyed your company; it's not often I get to speak to a human these days. In way of recompense, I'll tell you something you don't know: the Enchantress Widow captured your Death all those years ago and sealed it away somewhere in her fortress. She is the cause of your suffering . . . if such it is."

Julan frowned. "How do you know this?"

The spider shrugged by raising itself slightly on its eight black legs. "Common knowledge among spider-folk. Some of us are just about everywhere hereabouts, and have been since my ancestor's time. My kin saw what happened and passed the story along. If you really want to die, find your Death and set it free."

⟨≡⟩

> "I stood before the Enchantress Widow and, for almost too long, did nothing but gaze at her beauty."
> **—From the so-called "Memoirs of Julan the Lucky." Not considered authentic, or even very interesting.**

Julan considered what the spider had told him as he carefully picked his way through the rubble partially blocking the entrance to the fortress. It occurred to him that the spider had no real reason to lie to him. Or to tell him the truth, for that matter. Still, he had come to the Abandoned Lands because it was the only place he knew *to* go, and the part about Widow stealing his Death made sense of a sort, if anything did. That left a great many unanswered questions, including just how far he could trust what he had been told.

"There's only one way to find out. And it's not as if I would be doing something different if the spider had not come along."

All true enough. The fortress, he realized finally, had been his goal all along. He wanted to see it. He did not know why; that was another question needing an answer. Julan cleared the last pile of debris and came to the bridge.

The bridge, a stone arch reaching over the ring pit surrounding the fortress proper, was still standing, but the gates to the fortress itself, which Julan remembered being of ebony and rather magnificent, were broken and rotten. The timbers, massive as they had been, had all given way to either the weight of forty years or the loss of the Enchantress' magic. Either way they had fallen, and once past the bridge Julan's way into the fortress was clear. This, too, was much different than the last time. There were guards here too, as he recalled. Human guards, or something rather like a human. Their armor covered them almost entirely; Julan hadn't stopped to look at their faces once he'd killed them.

He stopped this time, at the rusty remnants where he recalled one of the guards had fallen. He lifted the visor, still in place all this time, and looked within. Nothing but spider's webs.

"Perhaps there was never anything there at all."

Or perhaps someone had come and taken the bodies away, leaving the armor. Julan didn't think so. The Abandoned Lands had remained the Abandoned Lands, even long after the mistress of this fortress had been destroyed. No one had been here in all this time. No one else would come after him. All the deeds were done—save one—and there was nothing here to call anyone as he had been called, for love and glory, so long ago.

And it had been long ago. Very long. Julan wasn't sure how much he could trust his memory, except where it showed him what he expected to find. That worried him, just a little. How would he know true memory from false? Did it matter now, after all these years? Julan wasn't sure.

"I think I killed her in the throne room," Julan said, and he went the way he remembered to go, through the ruined doorway and into the great echoing hall beyond.

Her servants scattered . . .

He remembered the screaming, the confusion. He wasn't supposed to reach them. Their mistress' power had failed, and they were afraid.

One opposed me here.

Julan looked down. He saw nothing but a rusting, broken sword, but it was enough. The servant had fled. They had all fled. He remembered no faces. It was all a blur. They didn't matter. The one who sat on the throne mattered.

She summoned her spiders against me.

They flew at him, conjured from Widow's outstretched fingers, trailing silken threads. They were not to small, not to large. His blade was a shining blue, there in that dim place. The threads parted, the spiders lay broken and dying. He looked down, saw nothing. Which was no more or less than what he did expect; there would be nothing left of them by now.

"So it begins," said the Enchantress Widow.

Julan had forgotten that detail; probably because it made no sense at the time or after. Nothing was beginning, save Julan's new life with Kalissa. He hadn't actually met Kalissa yet, but he knew where to find her, once the last obstacle was overcome. Widow was the last obstacle, and he did overcome her. He pinned her to the ebony throne with the point of his sword. He did hesitate before he killed Widow, and for almost too long; he remembered that bit. She was so beautiful.

She smiled at him. Why had she smiled at him? To make him forget why he had come? Well, it didn't work. At least, not for long.

Julan stood before the empty throne. No, not quite empty. A few bones lay on the rotting wood, a few more were scattered on the dusty stone floor. The skull had rolled some distance away but it regarded him now, with empty eyes, a few feet away beneath a rotting tapestry. Not so much left of her beauty now. No more than Julan would expect.

Except that it was all wrong.

"There was no body," Julan said aloud. "When I slew the Enchantress Widow her form, her flesh, all turned into spiders."

A man doesn't forget a detail like that, even after fifty years. Julan was sure of it: when the sword pierced her, her body rippled and came apart into thousands of scurrying black spiders. He'd stomped a few of them and the rest scattered into the stonework. He'd ignored them after that, going down into the dungeons to free Kalissa. He'd even forgotten the Enchantress Widow's beauty as he turned his attention to his memory of Kalissa's fair face and form, as his dreams and visions that led him to that desolate place had revealed to him. Kalissa was the goal, always had been . . .

The bones were gone.

First they were there, then they were not. Julan almost drew his sword then and there. He looked around, but nothing else had changed.

"There's more afoot here than I realized."

"You do have a way of stating the obvious."

It was the spider. She perched in the frame of a broken window. Being a spider, her face was pretty much unreadable, but Julan had the distinct impression that she would smile, if poison fangs and crushing mandibles were made for such.

"So. I wondered if your curiosity of me was satisfied yet. I also have the feeling you know more of this matter than you have revealed."

"I knew about your captive Death. Why should I not know other things as well? Yet did you ask? You did not. Action without sufficient consideration. Understandable in a child of twenty and five. Less so now. You still have a reckless streak in you."

"Still? You speak again as if you know me, and not just 'of' me as you said before. Where you here, then? When it all happened?"

"Perhaps I was. Perhaps I was a part of Enchantress Widow.

Perhaps a humble spinner in some crevice with a good view. Will I tell you? No. It doesn't matter."

"Well, then. Will you tell me where my Death can be found?"

The spider made a sound distinctly like a sigh. "In the dungeons somewhere. That's where she usually stored things not requiring a lot of thought. Didn't you assume as much yourself?"

Julan had, in fact, assumed exactly that. He wasn't sure why he'd asked the spider, except perhaps to verify what he already believed likely. He remembered the way. Julan paused a little while to light a torch with flint and steel from his pack, then pushed the rotting tapestry aside and went through the small door hidden there.

"What will you do with your Death when you find it?"

"I will set it free."

"If you do that, you will die. Yet you didn't say you wanted to die. In fact, I had the definite impression that you did not."

"It's right that I die. I can't go on like this."

"Why not?"

"I already told you. It's not right! When I think of what this has put my family through . . . "

"Unfortunate, but no longer a consideration. You left your home, and you did not plan to return. Your family will go on with your memory. Dying or not dying doesn't change that."

Julan stopped. "How do you know about that?!"

"No mystery. You said you came to find Death. Therefore it stands to reason you did not plan to return. Therefore any family remaining to you are grieving already. Think, Julan; you're dead to them now whatever happens."

Julan rubbed his forehead. Not for the first time, the thought occurred to Julan that the spider's voice seemed very familiar to him, and that was bothersome. The feeling had been growing in him that he should know her, that she was someone important, someone who mattered to him, but that was impossible. "Do be quiet. I'm really getting tired of your nonsense, spider."

The spider's eyes glittered. "Nonsense? If you wish to speak of nonsense, let's speak of you. Questing like an infant, so sure of what you think you want as if you were no more than the mewling babe you were fifty years ago. A seven score and more year old *child*."

"I know what I must do!"

"You don't know anything. Why did you come here, really? To seek Death? Or, perhaps, a reason to live?"

"I said be *silent*!"

Julan, furious, snatched the blade from its sheath and started to swing it at the spider, only the spider wasn't there. Julan couldn't believe it had moved so quickly, yet there was the evidence of his own eyes. Julan stood, sword in hand, feeling foolish.

"See that you stay absent, then, if you don't want your shiny black shell cracked!" Julan said finally to the empty air as he sheathed the blade again. He descended the stairway alone, and in blessed silence.

The torch really wasn't as much use as Julan had expected, or at least not for light. The dungeon may have been carved down into living rock but there were windows cut through to the daylight outside. It was dim, and full of floating dust, but Julan could see well enough. The torch was more useful for burning away the cobwebs that blocked the stairs now and then. Julan kept a wary watch for the spider and her smaller cousins, but all the spiders he saw on the stairwell were dead, desiccated and crumbling.

The silence, for its own part, was not so blessed now. It gave Julan time to think, and he did not want to think. His trip to the dungeon had been so different, before. The obstacles were gone, and Kalissa awaited. Now the obstacles were gone, and Death alone waited for him down in that dim, cold place.

As Julan passed open doorways and alcoves he saw bundles of web. Some were shaped like boxes, and chests, and books. One or two were shaped like men. All were still, unmoving, lifeless. Julan wondered, for a moment, if he would know what he sought if he found it, but that was a foolish thought. Even as a young man he had known Death when he saw it. Would he be so much blinder now?

The answer came soon enough. Julan came to a chamber much

larger than the others, much larger and also emptier. His footfalls echoed there in the silence, and on the far wall there were attached two bundles of webbing. The one on the left was totally obscured, wrapped snug in the web. The one on the right looked like a man, and the head was not covered. Rather, it looked like a specific man.

It looked like Julan.

Julan looked into the cold black eyes of the young man imprisoned there and knew him for who and what he was. He heard nothing, but the words were clear in his mind.

FREE ME.

Julan raised his sword to cut the webbing, hesitated. "Perhaps I have been reckless. Perhaps the spider was right. Maybe I should not be so quick to do what cannot be undone." Julan addressed his Death directly. "I know who you are." He pointed at the other bundle with his sword. "Who is that?"

DEATH, ALSO.

"I have two? That seems a bit excessive."

NOT YOURS, FOOL.

"I'm a fool? Well, I suspected as much. So. If not mine, whose?"

"Mine, of course."

Too late, Julan felt the kiss at his neck. He just had strength to turn around, but the sword fell from his nerveless fingers. It made a ringing, clanging sound as it struck the stones.

Enchantress Widow stood before him. She was exactly as he remembered: the long white hair, the pale face, luminous as the moon. She smiled at him.

"Yes, as you see. I live."

"I thought I killed you!"

"You tried but, like you, I cannot die. Yet."

Julan tried to reach for his sword, but he could not move. Widow simply shook her head.

"You haven't changed. Not in fifty years. I had hoped."

"What are you talking about? What evil have you planned for me?"

"I planned much for you, Julan. Fortunately for you, I am a patient woman. Part of my nature."

"Evil is your nature!"

"Is it? What have I done to you that you can say so?"

"I should have known you still lived. You blighted this land with your evil, and so it remains!"

"If you really believe that, then your knowledge of history is pathetic. The Abandoned Lands have always been the Abandoned Lands, and for good reason. I live here because no one else wants to, and because I value my privacy, that is all. You know that's true."

Julan did know it. He didn't want to, but he did. He searched for something else, found, much to his surprise, there was one other thing only to throw at her. "You kidnaped my beloved Kalissa! You would have drained the blood from her if I hadn't rescued her!"

Widow frowned. "Kalissa? That silly little blonde girl? Yes, I freely confess it: I did kidnap her. Drain her? I'm not a leech, Julan, whatever you may think. And who do you think sent you that nightly vision in the first place?"

Julan just stared at her for several seconds. "You . . . ?"

"What? You believed the fates or the purity of her spirit sent you a cry for help? Or did you think of it at all? I doubt it."

Julan didn't bother with more denials. There was no point. "Why did you do it?" Julan asked.

"I had heard of you, Julan the Lucky. I was curious, so I sent for you, and you did come."

"I don't believe you! I rescued Kalissa, and we were happy!"

"Thanks to me, Julan the Lucky. You had a choice, though you were too thick to realize it. No matter; you chose well enough. I think Kalissa was right for you then. You were a pair: two callow children playing at love, two parts of one not very substantial whole. Would she be so now, even had she lived? Was it always the spider's bite that made you dream of me?"

"I don't understand," Julan said, though it wasn't really true. He was beginning to understand.

"Then you haven't changed. At least, not enough. You seek Death, you who have yet to experience Life? Can you look at me now, and truly understand what you see? I doubt it." Widow sighed. "Go away, Julan. Come back in fifty more years, perhaps. Face me when you grow up. Not before."

"I can't leave. I can't move!"

The Widow made a clicking sound with her teeth. "You needn't bother."

The last thing Julan remembered was the sound of thousands of spider feet scuttling across the stone floor. It sounded like rain.

⚬

"Julan left his home and disappeared into the mists of time and legend. A proper fate for the hero-born; he will live in song forever."
   —From the Epilogue of The Ballad of Julan the Lucky, Revised Standard ed.

Julan awoke on the hard stone, the ashes of his campfires dead and cold beside him. He ached all over, and shivered from the chill. His neck felt numb and tingled a bit.

"Must have slept wrong . . . "

Julan felt the lump on his neck, felt how tender and swollen it was. He remembered the Widow's bite. He remembered what felt now like a dream. He also remembered that he'd been bitten before, on the nights of his dreams of Kalissa and the dark dread fortress in the Abandoned Lands.

"You should have shown yourself to me earlier, Widow."

Julan wasn't sure that he believed that. He couldn't change the past; nor, despite the turmoil he felt now, did he really want to. He had loved Kalissa dearly and would not have changed that bit for all the world.

Yet there was one thing he would have changed, perhaps, if

given the chance, but there was none. All he had to work with was the future, if there was to be one. Julan rolled up his blanket. He no longer thought of guides and help; he knew the way. Despite that, Julan wasn't terribly surprised to see the spider waiting, looking at him from the rocks.

Julan sighed. "I thought the voice was familiar. You were speaking though the spider all along, weren't you?"

"Which is only one of the things you would have realized much sooner, had you been paying attention. You really are a dolt, you know."

"Perhaps, but I am learning. I know what your venom can do, Widow. Did I dream it all? My return to your fortress, everything?"

"It's not my responsibility to tell you what's real and what isn't, Julan. You have to decide that for yourself; it's part of growing up."

"I'm not a child, Widow. At least, not now."

The spider shrugged. "As you say. So . . . questing again?"

Julan shook his head. "Not this time. More like traveling to a place I need to be."

"You're bringing your sword," she said.

He nodded, affably. "I may need that, too."

The spider clicked her mandibles. "I guarantee you will. So. What will you do this time? Rescue your Death? Mine? Both? Neither?"

Now Julan smiled. "You have all the answers, Lady — answer that one. Better yet, answer this one: not that it makes any difference, but I suppose I'll have to deal with the Guardian this time around? Will her fangs be as sharp? Her visage as terrible?"

"Oh, yes." The spider's eyes glittered. "Whatever you think, whatever you intend or believe, I won't make it easy for you. Just so you know—You're going to pay for making me wait."

He smiled at her. "Fair enough."

For fifty years all the folk of the known world had called Julan a hero. Now, so long after his greatest adventure supposedly ended, Julan the Lucky thought perhaps it was time to see if they were right.

COURTING THE LADY SCYTHE

Jassa son of Noban was a handsome young man of limited ambition, which was to say he had only one—to woo and to win the girl called Lady Scythe. It was a frustrating ambition, to say the very least.

It was noon on Culling Day and the crowd along the Aversan Way was barely a crowd at all, by the standards of the city. Most citizens kept off the streets of Thornall during this time if they could. Those who didn't were either the unfortunates who had friends and relatives given to Lady Scythe or the unfortunates with business that could not be delayed or the triply unfortunate with lives so wretched they enjoyed the spectacle of any sorrow they did not share. Whatever their reasons, they made way quickly for the Watchers, the traditional Guardians of the Emperor's Justice.

Jassa sat in a niche high up on the remnants of an ancient wall along the equally ancient street. Hardly anyone remembered why the Aversan Way had been named for a purely mythical creature or why there had once been a massive wall running alongside it. Jassa didn't know, any more than he knew the tale of how Lady Scythe's family had become the hereditary Executioners of the Emperor's Pleasure in Thornall. Nor did Jassa care. All that mattered was that Lady Scythe—whose proper name, rumor had it, was Aserafel—had outlived her father to become the sole descendent of her noble house. All its rights and burdens now fell to her, and today that meant he'd get to see her.

Jassa sighed a lover's sigh, and the thought returned like a revenant in a particularly stubborn haunting. *If only I could speak to her . . .*

It was not possible. The only time Aserafel left her family's holdings was on Culling Day and, by ancient decree, only representatives of the Emperor himself could approach her then. All others risked instant death. It was for her own protection, Jassa realized, but it certainly did complicate matters. As for appearing at the lady's door to present his suit, that was unthinkable.

Which is not to say Jassa didn't try it. The doorkeeper had looked Jassa up and down, made the only judgment possible, and sent him away. Now he sat and waited. Just to see her. It was all he could do.

"Make way!" shouted a Watcher, but his command wasn't really needed. The street was almost clear now. Most people left had moved off the road and now ringed the ancient common. The Watchers took up their positions at the four corners, gleaming in steel and bronze. Then came the Device, pulled by a matched team of black geldings along the Aversan Way and then into the center of the common by the monumental statue of Somna the Dreamer.

Jassa didn't have his blacksmith father's genius for iron and steel, but he had a fair eye for the practical applications of metalwork. The Device consisted of a platform raised to about shoulder height, with a smooth steel framework mounted just beneath a circular opening in the center. The mechanism itself was spring-loaded, though most of the actual working parts were hidden inside the platform itself. The mechanism was armed by a crank mounted on top of the platform near the driver. The victim placed his head within the metal frame underneath the opening and, when the mechanism was triggered, the unfortunate's neck would be at once stretched to its full length and then neatly severed at the base by a hidden blade. Painless, or at least so quick that it probably didn't matter. Not that anyone had been able to complain.

Not as clumsy as an axe nor requiring the skill of a swordsman. Consistent. Practical. The same for all who suffered the Emperor's Justice at Thornall, high or low born alike. The one thing you could say about a machine that you could say about almost nothing else—it was fair.

The condemned arrived first. Three today, two young and one old. That was two more than usual; the troubles in the coastal province at Darsa had raised the level of death across the entire Empire. All of the condemned had been stripped to their breeks, their arms bound behind them. They were paraded through the crowd by a contingent of four more Watchers, who brought them to the base of the Device and left them there, then took up their positions about the execution machine. The prisoners stood blinking in the sunlight, pale and frightened to a man, but they did not try to run. There was nowhere to go.

Jassa's breath caught in his throat. *Lady Scythe.*

She arrived riding a bone white stallion, her one nod to tradition. Jassa was old enough to remember her father making his entrance in a costume that matched the color of his mount, bearing a scythe of polished silver and wearing a death's-head mask and a crown of thornwood. None of this for Lady Scythe. Her hair was red gold and unbound; she was dressed in a plain flowing skirt and a laced bodice. A less discerning eye could have mistaken her for a barmaid, if it wasn't for the chain of gold about her neck and the fine leather boots and gilt spurs she wore as well.

She could make her work more of a spectacle, as her father did. I wonder why she does not.

Such trappings weren't required, but, when he thought of it, Jassa could see their value. Any ruler would take heads when the need arose. Do it too often—even at need—and discontent could follow. Wrap such in enough legal form, plus a little mystery and ritual and your subjects could almost forget that the real point of this show was to end the lives of three men. But when Lady Scythe was at work, there was no question of why the three wretches in question were present.

She drew rein on the common and said, in a clear sweet voice. "The Emperor has commanded. All will obey."

No one else spoke or made any more noise than a body must. The occasional cough, or a shifting of feet, or, here and there, muted sobs. The three condemned men turned to face her as she climbed down from her mount. A Watcher took the reins.

Aserafel's face was unreadable. She did not speak again. She walked briskly to the side of the machine and removed a small cloth that covered the trigger. A Watcher gave the command: "Set!"

The driver turned the crank until it would turn no more. Lady Scythe nodded at a Watcher and he led the first young man to the harness. The condemned man placed his head into the harness; the harness itself was mounted in such a way that the condemned looked full into the eyes of his executioner.

Will it happen?

It did, just as the mystery had occurred with all other executions he had seen his love perform. Just before she pulled the lever, Lady Scythe said something. Jassa did not hear; he could only see her lips move. He wondered if anyone did hear, except the condemned. Jassa was too far away to be sure, but he could almost swore that the man looked, well, *astonished.* Then Lady Scythe pulled the lever and the man's headless torso fell on the green. The body twitched once and was still. There was a low moan from the crowd. A young girl fell into the arms of an older woman, who stared with silent grief at the dead man.

"Set!"

Again the preparation was made, again the younger man was taken first, as was the custom. Lady Scythe's whisper, and then the second man's body fell alongside the first.

"Set!"

The old man had stood perfectly still all this time, but when the Watcher came for him, he did not move. The Watcher tugged at his arm and the old man pulled away. He stared at the machine, his eyes wild, and he would not take a step farther. The Watcher motioned to two of his comrades and they hurried forward, grabbing the old man from either side.

"No! I'm not ready!"

Jassa shook his head. *Do not resist, Old Man. It will only mean more pain for you and might cause my lady grief.*

The old man didn't seem to consider Lady Scythe's feelings. He was still attached to life and meant to stay that way. He struggled with more and more desperation as the guards pulled him closer and closer to death. He almost broke free, and one guard raised a mailed fist over the poor man's head.

"Stop!"

The fist halted in mid-strike. Even the condemned man ceased struggling. He watched with the others as Lady Scythe walked up to him and held out her slim hand. The Watchers glanced at each other, then at her, and they let go of the old man and stepped back.

The old man looked confused. He stood unmoving for a moment, then he took her hand and she stood on tiptoe to whisper something in his ear. He drew himself up to his full height; for a moment the years seemed to fall away and Jassa could imagine what he must have been like once. The old man smiled then and let the girl lead him very slowly to the machine. In a moment he was in the harness, stoic and patient as a stone. In another moment he was dead.

Lady Scythe climbed the steps to the top of the machine and the driver bowed low. She reached down and, one after another, lifted the severed heads and held them high for the crowd to see. Then all was done. She climbed down and reclaimed her mount and soon she had disappeared back down the Aversan Way with her execution machine and the Watchers following in her wake.

It was only then that the lamentations began, as the relatives and lovers and friends came to claim the bodies.

⟫

"I want what I can never have. It's foolish."

Jassa found himself wandering down the Aversan Way in the opposite direction from his love, out toward the ruins of the city walls, out toward the Weslan Gate. He was thinking, what little could be called thinking amidst the brooding, that he would take a long walk in the countryside to clear his head and his mood. It had been some time since Jassa had passed this way; he had quite forgotten about the Storytellers.

No one knew for how long the men and women who called themselves Storytellers had been meeting by the Weslan Gate. Idlers they were called by many, beggars by those who did not know them. In the late afternoon they would leave their homes and shops and forges and sit in groups on the grass by the ruined stone arch and tell stories. They did not ask for money; they did not ask for anything except time and attention. Needless to say, such were not in abundance. When listeners were scarce, as they often were, the Storytellers would form in circles and tell stories to each other.

They were not necessarily the kindest of listeners.

"Fah! You call that a tale, Lata?" An older man looked with disdain upon a young girl while the others of their circle, men and women, young and old, watched and smiled.

"I serve Somna as best I can, Tobas." The young girl spread her hands in supplication. There was a twinkle in her eye and she showed no signs of anger.

"You serve the goddess's aspect of bringer of sleep and ease," returned the man called Tobas. "A worthy goal, but personally I prefer my listeners to be awake."

"When was the last time you *had* a listener, Tobas?" Lata asked sweetly. Laughter all around. Tobas looked outraged, but it was clear that none of them meant a word.

Liars, of a sort. Jassa started to walk by.

"I have a listener now, friends," Tobas said. He looked right at Jassa. "Hello, young man. Have a seat."

Jassa blinked. "Ah . . . no, thank you. I was just out for a walk."

"But you *were* listening, at least for a bit." He smiled at Jassa. "So as long as you're here, I'd like you to help me settle a difference I'm having with this talentless lot—" he indicated the circle with a wave of his hand. "They say that no one appreciates stories anymore. What say you?"

"Well . . . I used to," Jassa answered frankly. "It's been some time."

"And why did you stop? Too busy? Too mature? Too much involved with the day to day burden of living your life?"

"All of that," Jassa said. "And the fact that they were almost never true."

"They're almost *always* true," Tobas corrected. "They just may not have actually happened. But there are true stories. If you would hear a story, you would rather it be a factual one?"

"Of course."

"Then let me grant your wish. Sit down."

Maybe because he really had nothing better to do, or maybe because there was no good reason *not* to, Jassa sat down. "May I choose the story, then?" he asked. He was feeling a little mischievous himself. Tobas nodded, and Jassa went on. "I want to know how the Aversan Way got its name."

"Well then—if the story will come to me, then I will tell it," Tobas said, and Jassa just smiled. Tobas returned that smile. "What troubles you, friend? The fact that no one alive knows that particular story?" Jassa nodded, and the girl shook her head. "You're wrong. Somna does."

"And does Somna speak to the Storytellers?" Jassa asked.

"Somna speaks to all," Tobas said. "But sometimes she speaks most clearly through us. Now be silent for a moment. I must see if there is a story for this young man."

Tobas closed his eyes while the murmur of voices from his circle quieted. Jassa watched, noting that Tobas's lips were moving.

Doubtless practicing the first lie . . . Jassa was ashamed of the thought from the moment it was born, for it was clear that Tobas wasn't trying on words for effect—he was praying. The other members of the circle, eyes closed, heads down, were doing the same. Jassa didn't move for several long moments from pure astonishment, and by the time it occurred to him to try and slip away, it was too late. Tobas opened his eyes.

"There is a story for you, young sir. A short one, but no less a thing for all that."

Jassa licked his lips, suddenly dry. "I would like to hear it."

Tobas nodded. "It was the dawn of the Third Age," he said, in a tone subtly different from his normal speech. "At this time, men and the Firstborn of Somna, the special ones that we call Aversa, were still sharing the world, although uneasily. Our ancestors' hate and fear of the Aversa had already begun to show itself, but together one of the Firstborn and those who were our distant fathers raised the stones that were to become Thornall."

"Why?" asked Lata.

"Because the Aversa knew that harmony is pleasing to Somna," Tobas replied. "She sought to serve. Our ancestors were content to let her."

"Why?" asked an old man across the circle.

"Because men knew that the powers of the Aversa would make their work go more quickly," Tobas said. "Then as now, they sought their advantage."

Jassa could see the stony expressions of the others in the circle and knew that whatever had touched that one storyteller had grasped them all. He spoke carefully. "Why did our people hate and fear the Aversa?"

"Because every one of them had more power than all of our distant fathers combined. Because there was nothing of them that was part of our fathers, save for Somna who created both. While Somna dreams she creates our world. The Aversa share a bit of that sleep, as well as the dream. Any one of them could remake the world, up to a point, and no one of our fathers knew what that point might be. Uncertainty breeds fear like cattle."

"What happened?"

"The walls were finished. The Temple of Somna was finished. Our distant fathers tried to slay the Aversa as soon as this was done. They failed. With a word she broke the temple and then walked out of the city, along the path still called the Aversan Way, through the Weslan gate. When she stood beneath it, the walls fell. All except the Weslan gate, where we gather to this very day."

"Where did the Aversa go?"

"To Loga's Well, at the foot the Gralat Mountains, which some call

Gahan's Spine—" Tobas shook himself, and his features relaxed. The others in the circle followed him as if on cue. Perhaps it was planned that way. Jassa did not think so.

"Did I go too far?" Tobas asked the others. He seemed to have forgotten about Jassa.

"The lad's question was unforeseen and ill-timed," said the old man who had spoken before. "but, if you were not meant to speak the answer, it would not have been spoken."

"You're a fatalist, Gos," said another. "I think it was a mistake."

"It doesn't matter, it's done," Lata said.

"What's done?" Jassa demanded.

Tobas shrugged. "If you don't know, then perhaps that's for the best. Thank you for listening."

The circle broke apart. Somna's Storytellers went off alone, in ones and twos and all in silence. After a while Jassa left, too, with the rather strange feeling that, as he passed beneath the Weslan Gate, he was leaving a temple.

Jassa did not go very far in his walk outside the city walls. He soon passed through the Weslan Gate, now deserted, and made his way home. There was no one there to greet him, had not been since his father's death the month before. The smithy attached to the building was locked tight and shuttered, the forge cold. Jassa gathered what he thought he would need and in the morning he left the city. As he passed the Weslan Gate, Jassa paused for a moment and smiled.

I need a miracle to win Lady Scythe. If there's any truth at all in what the Storytellers said, now I know where to find one.

It's not as if he had anything to lose.

⋖◆⋗

The Aversa laughed until Jassa was afraid the roof of the cave would come crashing down on both of them. She finally wiped tears from her eyes and grinned at Jassa. She had a lot of teeth. Sharp, too, he thought.

"They *still* tell that story in Thornall? Such a paradox, that men's lives should be so short and their memories so long. For all that they never seem to learn much from either."

"Then it's true?" he asked.

The Aversa shrugged. "Truth is a matter of interpretation; if the Storytellers failed to mention that, I will be amazed. Did it actually happen? More or less."

Jassa had followed the storyteller's directions and walked for two days, till he came to the foothills of Gahan's Spine. He followed the only road—more of a goat-path—and came to a freshwater spring near the end of a narrow box canyon. The cave was just a little farther in.

He found the Aversa sitting on a chair of stone about ten yards from the entrance, at a place where the entrance shaft widened into a high, echoing chamber. For a creature of myth and legend she was surprisingly easy to find and to recognize. She was slim and elegant, but her hair was white and the beautiful proportions of her face were nonetheless covered with skin almost translucent with age, marked with a fine network of lines almost as if she had been woven of spider-silk. Her eyes were larger than any human woman's, and the color of amber. She almost appeared to be waiting for him.

"It's true, then? You can reshape Somna's Dream?"

"We can make small changes in the world, if that's what you mean. Trifles. And at very high cost."

"I'm not a wealthy man, but I have some property to sell—"

The Aversa almost burst out laughing again, but she confined it to a brief chuckle, though it took obvious effort. She shook her head. "Let me show you something, Jassa of Thornall."

The world changed.

They weren't in the cave now. They stood in a perfumed garden at the base of a mountain that looked a little like the one where the Aversa made her home now. A waterfall cast rainbows into the air as it fell into a marble basin. Statues of exquisite artistry were set into niches carved in the living stone, in places Jassa remembered seeing

COURTING THE LADY SCYTHE

as eroded, crumbling rock just a few minutes before. The Aversa sat done on a white stone bench and patted the seat beside her. Jassa sat down, numbly.

"How do you like my home?" the Aversa asked.

"It's lovely."

"Yes." She sighed deeply. "It's also gone."

They were back in the cave. The Aversa wasn't smiling now. "Once all my people lived like that. But there never were very many of us, nor did living in peace with your kind work out very well. They'd have us greater demons than Gahan himself when the mood struck them. Use us when they could, kill us or drive us away when they could not. Until what few of us are left hang on in the empty places that no one else has found a use for."

"With your power, why did you allow this to happen?"

The Aversa smiled again ruefully. "Our power is in the Reshaping of Somna's Dream, the dream that is the world. But it is still Somna's dream, not ours. Do you know what happens when someone reshapes the dream in a way she does not like?"

Jassa shook his head, trying not to lose himself in her amber eyes. The Aversa continued. "It disturbs the Goddess's sleep. Do it often enough and brutally enough and she wakes. The world ends. Do you think the Aversa wanted to do what the Demon Gahan, with all his tricks, has so far failed to accomplish? Your folk have their place in Somna's dream or they wouldn't be here; I think ours will soon go away entirely."

"But . . . you are Beloved of Somna! First of all the races of the Dream!"

The Aversa looked around at the bare stone walls. "As I said—the cost is high. Only *we* pay it, Jassa. You do not. You choose your way, and that has its own consequences which have nothing to do with me. Now, then—do you still want me to help you?"

Jassa took a deep breath. "Yes."

"You're a fool, but I already knew that. This concerns Lady Aserafel of Thornall, yes?"

Jassa blinked. "How do you know that?"

"I can always tell when the Storytellers have been at work, and whom they've touched. Your dreams told me the rest. Call it a whim, but I will help you. What do you want?"

"If you've seen my dreams, you should already know."

The Aversa smiled again. "Clever boy. Dreams at once reveal and obscure. It's true I know what you want. Do you?"

Jassa shrugged. "I want Lady Scythe to love me. I want to have her lips on my brow. I want her to look into my eyes with such devotion that, in that instant, she is mine and only mine."

The Aversa nodded. "So I expected. Hand me that stone at your feet."

Jassa bent down and picked up a piece of dull limestone, little more than a pebble. He handed it to the Aversa, and in a moment she handed it back to him, only now it wasn't a stone. What she gave him was a small bronze medallion on a leather thong.

"Wear this," she said. "When you return to Thornall, show it to the Watcher at the gate. You will get your wish. Or . . . "

Jassa was already tying the cord around his neck. "Or?"

"Or you can toss it in the nearest river, or simply drop it here and now, go home, take up your father's profession or some other, and build a life for yourself without Lady Scythe. That would be my advice, if you'd asked for it."

"I can't do that. I love her."

The Aversa nodded, and she looked even older than she had before. Older, and infinitely more weary. "I know," she said.

⎯◆⎯

On the long walk back to Thornall, Jassa took a little time to think. He wondered if it were really possible to do as the Aversa had advised; he would always be a poor substitute for his father at the forge. Oh, he was well-trained, and Jassa was sure he could earn a decent living at the forge, but not like his father. The man worked art with his steel;

where Jassa would make a serviceable sword, Noban would create a master blade, perfect in balance and form. The same for anything Jassa had attempted; what his father had went beyond experience and practice, and Jassa knew that neither one would turn him into the smith his father was.

I could settle for less.

Only it was a lie. That was one thing Jassa could never do. Just as with Lady Scythe; there was no one to compare to her, and no point in trying. All or nothing; if there was a middle way he could never quite see it.

Jassa looked at the medallion. It was a simple disk of bronze with a carved sigil that looked like a closed eye. He dimly recognized it as one of the ancient symbols for Somna the Dreamer; beyond that it meant nothing to him. He wondered what it would mean to the Watcher.

He didn't have to wait long to find out. Jassa approached the gate and the Watcher on duty there. Jassa didn't show him the medallion; Jassa didn't have to. The Watcher glanced at it as Jassa approached and in an instant the man's sword was at Jassa's throat.

"In the Name of the Emperor, I apprehend thee."

In a dirty, damp cell that night Jassa reached fitful sleep. The Aversa was waiting for him in his dreams.

"You betrayed me!" he shouted, though no one not on the stage of dreams heard him.

The Aversa shook her head. "I have done something, yes, but not that."

"They wouldn't even tell me what the medallion *means*."

"To the Watchers it means you are a man who helped lead the revolt against the Emperor in the city of Darsa. A revolt that is spreading. Now they will stop looking for that man for a while. We all serve Somna with what we have, and the Emperor's reign has been bad for all of the Dream. You aren't the man they were looking for, of course, but the Watchers believe otherwise."

"Then I'll tell them!"

She nodded. "I suppose so."

They both knew it wouldn't make any difference. "Why?" he asked, finally. "What did I do to you?"

"You asked my help," she said. "And did not understand what that meant. That understanding is coming." Then Jassa was left alone in a dream that was no more than a dream. In the morning he did not remember.

⭑

Jassa walked with three younger men along the Aversan Way; his arms bound behind his back. In time he came into the presence of Lady Scythe.

Jassa almost smiled. *At least no one can deny me this much.*

One by one the others died. Soon it was his turn. He looked right at Lady Scythe and said, "I love you."

The Watchers just stared. Lady Scythe's sweet face had a quizzical look, but she didn't say anything. Jassa drew himself to his full height and waited for the Watchers to try and force him, as they had the old man. It didn't happen. Lady Scythe stepped forward immediately and took his hand. She led him to the device.

"You don't understand," he said. "I love you."

She smiled at him. "I do understand," she said, and then Jassa was in the harness. Her smiled flirted with madness. "Of all those I have loved, you were the only one to speak first of love to me. Thank you."

Lady Scythe took her place by the lever and then Jassa saw her lips move, as they always did. Only now he was close enough to hear. Now he was close enough to see the look of joy and devotion in his Lady's eyes; the *recognition* that was always there when she pulled the lever and looked into the eyes of Death itself. And, at that instant, it was all for Jassa.

"I love you," she said.

Jassa wanted to laugh, but he had no time.

When the Storytellers gather at the Weslan gate, every now and then someone tells the story of how Lady Scythe took an unclaimed head lying by the statue of Somna the Dreamer and made the skull into a gilt drinking cup. They would tell of how she would smile to herself as her lips brushed its cold brow and she gazed into its empty eyes. No one really knew if this actually occurred, but like any good story it grew enough in the telling that, in time, more than one good meaning found haven in the shade of it.

Such as the version in which, a few years later with both the Empire and the need for her services in decline, Lady Scythe married the governor of the frontier province of Lyrsa and moved far away from Thornall. Her clothes, her gold, and the skull cup were all she took from the city. The execution machine fell to rot and rust beneath the statue of Somna the Dreamer who, with closed eyes, saw all.

THE MAN WHO CARVED SKULLS

"I married your mother for her skull. It's no secret."

Jarak put aside his rasps and gouges for the moment, resting his eyes and mind from the precise, exacting work his trade demanded. He didn't mind his son's persistent questions at such times. Akan was at an age when he *should* be curious and, if curiosity was a duty, Akan was a dedicated boy. It wasn't as though Purlo the Baker, whose skull rested patiently on Jarak's workbench, was in a hurry.

Akan nodded. "Mother *is* pretty," he said. "Often men of the village speak about what a fortunate man Jarak the Skullcarver is."

"Letis is indeed the most beautiful woman in Trepa and for seven leagues around. But that's not the same thing. The ugliest man alive during your grandfather's time turned out to have a skull of exquisite beauty, as your grandfather knew all along. With time and practice and the aesthetic sense that *might* come with them, perhaps you'll understand and be able to see the difference for yourself. I hope so, if you're to take over for me some day."

"I hope so too, Father," Akan said very seriously.

The trumpet call echoed faintly from the south side of the village, opposite the temple of Somna the Dreamer. As a chance to satisfy his son's curiosity, it seemed a perfect opportunity. "They've started," Jarak said. "Let's go see, and maybe I'll tell you how I won your mother."

They walked out of the workshop, around Letis' herb garden, and out through the gate onto Trepa's main street. Other folk were stirring now as the trumpet sounded again, gathering in small groups that slowly grew and spread out until the entire cobbled street was lined with smiling people.

"Here they come!"

Three young girls led the procession, dropping daisy petals from willow baskets as they came. They all looked very solemn in their white muslim gowns and red ribbons. Jarak pointed to the dark-haired little girl in the middle. "That's Melyt, Theran's granddaughter. Your mother thinks she'd be a good wife for you. Isn't she pretty?"

Akan stuck out his tongue. "I'm not getting married, ever."

"You'll change your mind. And when you do, best not to leave the choosing of your bride to chance. That gives the Forces of Gahon too much room to play."

"You weren't betrothed to Mother," Akan pointed out. "She told me."

Jarak smiled. "Nonetheless . . . oh, there's Theran now."

At least, what was left of him. Four priests of Somna carried the skull on a raised dais. Jarak had decided to go with an historical motif for that skull; considering Theran's full and rich life, it had seemed more than fitting. The scenes of the old man's life were played out in bas-reliefs carved in a spiral that started at the top of his skull and ended just where the spine has once joined its base. They were too far away to see properly, but Jarak named them to Akan one by one.

Here was Theran traveling with the Wind People on the Great Grass Sea, smuggling weapons to Ly Ossia under the noses of the Watchers; here was Theran visiting the ruins of the Temple of the Dreamer in Darsa and bringing back the piece of the original altar that now resided in the local Temple. Here was Theran as all had known him, surrounded by his wife and children and grandchildren. Whether any of his stories were really true didn't matter; they were true now and would remain so as long as the House of Skulls stood.

Theran's widow Karta and his family came last. They did not grieve; grief was over and done long before. Now it was time for Theran to take his place in the House of Skulls, Now it was time for celebration. Karta beat a small drum and her steps were close to a dance; her daughters followed wearing small bells on straps about their wrists. Between the trumpets of the flanking priests and the din from Theran's family, Jarak was sure every Ancestor in that sacred place knew of Theran's coming. He said as much.

"They can't hear anything," Akan said solemnly.

Jarak raised an eyebrow. "Oh? And why not? Because they're dead?"

Akan shook his head and then hugged himself, nearly doubled over giggling. "No ears!"

Jarak put his arm around his son's shoulders. "Come on, you rogue. Let's follow."

Jarak and Akan fell into step behind the procession with the rest of the villagers, sharing the joy of Theran's family and adding to it as well. They came to the entrance to the Temple of the Dreamer, passing by the wooden statue and shrine that Jarak's father had carved years before. They did not stop at the shrine or the temple. Soon after Theran's death, his proper funeral had been held at the temple and offerings made at the shrine, and that had been the time for tears. Now it was Theran's Homecoming, and the procession did not pause until they reached the House of Skulls.

The procession broke apart; Theran's family went first into the stone building. Next season the masons would be summoned and another large room would be added to the House, and then again when that one filled. For now, there was still room in the main hall. Jarak and Akan followed the others into the echoing chamber, with rows and rows of intricately carved skulls staring down at them from niches evenly spaced in the walls.

"Theran Molka's Son, Beloved of Somna, has come home," said the senior priest. He carefully lifted the skull and handed it to Karta, placed it in the niche on the far wall that had been prepared for it, beside the skull of the small skull of his sister who died in childhood, beneath the skulls of their parents Molka and Derasee. Farther along the wall, the masons had already begun work on the niche for Purlo the Baker, for when his time came.

"Our father has come home," said each of Theran's children as they approached the skull in turn and paid their respects.

"Our grandfather has come home." Each of the grandchildren repeated the ritual, each looking very grave and serious, though

Melyt was clearly trying not to giggle. The ritual was repeated by all who had known Theran best or felt the desire to honor him; even Jarak took his turn.

"My friend has come home."

Then, finally, all was done. People broke apart into small groups and chatted, others drew apart to pay respects to the older residents of the House of Skulls. Jarak took Akan's hand and led him to a central column that was also full of niches like little doorways. Jarak pointed to one particular skull residing there.

"Do you know who that is?" Jarak asked.

Akan nodded somberly. "It's Great-Grandmother Laersa."

Jarak smiled. "You asked about how your mother and I got married—it's because of Laersa."

Akan's eyes got very big. "Did she tell you to get married?" he asked. "Weren't you frightened?"

"It wasn't like that. Your mother was the only daughter of the High Priest of Somna, and I no more than a skull-carver's apprentice. She had suitors from all over the village and far away, all well-favored young men of good family and prospects."

"Mother loves *you*," Akan said proudly.

Jaran grunted. "Not *then*, she didn't. I think she does now, but it was some time coming. I always loved her, of course. How could I not? But I had no chance, at least not until the Homecoming of her Aunt Telesa."

"What did you do?"

"I watched her. After most of the others had gone, she stayed. She came and stood about where you're standing now, looking at her Grandmother Laersa."

"*Great*-Grandmother Laersa," corrected Akan, looking as prim as Bol the Schoolmaster.

"*Her* Grandmother Laersa," said Jarak. "*Your* great-grandmother. So. She was alone, which almost never happened in those days. I could speak to her, but what would I say? So I watched her, and I noticed something. Something important."

"What was it?"

"It was the way she looked at Laersa. Not in grief, or even fond memory. The look on your mother's face was pure envy. You see, Laersa's skull was carved by a master, and he outdid himself. It is simply marvelous work."

Akan nodded. "Marvelous," he said, trying on the new word for size. "It's a very nice skull. But wasn't it wrong of Mother to envy someone?"

"Perhaps, but just then I thought it was a very endearing quality, because it gave me an idea. I went up to your mother, and I said that her grandmother's skull was the most beautiful in Trepa, and she agreed that this was so. Then I said 'I love you, Letis. Marry me and when the time comes I will make of your skull a work to eclipse even that of Laersa. Folk will look at you as you look at her now, and none will surpass you. Your name and your memory will live forever.' You see, I offered your mother immortality, and that's the one thing I had to give her that no other could."

"And she said 'yes'!" Akan clapped his hands in delight.

Jarak laughed. "Actually, she called me a presumptuous fool and stormed out. But, deep down, she believed I meant what I said. She held her suitors at bay, delaying her choice until she had time to see my apprentice work and even to speak, once, to my old master Boreth concerning me." Jarak winked. "She thinks I didn't know about that. Then, when the choice could be delayed no longer, she chose me."

"I'll offer to carve Melyt's skull," Akan said, grinning. "Will she like me then?"

Jarak snorted. "She'll more than likely box your ears. Every woman and every man has their own tale to unravel. If the Dreamer means for you and Melyt to share one, you'll have to untangle it yourselves."

"It's not such a bad thing," Letis said. "Beyond our island, I hear people actually bury their dead."

Akan looked at his mother. He knew she had aged, in the fifteen years since Theran's Homecoming, but the change had been so gradual that, to him, it was no change at all. Her hair was still the same rich shade of red-gold; the streaks of white were barely noticeable. Her eyes were still clear and bright, her face unlined and lovely.

The change that had come about in his father was quite different. Jarak was older than his years; the weakness in his heart had not been quite so gradual or so gently building. Jarak and Akan and Letis had long known the truth—Jarak would die first, and his promise to Letis would be unfulfilled. Letis was the first to speak of it. It was like a wall coming down.

Akan shook his head. "Why build a tomb when you can grow a garden? It makes no sense to me. The bone meal is good for the fields, the House of Skulls takes up far less room than a necropolis."

"At least the buried dead would never be seen . . . Akan, your mother is a vain woman. Jarak won me by that vanity, for all that I love him. But sometimes I think this is harder on him than me. He wants to fulfil his promise at least as much as I want him to." Letis sighed. "It is perhaps the Will of the Dreamer that both of us shall be . . . disappointed."

Akan looked grim. "Perhaps," he said, "the fulfillment of my father's promise will fall to me."

Letis looked up from her sewing, then reached up and patted his cheek. "You're a good son, and an excellent carver. But you are not your father. Where is he, by the way?"

Akan shrugged. "In his workshop, of course. And I know your meaning—I have not his skill."

Letis put the needle aside. "My 'meaning' is that your father's promise dies with your father. If my skull does come to you in time, I know I'll not disgrace my place in the House. It's wrong to want more than that."

"But you do want more."

"Yes, son. I do." Letis looked thoughtful. "I guess I just don't want it enough."

Akan stared at her, now afraid that he didn't understand her meaning, but more afraid that he did. "You would not—"

Letis smiled sadly. "I would." She showed her wrists and the faint red lines that marked them. "But I could not. Barely a scratch is all I managed. I'm a coward. I don't deserve immortality."

———◆———

Jarak was a sick man, but his grip on the gouge was still strong, his skill with the chisel still fine. The new skull was almost ready.

"I could finish that for you," Akan said.

His father shook his head. "It's not as if I'll have many more chances. This is what I love, Akan. This is what I've always wanted to do. You know that."

"I think you should speak to Mother," Akan said.

Jarak put his tools away for a moment. "Why? The sight of me adds to her suffering more than my words could assuage. Leave it be, Akan. There's nothing for it."

"She tried to kill herself."

Jarak nodded. "She failed. *We* failed. She wants to die in order to live forever, but she wants to live to be with me for as long as I have. She begged me to hold the knife myself, did she tell you that?" Akan shook his head, feeling numb. Jarak continued, "It's true. I could not. I'd sooner kill myself. And yet I always thought she would die first. We planned our lives around it, but we can't do the one thing necessary to make it happen. It's almost funny. I'm sure the Prince of Nightmares would appreciate the joke."

"It would be wrong," Akan said.

"I suppose so," Jarak said. "As excuses go, that one will have to do."

"Father—"

Jarak shook his head, and Akan fell silent. "Go find Melyt," Jarak said. "She'll be waiting for you."

———◆———

Melyt had grown into a lovely young woman, also so gradually that it was a long time before Akan noticed. By then he didn't need his parents wishes to push him in her direction. Melyt, sensible girl that she was, hadn't quite made up her mind about the matter yet, but she was perfectly willing to discuss it. Akan found her underneath a trailing willow on a bluff overlooking the river.

"You're late," she said.

"I'm sorry. I was delayed at home."

He sat down on the blanket Melyt had spread out there. She'd brought a willow basket for a picnic, and she began to unpack the food. "I'm sorry about your father's illness, Akan. He's a good man."

Akan sighed. "I just wish there was something I could do. There are . . . other problems between my mother and father now. I hate to see them like this."

Melyt handed him a meat pie and a bit of bread. "Have you consulted the Temple?"

Akan frowned. "What could they do? The only Temple Dreamers I know of are in Ly Ossia, and I'd need them for a proper oracle. Assuming I could make the journey and raise the gold I'd need for their fee, my father would be dead before I returned. I don't think he has very long."

"Then what about an improper oracle?" she asked. Akan just stared at her, and she went on, "Whenever I have a problem, I fast and then pray at the Temple. It soothes me. Sometimes I sleep on the Temple grounds, and the dreams are always useful, or at least strengthening. Your mother is related to the High Priest; I'm surprised she hasn't done that herself."

Akan thought of the times her mother had disappeared for long periods in the evening, and his father had said nothing of it. Akan's imagination had played with this knowledge with rather unsettling results, but once Melyt had spoken he knew that this is precisely what his mother had done. "Perhaps she has. Nothing has changed."

"It's not about 'changing,' Akan. It's about understanding. Try it; at least there's no harm in that."

Somna's presence in the world—since the world was, in fact, Somna's Dream—was something everyone just took for granted. Maybe it was time to see what meaning there was in that one fact. Akan considered.

"I think I will," he said, then added, "Thank you."

"You're welcome. Now try not to think about it for a bit. Your attention is required elsewhere."

Akan smiled and reached for her hand.

<hr>

The next evening Akan fasted, and then made a bed under the stars near the shrine of Somna the Dreamer. He dreamed, but it was not Somna who answered his dream. The creature was like a man and was not. It was part shadow, part pain, and all hunger, and the visage was the one carved in the base of the statue of Somna and painted on the temple walls.

Gahon the Destroyer. Gahon, Prince of Nightmares.

Akan tried to run, but there was nowhere to go, no part of the dream he could run to that did not also contain Gahon's shadow. Akan wanted to wake up, but he could not. Gahon waited, not threatening, not smiling, expressionless. He waited until Akan gave up and sat, trembling on the featureless floor of the night-stage.

"Mercy," Akan said.

"Too rare a thing," the demon said. "I'd like some for my own; can I get it? No. What else do you want of me, Akan Jarak's Son?"

"Want . . . ?"

"Certainly. You must want something. But will I give it? Ah, *there's* the question lying in ambush. Are you ready?"

"I don't know. I sought an oracle dream from Somna."

"Which you are now having, though you may be too thick to realize it. Don't you know who I am?"

"Gahon," Akan said. "Demon, Destroyer, the one who crouches

on Somna's breast in the form of nightmare and disturbs her dream. You shouldn't be here . . . "

"Nonsense. You dreamed me. It's the only way I can walk Somna's dream in my true form. Now . . . what is there about you that seeks the image of Somna and instead finds me?" Gahon poked Akan's ribs. His fingers were long and his fingernails like needles. "Eh? Think about it. You'll understand."

Akan did understand. In his heart, he had already decided what he was going to do. And Gahon clearly knew his heart. "Dreamer Forgive Me . . . "

Gahon shrugged. "She will. She's like that. Will you forgive yourself? Another pesky question. But if you ask my advice—and you did by virtue of being here—I'd say do it."

Akan shook his head. "It is sinful. Such evil would disturb the Dream—"

"How do you know that?" Gahon asked.

"You're trying to trick me; it won't work. I would cause much unhappiness to do as you suggest. And is not unhappiness poison to Somna's Dream? Does not the burdens of sorrow carried in the Dream disturb her sleep?"

Gahon grinned, showing teeth like a shark's. "It is. It does. So tell me—how much poison is coursing through the veins of your mother and father even as we speak? How much unhappiness is there between them, and how long will it last with your mother and then *you* to carry it on? How much damage to the Dream you prize so much? Oh, yes. It's spreading to you even now. Will you deny that?"

Akan shook his head. "No."

"Just so. Lancing a boil hurts, boy. That doesn't mean it shouldn't be done."

"Why would you help me? Why would the Sculptor of Lies speak truth? You seek to end the Dream!"

"I do. And why? Because Somna has spent too long in this one little world; her affection for her creation clouds her judgment. She could create much grander places than this. She could even forgo the

Divine Sleep for a bit and spare a moment and a smile for one who loves her."

Akan just stared. "You?"

Gahon smiled again. "I am what I am, and you simple manifestations of Somna's will don't know the smallest part of it. I want Somna to wake, yes. But I want the shock to be brief, the hurt fleeting. I would not chisel away at the dream piece by wretched piece, given a choice. We all serve Somna in our own way, Akan. We all sacrifice for what we want. You speak of poisons and unhappiness, but do you really know what it is to be happy?"

Akan shook his head, slowly. "No."

"Then I'll tell you." Gahon leaned close. "Sometimes," he said, "it's merely knowing what you can bear and what you cannot bear and living your life tailored to that understanding. You have to decide what you will do. The Dream continues or it does not. So do I, and as I plot and scheme I weigh Somna's pain in the balance with my own, always."

Akan sobbed. "What must I do?"

"What you already know to do. The only thing left is that you decide to act. Or not. Time is running out, either way."

Gahon the Destroyer held up a nearly-empty hourglass in his hands, and just when the last grains fell Akan awoke, cold and alone, by the statue of Somna the Dreamer.

⊷⬦⊶

The following afternoon, Akan found Letis his mother, knife in hand, standing under the willow tree by the river. She stared at the knife she held in disgust. She did not hear Akan approach until he spoke.

"Mother, if it is your will, I will hold the knife."

She looked at him. Akan was prepared for anything he saw there: rage, pain, contempt. He was not prepared for the love, the pure mad joy he saw in her eyes. "You love me as much as that?"

Akan took the knife from her. "Even more."

Two months later, Letis came home to the House of Skulls. She was a masterpiece, as Jarak had promised, easily outshining all who had gone before. Even Laersa. Jarak took to his bed soon after; his own Homecoming followed quickly.

———◆———

No one called what Akan had done murder, once Jarak had spoken for him, but understanding only went so far. Akan did not marry Melyt; that was impossible now. In time she married a fine young man from Tolbas and everyone thought that best; even Akan agreed. It was just one regret that he had to bear. Another was that he was not allowed to take his father's place as carver for Trepa, with only one exception—when Jarak died, Akan was the one who prepared the skull for Homecoming. It was Jarak's last request. The skull Akan did was fine work, his best up to that point. Not so fine as Jarak's but, still, showing promise for what might have been.

Afterwards Akan's freedom was given over to the Temple, and he was shackled with silver chains. Every morning till the day he died, Akan was led to the House of Skulls, there to watch the Homecomings in silence and then to tell his tale of vanity and selfish pride to any visitor who cared to listen.

Akan did not think of it as punishment; rather, he saw it as just another step in helping to secure his father's promise. He told the story with great feeling, and, with the skill of long practice, the tale became a wonder in itself and spread far and wide like some ancient legend that everyone knew. Akan never wearied of the telling, and every day he looked up at the remembered faces of his parents with great pride and love.

There were dark hours, of course. There always are. Yet even when such times forced Akan to place all his regrets in the scale against his one great joy, for him the balance remained true.

MOON VIEWING
AT SHIJO BRIDGE

In the early evening a tiny moth-demon was trying to batter its way into my room through a tear in the paper screen, no doubt attracted by the scent of poverty. I was debating whether to frighten the silly thing away or simply crush it, when the Widow Tamahara's delightful voice sent the poor creature fluttering away as fast as its little wings could carry it.

"Yamada-san, you have a visitor!"

Tamahara kneeled by the shoji screen that was the only door to my rooms. Besides the volume, there was an edge of excitement in the formidable old woman's voice that worried me just a little. The fact that aristocracy impressed her had worked to my advantage more than once when the rent was late, but her deference meant that just about anyone could get closer to me than might be healthy. That is, if they were of the right station in life. Anyone else giving a hint of trouble in her establishment she would throw out on their ear, if they were lucky.

"Who is it, Tamahara-san?"

"A messenger and that is all I know. She's waiting in the courtyard with her escort."

She?

Well, that explained why Widow Tamahara had not simply brought the person to my rooms. That would not have been proper, and the Widow Tamahara always did the right thing, to the degree that she understood what 'the right thing' was.

"Just a moment," I said.

After some thought I tucked a long dagger into my sleeve but left my *tachi* where it was. I wasn't wearing my best clothes, but my best would have been equally unimpressive. At least everything was clean.

I followed Tamahara out into the courtyard. The sun had set but there was light enough still.

The woman kneeled near a small pine tree, flanked on either side by her escorts. No rough provincial warriors these; the two men were polite, impassive, well-dressed and well-armed. The younger man wore the red and black clothing and bore the butterfly *mon* of the Taira Clan, the other wore plain black and bore no family crest or identification at all. I judged them as best I could. The escort wearing Taira livery I think I could have bested, if absolutely necessary and with a bit of luck. But the other . . . well, let's just say I didn't want any trouble. I also could not escape the feeling that we had met before.

I bowed formally and then kneeled in front of the woman. I noted the rightmost warrior's quick glance at my sleeve and how he inched almost imperceptibly closer, all the while not appearing to have noticed or moved at all. The man was even more formidable than I had suspected, but now my attention was on the woman.

Her *kimono* was very simple, as befitted a servant. Two shades of blue at most, though impeccably appropriate for the time of year. She wore a *boshi* with a long veil that circled the brim and hid her features. Naturally, she did not remove it. She merely bowed again from her seated position and held out a scroll resting on the palms of her small hands.

I took the offered scroll, all the while careful to make no sudden movements, and unrolled it to read:

The Peony bows
to no avail; the March wind
is fierce, unceasing.

Caught like a rabbit in a snare. And so damn easily. Just the first three lines of a *tanka*. The poem was not yet complete, of course; the rest was up to me.

I looked at the shadow of the woman's face, hidden behind the veil. "Are you instructed to await my reply?"

Again she bowed without speaking. The escort on her right produced a pen case and ink. I considered for a few moments, then added the following two lines:

The donkey kneels down to rest.
In his shadow, flowers grow.

My poetic skills—never more than adequate—were a little rusty and the result wasn't better than passable. Yet the form was correct and the meaning, like that of the first segment, more than clear to the one who would read it. The woman took the message from me, bowed again, then rose as one with her escort and withdrew quickly without further ceremony. The Widow Tamahara watched all this from the discreet distance of the veranda encircling the courtyard.

"Is this work?" she asked when I passed her on the way back to my room. "Will you be paid?"

"'Yes' seems the likely answer to both," I said, though that was mostly to placate the old woman. I was fairly certain that I would be the one paying, one way or the other.

Later that evening I didn't bother to prepare my bedding. I waited, fully clothed and in the darkness of my room, for my inevitable visitor. The summons was clear and urgent, but I couldn't simply answer it. The matter was much more complicated than that.

The full moon cast the man's shadow across the thin screen that was my doorway. It wasn't a mistake; he wanted me to know he was there. I pulled the screen aside, but I was pretty sure I knew who would be waiting.

He kneeled on the veranda, the hilt of his sword clearly visible. "Lord Yamada? My name is Kanemore."

"Lord" was technically correct but a little jarring to hear applied to me again. Especially coming from a man who was the son of an emperor. I finally realized who he was. "Prince Kanemore. You were named after the poet, Taira no Kanemore, weren't you?" I asked.

He smiled then, or perhaps it was a trick of the moonlight. "My mother thought that having a famous poet for a namesake might gentle my nature. In that I fear she was mistaken. So, you remember me."

"I do. Even when you were not at Court, your sister Princess Teiko always spoke highly of you."

He smiled faintly. "And so back to the matter at hand: Lord Yamada, I am charged to bring you safely to the Imperial compound."

The light was poor, but I used what there was to study the man a little more closely than I'd had time to do at our meeting earlier in the day. He was somewhat younger than I, perhaps thirty or so, and quite handsome except for a fresh scar that began on his left cheek and reached his jawline. He studied me just as intently; I didn't want to speculate on what his conclusions might be. Whether caused by my involvement or the situation itself—and I still didn't have any idea what that was—Kanemore was not happy. His face betrayed nothing, but his entire being was as tense as a bow at full draw.

"I am ready, Prince Kanemore."

"Just 'Kanemore,' please. With the Emperor's permission, I will renounce my title and found a new clan, since it is neither my destiny nor wish to ascend the throne."

"I am Goji. Lead on then."

The streets were dark and poorly lit. I saw the flare of an *onibi* down an alleyway and knew the ghosts were about. At this time of evening demons were a possibility too, but one of the beauties of Kyoto was that the multitude of temples and shrines tended to make the atmosphere uncomfortable for most of the fiercer demons and monsters. The rest, like that moth-demon, were used to skulking about the niches and small spaces of the city, unnoticed and deliberately so—being vulnerable to both exorcism and common steel.

We reached the Kamo River without incident and crossed at the Shijo Bridge. The full moon was high now, reflecting off the water.

Farther downstream I saw an entire procession of ghost lights floating above the water. I'm not sure that Kanemore saw the *onibi* at all. His attention was focused on the moon's reflection as he paused for a second or two to admire it. I found this oddly reassuring. A man who did not pause to view a full moon at opportunity had no soul. But the fact that his moon-viewing amounted to little *more* than a hesitation on Shijo Bridge showed his attention to duty. I already knew I did not want Kanemore as my enemy. Now I wondered if we could be friends.

"Do you know what this is about?" I asked.

"Explanations are best left to my sister," he said. "My understanding is far from complete."

"At this point I would be glad of scraps. I only know that Princess Teiko is in difficulty—"

He corrected me instantly. "It is her son Takahito that concerns my sister most. She always thinks of him first."

I didn't like the direction this conversation was taking. "Is Takahito unwell?"

"He is healthy," Kanemore said. "And still his half-brother's heir, at present."

That was far too ominous. "Kanemore-san, it was my understanding that the late Emperor only allowed the current Emperor to ascend on the condition that Takahito be named heir after him, and that Takahito in turn take his royal grandfather's nickname, Sanjo, upon his eventual ascent. Is Emperor Reizei thinking of defying his father's wishes?"

Kanemore looked uncomfortable. "There have been complications. Plus, the Fujiwara favor another candidate, Prince Norihira. He is considered more agreeable. I will say no more at present."

More agreeable because, unlike Princess Teiko, Norihira's mother was Fujiwara. I considered this. If the Fujiwara Clan supported another candidate, then this was bad news for Teiko's son. As the Taira and Minamoto and other military families were the might of the Emperor, so were the Fujiwara his administration. Court ministers and minor officials alike were drawn primarily from their ranks. All power was the Emperor's in theory, but in practice his role was mostly ceremonial. It was the Fujiwara who kept the government in motion.

Still, the politics of the Imperial Court and the machinations of the Fujiwara were both subjects I had happily abandoned years ago. Now it appeared that I needed to renew my understanding, and quickly. Despite my desire to question him further, I knew that Kanemore had said all he was going to say on the matter for now. I changed the subject.

"Did you see much fighting while you were in the north?"

"A bit," he admitted. "The Abe Clan is contained, but not yet defeated . . . " he trailed off, then stopped and turned toward me. "Goji-san, are you a seer in addition to your other rumored talents? How did you know I had been in the north?"

I tried to keep from smiling. "That scar on your jaw is from a blade and fairly new. Even if you were inclined to brawling—which I seriously doubt—I don't believe the average drunken *samuru* could so much as touch you. That leaves the northern campaigns as the only reasonable conclusion. It was an educated guess. No more."

He rubbed his scar, thoughtfully. "Impressive, even so. But the hour grows late and I think we should be on our way."

We had taken no more than a few steps when two *bushi* staggered out of a nearby drinking establishment. One collided with me and muttered a slurred curse and reached for his sword. I didn't give the fool time to draw it. I struck him with my open palm square on the chin and his head snapped back and collided with a very hard lintel post. Fortunately for him, since Kanemore's *tachi* was already clear of its scabbard and poised for the blow swordsmen liked to call 'the pear splitter,' because that's what the victim's bisected head would resemble once the blow was completed. I have no doubt that Kanemore would have demonstrated this classic technique on that drunken lout had I not been in the path of his sword. The drunk's equally inebriated companion had his own sword half-drawn, but took a long look at

Kanemore and thought better of it. He sheathed his sword, bowed in a rather grudging apology, and helped his addled friend to his feet. Together they staggered off into the night.

Kanemore watched them disappear before he put his sword away. "That, too, was impressive. But pointless. You should have let me kill him. One less provincial thug swaggering about the city. Who would miss him?"

I sighed. "His lord, for a start. Who would demand an explanation, and the man's companion would say one thing and we would say another and justice ministers would become involved and there would be time spent away from the matter at hand that I don't think we can afford. Or am I mistaken?"

Kanemore smiled. "I must again concede that you are not. I'm beginning to see why my honored sister has summoned you. May your lack of error continue, for all our sakes."

⇒

The South Gate to the Imperial compound was closest, but Kanemore led me to the East Gate, which was guarded by *bushi* in the red and black Taira colors, one of whom I recognized as the messenger's other escort. They stood aside for Kanemore and no questions were asked.

We weren't going to the Palace proper. The Imperial Compound covered a large area in the city and there were many smaller buildings of various function spread out through the grounds, including houses for the Emperor's wives and favorites. Considering our destination, it was clear we needed to attract as little attention as possible; Kanemore led me through some of the more obscure garden paths. At least, they had been obscure to other people. I remembered most of them from my time at Court. Losing access to the gardens was one of two regrets I had about leaving the Court.

Princess Teiko was the other.

Kanemore escorted me to a fine large house. A small palace, actually, and quite suitable for the widow of an Emperor. A group of very well-dressed and important-looking visitors was leaving as we arrived, and we stepped aside on the walkway to let them pass. There was only one I recognized in the lamplight before I kneeled as courtesy demanded: Fujiwara no Sentaro. It seemed only fitting— my one visit to the compound in close to fifteen years and I *would* encounter my least-favorite person at the Imperial Court. The coldness of Kanemore's demeanor as they walked by wasn't exactly lost on me either.

If Sentaro recognized me, he gave no sign. Possibly he'd have forgotten me by now, but then a good politician did not forget an enemy while the enemy still drew breath.

"I gather Lord Sentaro is not in your favor?" I asked after they had gone.

"To call him a pig would be an insult to pigs," Kanemore said bluntly. "But he is the Minister of Justice, a skilled administrator, and has our Emperor's confidence. The gods may decree that he becomes Chancellor after Lord Yorimichi, as luck seems to favor the man. My sister, for some reason I cannot fathom, bears his company from time to time."

I started to say something about the realities of court life, but thought better of it. While the saints teach us that life is an illusion, Sentaro's presence indicated that, sadly, some aspects of life did not change, illusion or not. We climbed the steps to the veranda.

"Teiko-hime is expecting us," Kanemore said to the *bushi* flanking the doorway, but clearly they already knew that and stepped back as we approached. A servant-girl pulled the screen aside, and we stepped into a large open room, impeccably furnished with bright silk cushions and flowers in artful arrangements and lit by several paper lanterns. There was a dais on the far wall, curtained-off, and doubtless a sliding screen behind it that would allow someone to enter the room without being seen. I had hoped to at least get a glimpse of Teiko, but of course that wasn't proper. I knew the rules, even if I didn't always follow them. Kanemore kneeled on a cushion near the dais, and I followed his example.

"My sister has been informed—" he started to say, but didn't get to finish.

"Your older sister is here, Kanemore-kun."

Two more maids impeccably dressed in layered yellow and blue *kimono* entered the room and pulled back the curtain. A veil remained in front of the dais, translucent but not fully transparent. I could see the ghostly form of a woman kneeling there, her long black hair down loose and flowing over her shoulders. I didn't need to see her clearly to know it was the same woman who had brought the message to me in the courtyard and whose face I had not seen then, either. No need— the way she moved, the elegance of a gesture, both betrayed her. Now I heard Teiko's voice again, and that was more than enough.

Kanemore and I both bowed low.

There was silence, and then that beautiful voice again, chiding me. "A *donkey*, Lord Yamada? Honestly . . . "I tried not to smile, but it was hard. "My poetry is somewhat . . . untrained, Teiko-hime."

"Teiko. Please. We are old friends."

At this Kanemore gave me a hard glance, but I ignored him. He was no longer the most dangerous person in my vicinity, and I needed all my attention for the one who was.

"I think there is something you wish to discuss with me," I said. "Is this possible?" It was the most polite way I knew to phrase the question, but Teiko waved it aside.

"There is no one within hearing," she said, "who has not already heard. You may speak plainly, Lord Yamada. I will do the same—I need your help."

"You have read my answer," I said.

"True, but you have not heard my trouble," Teiko said, softly. "Listen, and then tell me what you will or will not do. Now then—do you remember a young Fujiwara named Kiyoshi?"

That was a name I had not heard in a long time. Kiyoshi was about my age when I came to the Court as a very minor official of the household. Since he was handsome, bright, and a Fujiwara, his destiny seemed fixed. Like Kanemore he chose the *bushi* path instead and died fighting the northern barbarians. He was one of the few of that clan I could tolerate, and I sincerely mourned his death.

"I do remember him," I said.

"There is a rumor going around the Court that Kiyoshi was my lover, and that my son Takahito is his issue, not my late husband's."

For a moment I could not speak. This matter was beyond serious. Gossip was close to the rule of law at Court. If this particular gossip was not silenced, both Takahito's and Teiko's positions at court were in peril, and that was just for a start.

"Do you know who is responsible for the slander?"

"No. While it's true that Kiyoshi was very dear to me, we grew up together at court and our affections to each other were as brother and sister, as was well understood at the time. You know this to be true."

I did. If I knew anything. "And you wish for me to discover the culprit? That will be . . . difficult."

She laughed softly then, decorously covering her face with her fan even through the veils prevented me from seeing her face clearly. "Lord Yamada, even if I knew who started the rumors it would do little good. People repeat the gossip without even knowing who they heard it from. What I require now is tangible and very public proof that the rumors are false."

I considered. "I think that will be difficult as well. The only one who could swear to your innocence died fifteen years ago. Or am I to pursue his ghost?"

She laughed again. The sound was enchanting, but then everything about her was enchanting to me. There was a reason Princess Teiko was the most dangerous person in that room. I found myself feeling grateful that the screen was in place as I forced myself to concentrate on the business at hand.

"Nothing so distasteful," she said. "Besides, Kiyoshi died in loving service to my husband the late Emperor, and on the path he himself chose. If he left a ghost behind I would be quite surprised. No, Lord Yamada, Kiyoshi left something far more reliable—a letter. He sent it to me when he was in the north, just before . . . his final battle. It was intended for his favorite and was accompanied by a second letter for me."

I frowned. "Why didn't he send this letter to the lady directly?"

She sighed then. "Lord Yamada, are you a donkey after all? He couldn't very well do so without compromising her. My friendship with Kiyoshi was well-known; no one would think twice if I received a letter from him, in those days. In his favorite's case the situation was quite different. You know the penalty for a Lady of the Court who takes a lover openly."

I bowed again. I did know, and vividly. Banishment, or worse. Yet for someone born for the Court and knowing no other life, there probably *was* nothing worse. "Then clearly we need to acquire this letter. If it still exists, I imagine the lady in question will be reluctant to part with it."

"The letter was never delivered to her." Teiko raised her hand to silence me before I even began. "Do not think so ill of me, Lord Yamada. News of Kiyoshi's death reached us months before his letter did. By then my husband had given the wretched girl in marriage to the *daimyo* of a western province as reward for some service or other, so her romantic history is no longer at issue. Since Kiyoshi's letter was not intended for me I never opened it. I should have destroyed it, I know, but I could not."

"Perhaps foolish, but potentially fortunate. Yet I presume there is a problem still or I would not be here."

"The letter is missing, Lord Yamada. Without it I have no hope of saving my reputation and my son's future from the crush of gossip."

I let out a breath. "When did you notice the letter was stolen?"

"Lord Sentaro says it disappeared three days ago."

Now I really didn't understand and, judging from the grunt to my immediate right, neither did Kanemore. "What has Lord Sentaro to do with this?"

"He is the Emperor's Minister of Justice. In order to clear my reputation, I had to let him know of the letter's existence and arrange a time for the letter to be read and witnessed. He asked that it be given to him for safekeeping. Since he is also Kiyoshi's uncle I couldn't very well refuse."

She said it so calmly, and yet she had just admitted cutting her own throat. "Teiko-hime, as much as this pains me to say, the letter has surely been destroyed."

There was nothing but silence on the other side of the veil for several seconds, and then she simply asked, "Oh? What makes you think so?"

I glanced at Kanemore, but there was no help from that direction. He looked as confused as I felt.

"Your pardon, Highness, but it's my understanding that the Fujiwara have their own candidate for the throne. As a member of that family, it is in Lord Sentaro's interest that the letter never resurface."

"Lord Sentaro is perhaps overly ambitious," Teiko said, and there was a more than hint of winter ice in her voice. "But he is also an honorable man. He was just here to acquaint me with the progress of the search. I believe him when he says the letter was stolen; I have less confidence in his ability to recover it. Lord Yamada, Will you help me or not?"

I bowed again and made the only answer I could. "If it lies within my power, I will find that letter for you."

<hr />

"That," said Kanemore later after we passed through the eastern gate, "was very strange."

The man, besides his martial prowess, had quite a gift for understatement. "You didn't know about the letter?"

"Teiko never mentioned it before, though it doesn't surprise me. Yet . . . "

"The business with the Minister of Justice does surprise you, yes?"

He looked at me. "Since my sister trusts you I will speak plainly—Lord Sentaro is Chancellor Yorimichi's primary agent in the Fujiwara opposition to Takahito. If I had been in Lord Sentaro's place I would have destroyed that letter the moment it fell into my hands and danced a tribute to the gods of luck while it burned."

I rubbed my chin. "Yet Teiko-hime is convinced that the letter was not destroyed."

Kanemore grunted again. "Over the years I've gone where my Emperor and his government have required. My sister, on the other hand, knows no world other than the Imperial Court. If Teiko were a *koi*, the Court would be her pond, if you take my meaning. So why would something that is immediately obvious to us both be so unclear to her?"

"Perhaps we're the ones who aren't clear," I said. "Let's assume for the moment that your sister is right and that the letter was simply stolen. That would mean that Lord Sentaro had a good reason for not destroying it in the first place."

"That makes sense. Yet I'm having some difficulty imagining that reason," Kanemore admitted.

"As am I."

I looked around. Our path paralleled the river Kamo for a time, then turned south-west. Despite the lateness of the hour there were a few people on the road, apparently all in a hurry to reach their destinations. Demons were about at this time of night, and everyone's hurry and wariness was understandable. Kanemore and I were the only ones walking at a normal pace by the light of the setting moon.

"Your escort duties must be over by now and, as I'm sure you know, I'm used to moving about the city on my own," I said.

Kanemore looked a little uncomfortable. "It was Teiko's request. I know you can take care of yourself under most circumstances," Kanemore said, and it almost sounded like a compliment. "But if someone *did* steal the letter, they obviously would not want it found, and your audience with my sister will not be a secret. Sentaro himself saw you, for one."

"I didn't think he recognized me."

"I would not depend on that," Kanemore said drily. "The man forgets nothing. His enemies, doubly so."

"You flatter me. I was no threat to him, no matter how I might have wished otherwise."

"Why did you resign your position and leave the Court? If I may be so impolite as to ask. It could not have been easy to secure the appointment in the first place."

I had no doubt he'd already heard the story from Teiko, but I didn't mind repeating events as I remembered them.

"Your sister was kind to me, in those early days. Of course there would be those at Court who chose to misinterpret her interest. I had become a potential embarrassment to Princess Teiko, as Lord Sentaro delighted in making known to me."

"Meaning he would have made certain of it," Kanemore said. "I wondered."

I shrugged. "I made my choice. Destiny is neither cruel nor kind. So. Kanemore-san, I've answered a personal question of yours. Now I must ask one of you: what are you afraid of?"

"Death," he said immediately, "I've never let that fear prevent me from doing what I must, but the fear remains."

"That just means you're not a fool, which I already knew. So, you fear death. Do you fear things that are already dead?"

"No . . . well, not especially," he said, though he didn't sound completely convincing or convinced. "Why do you ask?"

"Because I'm going to need help. If the letter is in the Imperial Compound, it's beyond even your reach. Searching would be both dangerous and time-consuming."

"Certainly," Kanemore agreed. "Yet what's the alternative?"

"The 'help' I spoke of. We're going to need several measures of uncooked rice."

He frowned. "I know where such can be had. Are you hungry?"

"No. But I can assure you that my informant is."

About an hour later we passed through Rashamon, the south-west gate. There was no one about at this hour. The south-west exit of the city, like the north-east, was not a fortunate direction, as the priests often said these were the directions from which both demons and trouble in general could enter the city. I sometimes wondered why anyone bothered to build gates at such places, since it seemed to be asking for trouble, yet I supposed the demands of roads and travelers outweighed the risks. Even so, the most hardened *bushi* would not accept a night watch at the Rasha Gate.

The bridge I sought was part of a ruined family compound just outside the city proper, now marked by a broken-down wall and the remnants of a garden. In another place I would have thought this the aftermath of a war, but not here. Still, death often led to the abandonment of a home; no doubt this family had transferred their fortunes elsewhere and allowed this place to go to ruin. Wasteful, but not unusual.

The compound was still in darkness, but there was a glow in the east; dawn was coming. I hurried through the ruins while Kanemore kept pace with me, his hand on his sword. There were vines growing on the stone bridge on the far side of the garden, but it was still intact and passable, giving an easy path over the wide stream beneath it. Not that crossing the stream was the issue. I pulled out one of the small bags of uncooked rice that Kanemore had supplied and opened it to let the scent drift freely on the night breezes.

The red lantern appeared almost instantly. It floated over the curve of the bridge as if carried by someone invisible, but that wasn't really the case—the lantern carried itself. Its one glowing eye opened, and then its mouth.

I hadn't spoken to the ghost in some time, and perhaps I was misremembering, but it seemed much bigger than it had been on our first meeting. Still, that wasn't what caught my immediate attention: it was the long, pointed teeth.

Seita did not have teeth—

"Lord Yamada, drop!"

I didn't question or hesitate but threw myself flat on the ground just as the lantern surged forward and its mouth changed into a gaping maw. A shadow loomed over me and then there was a flash of silver in the poor light. The lantern shrieked and then dissolved in a flare of light as if burning to ashes from within. I looked up to see the neatly sliced-open corpse of a *youkai* lying a few feet away from me. The thing was ugly, even for a monster. A full eight feet tall and most of that consisting of mouth. The thing already stank like a cesspit, and in another moment it dissolved into black sludge and then vanished. I saw what looked like a scrap of paper fluttering on a weed before it blew away into the darkness.

Where did the creature go?

I didn't have time to ponder; another lantern appeared on the bridge and Kanemore made ready, but I got to my feet quickly. "Stop. It's all right."

And so it was. Seita came gliding over the bridge, with his one eye cautiously watching the pair of us. Now I recognized the tear in the paper near his base and his generally tatty appearance, things that had been missing from the imposter's disguise.

"Thank you for ridding me of that unpleasant fellow," he said, "but don't think for a moment that will warrant a discount."

Kanemore just stared at the ghost for a moment, then glanced at me, but I indicated silence. "Seita-san, you at least owe me an explanation for allowing your patron to walk into an ambush. How long has that thing been here?"

I think Seita tried to shrug, but that's hard to do when your usual manifestation is a red paper lantern with one eye and one mouth and no arms, legs, or shoulders. "A day or so. Damned impertinent of it to usurp my bridge, but it was strong and I couldn't make it leave. I think it was waiting on someone. You, perhaps?"

"Perhaps? Almost certainly, yet that doesn't concern me now. I need your services."

"So I assumed," said the lantern. "What do you want to know?"

"A letter was stolen from the Imperial Compound three days ago. I need to know who took it and where that letter is now. It bears the scent of Fujiwara no Kiyoshi, among others."

Kanemore could remain silent no more. He leaned close and whispered, "Can this thing be trusted?"

"That 'thing' remark raises the price," Seita said. "Four bowls."

"I apologize on behalf of my companion. Two now," I countered. "Two more when the information is delivered. Bring the answer by tomorrow night and I'll add an extra bowl."

The lantern grinned very broadly. "Then you can produce five bowls of uncooked rice right now. I have your answer."

That surprised me. I'd expected at least a day's delay. "Seita-san, I know you're good or I wouldn't have come to you first, but how could you possibly know about the letter already? Were the *rei* involved?"

He looked a little insulted. "Lord Yamada, we ghosts have higher concerns than petty theft. This was the work of *shikigami*. The fact that they were about in the first place caught my attention, but I do not know who sent them. That is a separate question and won't be answered so quickly or easily."

"Time is short. I'll settle for the location of the letter."

Seita gave us directions to where the letter was hidden. We left the rice in small bags, with chopsticks thrust upright through the openings as proper for an offering to the dead. I offered a quick prayer for Seita's soul, but we didn't stay to watch; I'd seen the ghost consume an offering before and it was . . . unsettling.

"Can that thing be trusted?" Kanemore repeated when we were out of earshot of the bridge, "and what is this *shikigami* it was referring to?"

"As for trusting Seita, we shall soon know. That thing you killed at the bridge was a *shikigami*, and it's very strange to encounter one here. Thank you, by the way. I owe you my life."

Kanemore grunted. "My duty served, though you are quite welcome. Still, you make deals with ghosts, and encountering a simple monster is strange?"

"A *shikigami* is not a monster, simple or otherwise. A *youkai* is its own creature and has its own volition, nasty and evil though that may be. A *shikigami* is a created thing; it has no will of its own, only that of the one who created it."

He frowned. "Are you speaking of sorcery?"

"Yes," I said. "And of a high order. I should have realized when the thing disappeared. A monster or demon is a physical creature and, when slain, leaves a corpse like you or I would. A *shikigami* almost literally has no separate existence. When its purpose is served or its physical form too badly damaged, it simply disappears. At most it might leave a scrap of paper or some element of what was used to create it."

"So one of these artificial servants acquired the letter and hid it in the Rasha Gate. Fortunate, since that's on our way back into the city."

"Very fortunate."

Kanemore glanced at me. "You seem troubled. Do you doubt the ghost's information?"

"Say rather I'm pondering something I don't understand. There were rumors that Lord Sentaro dabbled in Chinese magic, even when I was at Court. Yet why would he choose *shikigami* to spirit the letter away? It was in his possession to begin with; removing it and making that removal seem like theft would be simple enough to arrange without resorting to such means."

Kanemore shrugged. "I've heard these rumors as well, but I gave them no credence. Even so, it is the letter that concerns me, not the workings of Lord Sentaro's twisted mind."

Concentrating on the matter at hand seemed a very sensible suggestion, and I abandoned my musings as we approached the deserted Rasha Gate. At least, it had seemed deserted when we passed through it earlier that evening. I was not so certain of that now. I rather regretted having to leave my sword behind for my audience with Teiko-hime, but I still had my dagger, and I made certain it was loose in its sheath.

The gate structure loomed above us. We checked around the base as far as we could but found no obvious hiding places. Now and then I heard a faint rustle, like someone winding and unwinding a scroll.

Kanemore was testing the looseness of a stone on the west side of the gate. I motioned him to be still and listened more closely. After a few moments the sound came again.

From above.

This time Kanemore heard it, too. He put his sword aside in favor of his own long dagger, which he clenched in his teeth like a Chinese pirate as he climbed the wooden beams and cross-bars that supported the gate. I quickly followed his example, or as quickly as I could manage. Kanemore climbed like a monkey, whereas I was not quite so nimble. Still, I was only a few seconds behind him when he reached the gap between the gate frame and the elaborate roof.

"Goji-san, they are here!"

I didn't have to ask who "they" were. The first of the *shikigami* plummeted past, missing me by inches before it dissolved. If the body survived long enough to strike the flagstones, I never heard it, but then I wasn't listening. I hauled myself over the top beam and landed in a crouch.

I needn't have bothered; the gap under the roof was quite tall enough for me to stand. Kanemore had two other lumbering *shikigami* at bay, but a third moved to attack him from the rear. It was different from the other two. Snakelike, it slithered across the floor, fangs bared and its one yellow eye fixed on Kanemore's naked heel.

I was too far away.

"Behind you!"

I threw myself forward and buried my dagger in the creature near the tip of its tail, which was all I could reach. Even there the thing was as thick as my arm, but I felt the dagger pierce the tail completely and bury its tip in the wood beneath it. My attack barely slowed the creature; there was a sound like the tearing of paper as it ripped itself loose from my blade to get at Kanemore.

Kanemore glanced behind him and to my surprise took one step backward. Just as the creature's fangs reached for him he very swiftly lifted his left foot, pointed the heel, and thrust it down on the creature's neck just behind the head. There was a snap! like the breaking of a green twig and the serpent began to dissolve. In that instant the other two *shikigami* seized the chance and attacked, like their companion, in utter silence.

"Look out!"

I could have saved my breath. Kanemore's dagger blade was already a blur of motion, criss-crossing the space in front of him like a swarm of wasps. Even if the other two creatures intended to scream they had no time before they, too, dissolved into the oblivion from whence they came. Kanemore was barely breathing hard.

"Remind me to never fight on any side of a battle opposite yourself," I said as I got back off the floor.

"One doesn't always get to choose one's battles," Kanemore said drily. "In any case it seems you've returned the favor for my earlier rescue, so we my call our accounts settled in that regard."

I picked up a ragged bit of mulberry-paper, apparently all that remained of our recent foes. There were a few carefully printed *kanji*, but they were faded and impossible to read. "Fine quality. These servitors were expensive."

"And futile, if we assume they were guarding something of value."

It didn't take long to find what we were searching for; I located a small pottery jar hidden in a mortise on one of the beams and broke it open with my dagger hilt. A scroll lay within. It was tied with silk strings and the strings' ends in turn were pressed together and sealed with beeswax impressed with the Fujiwara *mon*. I examined it closely as Kanemore looked on.

"Your sister will have to confirm this," I said at last, "but this does appear to be the missing letter."

The relief on the man's face was almost painful to see. "And now I am in your debt again, Lord Yamada. It has been a long night and we are both weary, yet I do not think that this can wait. Let us return to the Palace now; it will be stirring by the time we arrive."

The lack of sleep plus the sudden stress of the fight, now relieved, had left me feeling as wrung out as a washerwoman's towel. I knew

Kanemore must have been nearly as bad off, even though from his stoic demeanor I'd have thought he could take on another half-dozen *shikigami* without breaking a sweat.

"We'll go directly," I said, "but I'm going to need a breath or two before I try that climb again. You could do with some rest yourself."

He nodded and only then allowed himself to sit down in that now empty place. "I am too tired to argue, so you must be right."

We greeted the dawn like two roof-dragons from the top of the Rasha Gate and then made our way back into the city. The Imperial Compound was already alive with activity by then, but Kanemore didn't bother with circuitous routes. We proceeded directly to Teiko-hime's manor and at the fastest speed decorum allowed. We probably attracted more attention than we wanted to, but Kanemore was in no mood for more delays.

Neither was I, truth to tell, but Teiko-hime had not yet risen, and I had to wait on the veranda while Kanemore acquainted his sister with the news. I waited. And I waited. I was starting to feel a little insulted by the time Kanemore finally reappeared. But he did not come from the house; he came hurrying through the garden path, and his face . . . well, I hope I never see that expression again on a human being.

"I am truly sorry . . . to have kept you waiting, Lord Yamada. This . . . I was to give you this . . . "

"This" was a heavy pouch of quilted silk. Inside were half a dozen small cylinders of pure gold. I take pride in the fact that I only stared at them for a moment or two.

"Kanemore-san, what has happened?"

"I cannot . . . "

"I think you can. I think I will have to insist."

His eyes did recover a little of their old fire then, but it quickly died away. "My sister was adamant that we deal with the matter at once. I escorted her to the Ministry of Justice as she insisted. I guess the burden of waiting had been too much; she did not even give me time to fetch you . . . oh, how could she be so reckless?"

I felt my spirit grow cold, and my own voice sounded lifeless in my ears. "The letter was read at the Ministry? Without knowing its contents?"

"Normally these matters take weeks, but considering what had happened to the letter under his care, Lord Sentaro couldn't very well refuse Teiko's demand for an audience. I must say in his favor that he tried to dissuade her, but she insisted he read it before the court. We all heard, we all saw . . . "

I put my hands on his shoulders, but I'm not even sure he noticed. "Kanemore?"

He did look at me then, and he recited a poem:

"The Wisteria pines
alone in desolation,
without the bright Peony."

I could hardly believe what I was hearing. Three lines of an incomplete *tanka*. Like the three that Teiko had used to draw me back to court, these three in turn had damned her. Wisteria was of course a reference to the Fujiwara family crest, and "Peony" had been Teiko's nickname at Court since the age of seven. Clearly, the poem had been hers to complete and return to Kiyoshi. The imagery and tone were clear, too. There was no one who could hear those words and doubt that Kiyoshi and Teiko had been lovers. For any woman at court it would have been indiscreet; for an Imperial Wife it amounted to treason.

"What is to be done?" I asked.

"My sister is stripped of her titles and all Court honors. She will be confined and then banished . . . " and here Kanemore's strength failed him, and it was several heartbeats before he could finish. "Exiled. To the northern coast at Suma."

Say, rather, to the ends of the earth. It was little short of an execution.

"Surely there is—"

"Nothing, Goji-san. In our ignorance we have done more than enough. The writ is sealed."

He left me there to find my own way out of the compound. It was a long time before I bothered to try.

⸺⸺

It took longer to settle my affairs in Kyoto than I'd hoped, but the gold meant that the matter would be merely difficult, not impossible. The Widow Tamahara was, perhaps, one of the very few people genuinely sorry to see me leave. I sold what remained of my belongings and kept only what I could carry, along with my new traveling clothes, my sword, and the balance of the gold which was still quite substantial.

On the appointed day, I was ready. Teiko's party emerged from the eastern gate of the compound through the entrance still guarded by the Taira. Yet b*ushi* of the Minamoto Clan formed the bulk of her escort. Kanemore was with them, as I knew he would be. His eyes were sad but he held his head high.

Normally a lady of Teiko's birth would have traveled in a covered ox-cart, hidden from curious eyes, but now she walked, wearing the plain traveling clothes that she'd used to bring that first message in disguise, completing her disgrace. Still, I'd recognized her then as I did now. When the somber procession had moved a discreet distance down the road, I fell in behind, just another traveler on the northern road.

I was a little surprised when the party took the northeast road toward Lake Biwa, but I was able to learn from an attendant that Teiko wished to make a pilgrimage to the sacred lake before beginning her new life at Suma. Since it was only slightly out of the way, her escort had seen no reason to object. Neither did I, for that matter, since I was determined to follow regardless. The mountains surrounding the lake slowed the procession's progress and it took three days to get there. When the party made camp on the evening of the third day, I did the same nearby.

I wasn't terribly surprised to find Kanemore looming over me and my small fire within a very short time.

"I was just making tea, Kanemore-san. Would you care for some?"

He didn't meet my gaze. "My sister has instructed me to tell you to go home."

"I have no home."

"In which case I am instructed to tell you to go someplace else. I should warn you that, should you reply that where you are now *is* 'someplace else,' she has requested that I beat you senseless, but with affection."

I nodded. "Anticipated my response. That's the Teiko I always knew. So. Are you also instructed to kill me if I refuse your sister's order?"

Now he did look me squarely in the eye. "If killing you would atone for my own foolishness," Kanemore said, "I'd do it in a heartbeat. Yet I cannot blame you for what happened, try as I might. You only did as my sister bid —"

"As did you," I pointed out.

He managed a weak smile. "Even so, we still share some of the responsibility for what happened. I could not prevent her disgrace, so I am determined to share it."

"That is my wish as well," I said.

"You have no—" he began but did not finish.

"Exactly. My failure gives me that right, if nothing else does. Now consider: what about Prince Takahito? Your nephew? Where is he?"

"At Court. Takahito of course asked to accompany his mother, but permission was refused."

"Indeed. And now he remains at Court surrounded by his enemies. Who will look after him?"

"Do not lecture me on my duties! Who then, shall look after my sister? These men are to escort her to Suma. They will not remain and protect her afterward."

I waved that aside. "I well understand the burden of conflicting obligations. Your instinct for love and loyalty is to protect both your sister and her son. How will you accomplish this when they are practically on opposite ends of the earth? Which path would Teiko choose for you?"

His face reddened slightly; I could tell that the subject had already come up. Repeatedly, if I knew Teiko.

"We've spoken our minds plainly to each other in the past, Kanemore-san, and I will do the same now: your sister is going to a place where life is harsh and she will be forced to make her own way. Despite her great gifts, neither she nor her two charming and loyal attendants have the vaguest idea of how to survive outside the shelter of the Imperial Court. I do."

Kanemore didn't say anything for several long moments. "My sister is the daughter of an Emperor. She was born to be the mother of an Emperor," he said finally.

"If that were the case, then it would still be so," I said. "Life does not always meet our expectations, but that should not prevent us from seeking what happiness we can."

"You are unworthy of Princess Teiko," Kanemore said, expressionless, "and I say that as someone who holds you in high regard. Yet you are also right. For what little it may be worth, I will speak to my sister."

"When I finish my tea," I said, "and with your sister's permission, so will I."

Teiko agreed to see me, perhaps because she saw no good way to prevent it. After fifteen years I did not care what her reasons might be. The fact that she did agree was enough.

I found her sitting by herself in a small clearing. She gazed out at a lovely view of Lake Biwa beyond her. The sun had dipped just below the mountains ringing the lake and the water had turned a deep azure. Teiko's escort was present but out of earshot, as were both of her attendants. She held an empty teacup; the rice cakes beside her looked hardly touched. She still wore her *boshi*, but the veil was pulled back now to reveal her face. It was a gift, I knew, and I was grateful.

I can't say that she hadn't changed at all in fifteen years: there might have been one or two gray strands among the glossy black of her hair, perhaps a line or two on her face. I can say that the changes didn't matter. She was and remained beautiful. She looked up and smiled at me a little wistfully as I kneeled not quite in front of her but a little to the side, so as not to spoil her view.

"So. Have you come to lecture me on my recklessness as well? Please yourself, but be warned—my brother has worried the topic to exhaustion."

"Your brother thinks only of you. Yet what's done cannot be undone."

"Life is uncertain in all regards," Teiko said very seriously, then she managed a smile and waved a hand at the vast stretch of water nearby. "An appropriate setting, don't you think? I must look like a fisherman's wife now. What shall I do at Suma, Lord Yamada? Go bare-breasted like the abalone maidens and dive for shells? Learn to gather seaweed to make salt, like those two lovers of the exiled poet? Can you imagine me, hair loose and legs bared, gleaning the shore?"

"I can easily so imagine," I said.

She sighed. "Then your imagination is better than mine. I am a worthless creature now."

"That is not possible."

She smiled at me. There were dimples in her cheeks. "You are kind, Goji-san. I'm glad that the years have not changed this about you."

She offered me a cup of tea from the small pot nearby, but I declined. She poured herself another while I pondered yet again the best way to frame one of the questions that had been troubling me. I finally decided that there simply was no good way, if I chose to ask.

"No lectures, Teiko-hime, but I must ask about the letter."

Her expression was unreadable. "Just 'Teiko,' please. Especially now. So. You're curious about Kiyoshi's letter, of course. That poem was unexpected."

"You weren't Kiyoshi's lover," I said.

Teiko smiled a little wistfully. "You know I was not," she said. "But at the moment there is no explanation I can offer you."

"I'm not asking for one. What's done is done."

She sipped her tea. "Many things have been done, Goji-san. There is more to come, whatever our place in the order of events may be. Speaking of which, my brother in his own delicate way hints that there is another matter you wish to speak to me about."

"I am going to Suma," I said.

"That is noble, but pointless. Your life is in Kyoto."

"My life is as and where it is fated to be, but still I am going to Suma," I repeated. "Do you require me to say why?"

She actually blushed then, but it did not last. "You say that what's done cannot be undone. Perhaps that is true, but you do not yet know all that has been done. As at our last meeting, I must ask you to listen to me, and then decide what you will or will not do. Please?"

"I am listening."

"You left Court because people were starting to talk about us."

"Yes. When the Emperor bestowed his favor on you, Lord Sentaro—"

"Did no more or less than what I asked him to do."

For a little while I forgot to breathe. I idly wondered, somewhere above the roar in my ears, whether I ever would again. "What you . . . ?"

"It's unforgivable, I know, but I was not much more than a child, and both foolish and afraid. Once I had been chosen by the former Emperor there could be nothing between us nor even the rumor of such. I knew that you would do what you did, to protect my reputation."

"I would have done anything," I said, "if you had asked me."

"That is the true shame I have born these past fifteen years," Teiko said softly. "I let this person you detest be the one to break your heart because I lacked the courage to do it myself. I heard later that he took undue pleasure in this. I must bear the blame for that also."

Fifteen years. I could feel the weight of every single one of them on my shoulders. "Why are you telling me this now?"

"Because I needed to tell you," she said. "More importantly, you needed to hear it, and know just how unworthy I am of your regard before you choose to throw your life away after mine. Or do you still wish to speak to me of things that cannot be undone?"

Perhaps it was a test. Perhaps it was a challenge. Perhaps it was the simple truth. I only knew what remained true for me. "My decision is not altered," I said. "I would like to know yours."

There were tears in her dark eyes. "There are things we may not speak of, even now. If it is our fate to reach Suma together, speak to me then and I will answer you."

⟡

The demons were teasing me in my dreams. At least, so I believe. In a vision I saw myself and Teiko on the beach at Suma. The land was desolate but the sea was beautiful and it met most of our needs. We walked on its shore. Teiko was laughing. It was the most exquisite of sounds, at least until she started laughing at me, and it wasn't Teiko at all but some ogress with Teiko's smile.

"What have you done with Teiko?" I demanded, but the demon just mocked me. I drew my sword but the blade was rusted and useless; it would not cut. I looked around frantically at the sea but there was nothing but gigantic waves, one after another racing toward the beach. Sailing against them was one small boat. I could see Teiko there, her back turned to me, sailing away. I ignored the demon and chased after her, but the sea drove me back again and again until her boat was swallowed by the attacking sea.

"—amada!"

Someone was calling me. The ogress? I did not care. Teiko was gone.

"Lord Yamada!"

I was shaken violently awake. Kanemore kneeled beside my blankets, looking frantic.

"What-what's happened?" I said, trying to shake off the nightmare.

"My sister is missing! Help us search!"

I was awake now. "But . . . how? Her guards worked in paired shifts!"

Kanemore looked disgusted as I scrambled to my feet. "The fools swear they never took their eyes off of her, that Teiko and her maids were sleeping peacefully, and then suddenly Teiko wasn't there! Nonsense. They must have been playing *Go* or some such rot. I'll have their heads for this!"

"We'll need their heads to help us search. She could not have gotten far. Go ahead. I will catch up."

Kanemore ran through the camp with me not far behind, but when I came to the place where I knew Teiko and her ladies had been sleeping, I paused. The two maidservants were huddled together looking confused and frightened, but I ignored them. There was a small screen for some privacy, but no way that Teiko could have left the spot without one of the guards seeing her. I looked in and found her bedding undisturbed, but empty. I pulled her coverlet aside and found a crumpled piece of paper.

"She's up there!"

I heard Kanemore call to me from the shore of the lake and I raced to join him. Just a little further down the shoreline was a place where the mountains dropped sheer to the water. On the very edge of that high promontory stood a small figure dressed in flowing white, as for a funeral.

"Teiko, no!"

I started to shout a warning to Kanemore, but he was already sprinting ahead looking for the quickest route up the slope and I followed hot on his heels, but it was far too late. In full sight of both of us, Teiko calmly stepped off the edge.

With her broad sleeves fluttering like the wings of a butterfly, one could almost imagine her fall would be softened, but the sound of her body striking the water carried across the lake like the crack of ice breaking on the Kamo River in spring.

One could also imagine, first hope having failed, that there would be nothing in the water to find except, perhaps, a few scraps of paper.

One tried very hard to hold on to this hope and only relented when the fishermen from a nearby village helped us locate and remove the cold, broken body of former Princess Teiko from the deep dark waters of the sacred lake.

⟨⬩⟩

The moon was high again and cast its reflection on the river. The modest funeral rites for Teiko were well under way, and once more I stood on the Shijo bridge, staring down at the moon and the dark water beneath it. Again I saw the *onibi* flare out on the water. I knew that, if I waited long enough, the ghost lights would be followed by the graceful spirits of women who had drowned themselves for love.

I had seen them before; they would soon appear just above the water in solemn procession, drifting a bit as if with the currents below. The legend was that men unfortunate enough to stare at them too closely would drown themselves out of love as well. I wondered if I, too, before I drowned myself in turn, might see one small figure with the face of Princess Teiko.

I didn't know what Kanemore intended when he appeared beside me on the bridge. At that moment I did not care. I simply gazed at the moon's reflection and waited for whatever might come.

He placed a small scroll on the railing in front of me. "This is for you, Lord Yamada," he said formally.

I frowned. "What is it?"

"A letter," he said. "From my sister. I have already opened and read the one intended for me."

I didn't move or touch the letter. "Meticulous. She had this planned before we even left the city. She never intended to go to Suma."

"The shame of her disgrace was too much to bear," he said. He sounded about as convinced as I was.

"I rather doubt," I said, "that there was anything your sister could not bear, at need."

"Then why did she do it?" he asked softly.

A simple question that covered so much, and yet at the moment I didn't have a clear answer. I think I understood more of what had happened than Kanemore did, but the "why" of it all was as big a mystery to me as it was to him. I shared the one thing I thought I knew for certain.

"I've only been able to think of one clear reason. I have been drinking for the past day or so to see if I could perhaps forget that reason."

"Have you succeeded?"

"No."

He leaned against the rail with me. Out on the water, the mists were forming into the likenesses of young women. Kanemore glanced at them nervously. "Then share that reason with me. Preferably someplace else."

I smiled. "You must drink with me then."

"If needs must then let's get to it."

I picked up Teiko's letter and we left the ghostly women behind. From there we went to the Widow Tamahara's establishment, as it was the closest. Usually it was filled with drinking *samuru*, but for the moment all was quiet. We found an unused table, and Kanemore ordered saké, which the smiling Widow Tamahara delivered personally. Kanemore poured out two generous measures, and we drank in companionable silence until Kanemore could stand it no longer. "So. What is the answer you drink to forget?" he asked, as he topped off his cup and my own. "Why did Teiko kill herself?"

"The only obvious and immediate answer is that, upon her death, you would be free to return to the capital and look after Takahito."

He frowned. "But you were going to be with her."

I sighed deeply. "Which did not alter her plans in the slightest, as apparently I was not an acceptable alternative."

"That is a very sad thing to bear," he said after a while, "and also very odd. I know my sister was fond of you."

"Maybe. And yet . . . "

"Yet what?"

I took a deep breath and then an even deeper drink. "And yet there is a voice deep in my brain that keeps shouting that I am a complete and utter ass, that I do not understand anything, and the reason Teiko killed herself had nothing to do with me. Try as I might, *drink* as I might, that troublesome fellow only shouts louder."

"You have suffered greatly because of my family," Kanemore said. "And I know that I have no right to ask more of you. Yet it was my sister's wish that you read her letter. Will you grant her last request?"

I didn't answer right away. "I once asked what you were afraid of, Kanemore-sama. I think it only fair to tell you what *I* am afraid of. I am very afraid of what Princess Teiko will say to me now."

Yet there was never really any question of refusing. I took out the letter. After hesitating as long as I dared I broke the seal. In doing so I discovered that, when I feared the very worst, I had shown entirely too little imagination.

And, yes, I was in fact a complete and utter ass.

The letter was very short, and this is most of what it said:

"The crane flies above
The lake's clear shining surface.
White feathers glisten,
Made pure by sacred water,
As the poet's book was cleansed."

At the end of the poem she had simply written: "Forgive me—Teiko."

I thought, perhaps, if one day I was able to forgive myself, maybe then I would find the strength to forgive Teiko. Not this day, but that didn't matter. I had other business. I put the letter away.

"*Kampai*, Kanemore-sama. Let us finish this jar of fine saké."

I knew Kanemore was deeply curious about the letter but too polite to ask, for which I was grateful. He hefted the container and frowned. "It is almost empty. I'll order another."

"No, my friend, for this is all we will drink tonight. From here we will visit the baths, and then go to sleep, for tomorrow our heads must be clear."

"Why? What happens tomorrow?"

"Tomorrow we restore your sister's honor."

⟞⟝

The Imperial Court was composed more of tradition and ritual than people. Everything in its time, everything done precisely so. Yet it was astonishing to me how quickly matters could unfold, given the right impetus.

Kanemore kneeled beside me in the hall where justice, or at least Fujiwara no Sentaro's version of it, was dispensed. The Minister had not yet taken his place on the dais, but my attention was on a curtained alcove on the far side of the dais. I knew I had seen that curtain move. I leaned over and whispered to Kanemore.

"His Majesty Reizei is present, I hope?"

"I believe so, accompanied by Chancellor Yorimichi I expect. He will not show himself, of course."

Of course. The acknowledged presence of the Emperor in these proceedings was against form, but that didn't matter. He was here, and everyone knew it. I was almost certain he would be, once word reached him. Kanemore, through another relative in close attendance on His Majesty, made sure that word did so reach him. I think Lord Sentaro convened in such haste as a way to prevent that eventuality, but in this he was disappointed. He entered now, looking both grave and more than a little puzzled.

Kanemore leaned close, "I've sent a servant for a bucket of water, as you requested. I hope you know what you're doing."

Kanemore was obviously apprehensive. Under the circumstances I did not blame him. Yet I was perfectly calm. I claimed no measure of courage greater than Kanemore's; I simply had the distinct advantage that I no longer cared what happened to me.

"What is this matter you have brought before the Imperial Ministry?" Lord Sentaro demanded from the dais.

"I am here to remove the unjust stain on the honor of the late Princess Teiko, daughter of the Emperor Sanjo, Imperial Consort to the late Emperor Suzaku II," I said, clearly and with more than enough volume to carry my words throughout the room.

There was an immediate murmur of voices from the clerks, minor judges, members of the Court, and attendants present. Lord Sentaro glared for silence until the voices subsided.

"This unfortunate matter has already been settled. Lady Teiko was identified by my nephew, who died a hero's death in Mutsu province. Consider your words carefully, Lord Yamada."

"I choose my words with utmost care, Your Excellency. Your nephew was indeed a hero and brought honor to the Fujiwara family. He did not, however, name Princess Teiko as his lover. This I will prove."

Lord Sentaro motioned me closer, and when he leaned down his words were for me alone. "Shall I have cause to embarrass you a second time, Lord Yamada?"

Up until that point I almost felt sorry for the man, but no longer. Now my blade, so to speak, was drawn. "We shall soon see, Lord Minister of Justice. May I examine the letter?"

He indicated assent and I returned to my place as Lord Sentaro's stentorian voice boomed across the room. "Produce my nephew's letter so that Lord Yamada may examine it and see what everyone knows is plainly written there."

A few snickers blossomed like weeds here and there in the courtroom despite the seriousness of the proceedings, but I ignored them. A waiting clerk hurried up, bowed low, and handed me the letter in question. I unrolled it and then signaled Kanemore who in turn signaled someone waiting at the back of the room. A young man in Taira livery came hurrying up with a bucket of clear water, placed it beside me, and then withdrew.

Lord Sentaro frowned. "Lord Yamada, did you neglect to wash your face this morning?"

More laughter. I was examining the poem closely and did not bother to look up. "The water is indeed to wash away a stain, Lord Sentaro. Not, however, one of mine."

The letter was not very long, and mostly spoke of the things Kiyoshi had seen and the hardships of the camp. The poem actually came after his personal seal. I unrolled the letter in its entirety, no more than the length of my forearm, and carefully dipped the paper into the water.

There was consternation in the court. Two guards rushed forward, but one glare from Prince Kanemore made them hesitate, looking to Lord Sentaro for instruction.

"Lady Teiko's sin dishonors us all," Lord Sentaro said, and his voice was pure sweet reason, "but the letter has been witnessed by hundreds. Destroying it will change nothing."

"I am not destroying the letter, Lord Sentaro. I am merely cleansing it. As the poet Ono no Komachi did in our great-grandsires' time."

Too late the fool understood. A hundred years before, a Lady of the Court had been accused by an enemy of copying a poem from an old book and presenting the piece as her own work. She faced her accuser and washed the book in question in clear water, just as I was doing now, and with the same result. I held the letter up high for all to see. Kiyoshi's letter was, of course, perfectly intact.

Except for the poem. That was gone.

More consternation. Lord Sentaro looked as if someone had struck him between the eyes with a very large hammer. I didn't wait for him to recover.

"It is a sad thing," I said, again making certain my voice carried to every corner—and alcove—of the court, "that a mere hundred years after the honored poet Ono no Komachi exposed this simple trick we should be deceived again. The ink in Fujiwara no Kiyoshi's letter is of course untouched, for it has been wedded to this paper for the past fifteen years. Clearly, the poem slandering Princess Teiko was added within the month."

"Are you accusing me —" Lord Sentaro stopped, but it was too late. He himself had made the association; I needed to do little else.

"I accuse no one. I merely state two self-evident facts: That Teiko-hime was innocent, and that whoever wrote the poem accusing her had both access to the letter," and here I paused for emphasis, "and access to a Fujiwara seal. These conclusions are beyond dispute, Excellency. At the present time the identity of the person responsible is of lesser concern."

The man was practically sputtering. "But . . . but she was here! Why did Princess Teiko not speak up? She said nothing!"

I bowed low. "How should innocence answer a lie?"

The murmuring of the witnesses was nearly deafening for a time. It had only just begun to subside when a servant appeared from behind the alcove, hurried up to the dais, and whispered briefly in Lord Sentaro's ear. His face, before this slowly turning a bright pink, now turned ashen gray. Kanemore and I bowed to the court as the official proceedings were hastily declared closed. The proceedings that mattered most, I knew, had just begun.

That evening Kanemore found me once more on Shijo Bridge. The moon was beginning to wane, now past its full beauty, but I still watched its reflection in the water as I waited for the ghosts to appear. Kanemore approached and then leaned against the rail next to me.

"Well?" I asked.

"Teiko's honors and titles are to be posthumously restored," he said. "Lord Sentaro is, at his own expense and at Chancellor Yorimichi's insistence, arranging prayers for her soul at every single temple in Kyoto."

"If you'll pardon my saying so, Kanemore-sama, you don't sound happy about it."

"For the memory of my sister, I am," he said. "Yet one could also wish we had discovered this deception soon enough to save her. Still, I will have satisfaction against Lord Sentaro over this, Minister of Justice or no."

I laughed. "No need. Even assuming that the expense of the prayers doesn't ruin him, Lord Sentaro will be digging clams at the beach at Suma or Akashi within a month, or I will be astonished," I said. "It's enough."

"Enough? It was *his* slander that killed my sister! Though I must ask, while we're on the subject—how did you know?"

I had hoped to spare us both this additional pain, but clearly Kanemore wasn't going to be content with what he had. There was that much of his sister in him.

"Lord Sentaro did not kill your sister, Kanemore-sama. We did."

One can never reliably predict a man's reaction to the truth. I thought it quite possible that Kanemore would take my head then and there. I'm not sure what was stopping him, but while he was still staring at me in shock, I recited the poem from his sister's letter. "I trust you get the allusion," I said when I was done.

From the stunned look on the poor man's face it was obvious that he did. "Teiko *knew* the poem was a forgery? Why didn't she—"

At that moment Kanemore's expression bore a striking resemblance to Lord Sentaro's earlier in the day. I nodded.

"You understand now. Teiko knew the poem was forged for the obvious reason that she did it herself. She used a carefully chosen ink that matched the original for color but was of poorer quality. I don't know how she acquired the proper seal, but I have no doubt that she did so. It's likely she started the original rumors as well, probably through her maids. We can confirm this, but I see no need."

Kanemore grasped for something, anything. "If Lord Sentaro thought the letter was genuine, that does explain why he didn't destroy it, but it does *not* explain why he didn't use it himself! Why didn't he accuse Teiko openly?"

"I have no doubt he meant to confront her in private if he'd had the chance, but in court? Why should he? If Takahito was Kiyoshi's son, then the Emperor's heir was a Fujiwara after all, and with Teiko the Dowager Empress under Sentaro's thumb, thanks to that letter. Until that day came he could continue to champion Prince Norihira, but he won no matter who took the throne, or so the fool thought.

Teiko was not mistaken when she said Sentaro was searching for the letter—he wanted it back as much as she did."

Kanemore, warrior that he was, continued to fight a lost battle. "Rubbish! Why would Teiko go to such lengths to deliberately dishonor herself?"

I met his gaze. "To make her son Emperor."

Despite my sympathy for Kanemore, I had come too far alone. Now he was going to share my burden whether he liked it or not. I gave him the rest.

"Consider this—so long as the Fujiwara preferred Prince Norihira, Takahito's position remained uncertain. Would the Teiko you knew resign herself to that if there was an alternative? *Any* alternative?"

Kanemore looked grim. "No. She would not."

I nodded. "Just so. Teiko gave Sentaro possession of the letter solely to show that he *could* have altered it. Then she likewise arranged for the letter to disappear and for us to find it again. In hindsight I realize that it had all been a little too easy, though not so easy as to arouse immediate suspicion. Those *shikigami* might very well have killed me if I'd been alone, but Teiko sent you to make certain that did not happen. Her attention to detail was really astounding."

Kanemore tried again. "But . . . if this was her plan, then it worked perfectly! Lord Sentaro was humiliated before the Emperor, the Chancellor, the entire Court! His power is diminished! She didn't have to kill herself."

I almost laughed again. "Humiliated? *Diminished*? Why should Teiko risk so much and settle for so little? With the responsibility for her death laid solely at his feet, Lord Sentaro's power at Court has been *broken*. The entire Fujiwara clan has taken a blow that will be a long time healing. No one will oppose Prince Takahito's claim to the Throne now, or dare speak ill of your sister in or out of the Imperial Presence. It was Teiko's game, Kanemore-san. She chose the stakes."

Kanemore finally accepted defeat. "Even the *shikigami* . . . Goji-san, I swear I did not know."

"I believe you. Teiko understood full well what would have happened if she'd confided in either of us. Yet we can both take comfort in this much—we did not fail your sister. We both performed exactly as she hoped."

Kanemore was silent for a time. When he spoke again he looked at me intently. "I thought my sister's payment was in gold. I was wrong. She paid in revenge."

I grunted. "Lord Sentaro? That was . . . satisfying, I admit, but I'd compose a poem praising the beauty of the man's hindquarters and recite it in front of the entire Court tomorrow if that would bring your sister back."

He managed a brief smile then, but his expression quickly turned serious again. "Not Sentaro. I mean you could have simply ignored Teiko's final poem, and her death would have been for nothing and my nephew's ruin complete and final. She offered this to you."

I smiled. "She knew . . . Well, say in all fairness that she left the choice to me. Was that a choice at all, Kanemore-san?"

He didn't answer, but then I didn't think there was one. I stood gazing out at the moon's reflection. The charming ghosts were in their procession. I think my neck was extended at the proper angle. The rest, so far as I knew or cared, was up to Kanemore.

I felt his hand on my shoulder. I'm not sure if that was intended to reassure me or steady himself.

"You must drink with me, Goji-san," he said. It wasn't a suggestion.

"I must drink," I said. "With or without you."

We returned to the Widow Tamahara's establishment. I wondered if we would drink to the point of despair and allow ourselves to be swallowed up by the darkness. Or would we survive and go on, as if I had said nothing at all on Shijo Bridge? While we waited for our saké, I think I received an answer of sorts as Kanemore's attention wandered elsewhere in the room. He watched the *samuru* laughing and drinking at the other low tables, and his distaste was obvious.

"A sorry lot. Always drinking and whoring and gambling,

when they're not killing each other." Kanemore sighed deeply and continued, "And yet they are the future."

I frowned. "These louts? What makes you think so?"

Our saké arrived and Kanemore poured. "Think? No, Goji-san—I know. Year by year the power and wealth of the provincial *daimyos* increases, and their private armies are filled with these *samurai*," he said, now using the more common corrupted word, "whose loyalties are to their lords and not the Emperor. They are the reason upstarts like the Abe Clan are able to create so much trouble in the first place."

"Dark days are ahead if you are correct."

Kanemore raised his cup. "Dark days are behind as well."

So. It seemed we had chosen to live, and in my heart I hoped that, at least for a while, things might get better. To that end I drank, and as the evening progressed I used the saké to convince myself that all the things I needed desperately to believe were really true.

I told myself that Teiko was right to do as she did. That it wasn't just family scheming or royal ambition. That Kanemore and I, though mostly unaware, had helped her to accomplish a good thing, a noble thing, and time would prove it so. First, in the continued decline of the power and influence of the Fujiwara. Second, in the glory to come under the reign of Crown Prince Takahito, soon to be known to history as His Imperial Majesty, Sanjo II.

My son.

PUBLICATION HISTORY

"On the Banks of the River of Heaven"
Realms of Fantasy, April 2008

"The Finer Points of Destruction"
Fantasy Magazine #1, November 2005

"A Pinch of Salt"
Mythic #2, 2006

"A Garden in Hell"
Fantasy Magazine #5, 2006

"The Twa Corbies, Revisited"
First Publication

"Lord Goji's Wedding"
Lady Churchill's Rosebud Wristlet #15, January, 2005

"The Feather Cloak"
First Publication

"Skin Deep"
Eclipse #2, November 2008

"Brillig"
Jabberwocky #2, 2006

"On the Wheel"
The Hub #41, January 2008

"Soft As Spider Silk"
First Publication

"Courting the Lady Scythe"
Paper Cities, April 2008

"The Man Who Carved Skulls"
Weird Tales #344, 2007

"Moon Viewing at Shijo Bridge"
Realms of Fantasy, April 2006